Passage Through Gehenna

Passage Through Gehenna

MADISON JONES

LOUISIANA STATE UNIVERSITY PRESS

Baton Rouge and London

Designer: Albert Crochet
Type face: VIP Primer
Typesetter: Graphic Composition, Inc., Athens, Georgia
Printer and Binder: Kingsport Press, Inc., Kingsport, Tennessee

LIBRARY OF CONGRESS CATALOGING IN PUBLICATION DATA
Jones, Madison, 1925–
    Passage through Gehenna.

    I. Title.
PZ4.J775Pas [PS3560.0517] 813'.5'5   77–13724
ISBN 0–8071–0376–4

The author gratefully acknowledges the financial assistance
of the John Simon Guggenheim Memorial Foundation.

It is profitable for thee that one of thy
members should perish, and not thy whole
body go into Gehenna.
Matthew 5:29

Part ONE

1

HIS NAME WAS JUD, JUDSON RIVERS. WHEN HE WAS growing up, in the Bethel hills ten or twelve miles from town, the religion still had a great deal of the old starch left in it. So this fact is some part of an explanation for Jud's turn of mind at so young an age. At least there was nothing much in the air around to weaken his grip on the ambition he had got hold of—or that had got hold of him. The ambition was to become a man of God, a preacher.

It was not just an ordinary ambition, of the kind children often have. It was more like a sense of destiny. As far back as he could remember, but especially from the time his mother died, it had been there like a little wick at the back of his mind—out sometimes but always ready to catch any spark struck close by. How it came there in the first place was no wonder, given the mother he had. She was an intensely pious, stern woman, even for that community up there, and in her heart she believed that, for a man, there was nothing really worth being but a preacher. If the man was smart, that is, and obviously Jud was going to be a smart one. She died when he was only nine, but with his kind of training and natural disposition, this was the very thing to brand the idea into his mind. From the day in that little sloping graveyard next to the Bethel Church of Christ, when he watched, over the coffin, Brother Campbell with uplifted arms committing his mother to heaven, he was convinced that this life was nothing but a sad and troublesome journey on to the next one.

Jud's father, Coleman, was not quite so sure about this view of things—not in his heart, anyway. He was a fairly steady churchgoer all right, and professed all the necessary beliefs with a good deal of firmness in his voice, but his life did not entirely bear out his professions. Not far enough for Jud, at least, and especially after Annie Rivers died. After that, Coleman relaxed in ways that shocked Jud, neglecting his Bible and sometimes a church service and once in a while even coming home drunk from some dark place unknown to Jud. Jud prayed for his father. As young as he was, he tried to lecture him. Coleman took this quietly, as he would not have done from his daughter who was four years older than Jud, and in fact seemed repentant more commonly than not. Already he thought of Jud as something special, with a certain license to reprimand him. One of the reasons was Jud's piety, which shamed Coleman, as if Jud spoke for his dead wife and God at the same time. But another reason was the fact that Jud was so smart.

Coleman had had only a little education, and he never could do much more than spell his way through the Bible. Yet here was his boy, at nine and ten years old, who could read and figure in a way to make a grown man's head swim. And when it came to knowledge of the Bible, this boy, this child, was as dazzling as a miracle. He knew all the books of the Old and New Testaments and, starting anywhere, could rattle them off on call. He knew the Ten Commandments in order, and the Beatitudes, and the Prophets of Israel, and he could tell the stories of Moses and Joseph and David more clearly and accurately than most preachers could. Altogether he was a good deal of a wonder in his father's eyes. But if Coleman was awed and later intimidated by him, he was also proud and showed him off in public whenever he could. The only thing about Jud that worried him—early on, that is—was the fear that the devil might use this brilliance to puff Jud up.

But Jud was alert to the devil. He heeded the Scripture about the devil's ways, and he was sure there was no danger of his ever getting puffed up. He minded his father according to Scripture and listened to his father's wisdom just as if he thought it came like the voice from the Burning Bush. He worked hard on the farm, too, without complaining. Milking and cutting wood and keeping the garden hoed clean was just part of it. He was right there with his father in the tobacco patch on the steep hillside, setting or topping or suckering the plants in the row next to Coleman's, trailing just a little way behind him. The heat would flare up from the big fleshy leaves under his face and the stinging gum got into his eyes. But he always kept his martyred tongue still. Whenever he was tempted to complain he would think about Ruth far away from home gleaning the fields and he would keep on in silence. He rested when his father told him to and sat there in the shade listening to the arguments of crows or the squawking of jays down along the hollow branch as if they had something to tell him that came from the Lord. You can already tell, as Jud himself once observed ironically to me, what a model of a Christian boy he was. You see, years later, in a place far removed from his old home, I became his minister and friend and he finally told me all this.

Jud did begin to worry his father, though, in a way that Coleman thought was more serious than the danger of getting puffed up by the devil. "You need to get off and have some fun sometimes, son," he would say. "A boy ought to be with other boys part of the time. What if Jesus had of stayed off by his self?"

There were other boys on other farms in easy walking distance of Coleman's little place, but Jud hardly ever sought them out. Most of the time, including days when there was no work left to be done, he acted as if he was the only boy in all the Bethel hills. His father's urging did no good. Jud would hint, and sometimes say outright, that those boys did not have much of God's grace in them. He did not mean to risk corruption. Even when he was sixteen and already taller and a whole world smarter and better looking than his father, things were not much different with him. Except his sister he would not look at a girl, though the girls liked him. In fact at school and even at church, as his father also noticed, they were always after him. No use, though. Coleman would shake his little bald head. But Jud had business in this world, and girls to tempt him were not any part of it. Finally Coleman stopped shaking his head and settled for thinking, though uneasily, that this was all another sign. By now even he was practically convinced that Jud had warning, maybe like the sound of a great breath being sucked in slowly, of God's call preparing to fall on him. Jud was certain of it.

When one evening late in the summer Jud was suddenly taken sick, both his father and he thought at first that this was it. It was laid on like a hand, inflaming Jud's head and making his eyes dark, and he seemed to hear a voice calling his name. Soon, though, it was clear that this was a fever, the raging kind. Coleman never had put much store in doctors. But to see Jud lying there looking as if he was being slowly burnt up from the inside out was too much for his notions, and he took the truck and fetched a doctor from down at Hallsboro. The doctor did what he could, but his manner said that it was too late now, even for a hospital to help. This was what Jud thought, too.

He was going to die. This was the meaning of the hand he felt laid on and of the call he had heard. It was also the meaning of the round frightened eyes of his father and sister that he saw about him in the darkened room. He had seen his mother die and put into the grave in the little hillside graveyard, and he kept thinking that one of these long cold soaring flights into darkness would end by setting him down there beside her. The gravestones frightened him. Not all his shuddering spasms came from the cold. His room changed its shape by the moment, contracting as if it would crush the breath from his body, then swelling out to the size of a circus tent. He lay outstretched inside a bellows. Sometimes the faces of his father and sister were as big as the moon, but soon again they were tiny, like faces seen through the wrong end of a telescope. And always there was his thirst and swollen tongue and his lips burning hot and cold. For all his prayers, that hand laid on him would not ease its pressures.

There actually was a hand, a fleshly hand. At the time Jud was confused about the sequence of things, but later he understood that the hand's presence had followed an interval when one of the two faces hovering over him had been absent. He did not want this hand removed. It was on his forehead and the thumb, impressed in his temple, felt as if it was transmitting coolness like green sap into his brain. A strange voice was praying, a strange unclear face. Already he knew that his fever was in retreat. He remembered very well how it went away—in stages marked by intervals of his father's or his sister's voice, and slowly, like something walking backward with a rueful scowling face into the dark. Then it was gone. It was full daylight, and his body was like a shell or a husk that the wind had dropped. But it also felt as though it had been washed clean and left suspended in an air that was neither hot nor cold. Only one clear thing was left over. It was the impress of that hand on his forehead.

Looking down at him Coleman said, "I reckon I'm in for a hard time doubting him now."

"The Lord?" Jud thought. But the Lord was not who his father meant just then. "Who?" Jud said.

"Old Salter. The Lord's ways is a mystery no man can't plumb."

Salter? Jud groped for a while and finally unearthed it. It was all tales and gossip and passing glimpses he had had. The man's name was Virgil Salter. Some people said he was just a crank, but others said no, he could heal the sick. The first thing was what most people, including Coleman, said, and Jud had always accepted this. It was different now.

In the slow, buzzing autumn days of his convalescence Jud sat and thought. He sat in the nearly bare front yard against a hickory tree and looked down into the woods where the russet and yellow leaves were falling. He hardly noticed when the chickens, clucking and purring around him, came up and pecked at his bare toes, or when his sister came out on the creaking porch to shake the dust from a mop or a rug. He was thinking about Salter. He kept envisioning the big desolate field of sassafras and briers and buckberry bushes, and the shack and the scarred, peeling house trailer parked by a shed under a single oak tree. There was nothing else in sight. But the Lord was there. He was everywhere, but He was there especially. Even Coleman had to admit this now, though with reluctance. "I reckon the Lord can use any kind of a tool he wants to for His business. But Salter ain't Church of Christ, son. Or none other, neither. He's a man alone." Salter made him nervous.

But Jud ignored his father. To his mind, that place— the field with the trailer and tree and shack—came bathed in the kind of light that the Pillar of Fire must have shed on the fleeing Children of Israel. He dreamed about it, and on his first day back at school he let the school bus leave without him and walked. The place was a whole mile out of his way, down the turnoff beyond Zion Church, the one building you passed after you came out of Bethel Community. He did not get quite there. Along with his tiredness, a feeling of awe stopped him at a distance from the place. But the ridgetop ahead of him was flat and he could see the roofs of the two buildings and the top of the trailer under the tree. All the way to the skyline that was inflamed with sunset just then, there was nothing else to see. There was not one movement. There was not even the sound of a rooster anywhere. He supposed it was finally his exhaustion that made the place look so much like his dreams about it and kept him from going any closer. When he got home that night he all but fell down on the porch steps, while Coleman, learning where Jud had come from, shook his head.

A few days later Jud went back. He went closer, this time, almost to the turn-in through the heavy brush, because he saw that the trailer was no longer there. If the Israelites had one day found the holy Ark gone from the tabernacle, they would have felt about as he felt. But on reflection he knew where the trailer was. It was gone to carry faith and healing to the sick and the lost out there. When Jud came back the third time, the trailer was under the oak tree once again.

9

He found the courage somewhere. Driving himself he followed the wheel tracks through the brush and stepped out into the clearing. He believed that the light really was unusual that evening. It looked as if the sun had been melted like so much copper and smeared across the whole western sky.

"Come here, son."

Jud was sure his heart had stopped. Salter was sitting under the tree, holding an open bean can between his knees. He was chewing slowly, the way cattle chew, and as Jud approached, Salter kept his gaze on him. Jud thought of cattle, a cow's eyes. Salter's were liquid brown like that and swallowed up what they saw. They were not old, either, though his face, too narrow for them, looked as if he had spent a good part of his life in bitter gnawing wind.

"Plumb healed now, ain't you?" Salter said kindly.

"Yes sir." Jud's voice was above its normal range. "I came to thank you."

Without moving his eyes Salter put his spoon back in the can. "Son, don't you know it wasn't none of me." He raised one thumb, pointing upward. The thumb was flat and gray like dried-out loam. "You know who to thank for your life. He done a miracle."

There was something wrong with Salter's hand. As if to answer Jud's thought, Salter opened his fingers, exposing the hand, turning it back and forth for Jud's inspection. It was badly scarred. Clear up into the flesh of his wrist there were ridges of tissue that made Jud think of fat pale worms half buried in the skin.

"Look at it good. Wasn't no dirtier hand in God's world till He burnt it clean. For His use, and not none of mine."

All Jud could do was blink at the hand.

"Get down on your knees and thank Him. And pray you

10

keep them hands of yours clean. He ain't brought you back from the dead for nothing."

Jud knelt down. With his eyes shut tight and his lips shaping the words, he gave thanks with all his might and prayed that the hands he was holding clenched in fists against the world's dirt might be kept clean always in the Lord's service.

If there had been any question before, there was not one now. Jud knew beyond any chance of a doubt what he, and all men, were made for. The business of man was the service of God. But it was especially Jud's business, who had been brought back by a miracle and now could see God's hand everywhere working His big and little miracles in the world. It was all miracles. What else could have kept the world around and around on its track and kept night and day from mixing and showed the sap the time to rise and the geese which way was south. All things spoke of Him. His print was there on everything created. Jud wondered how there were people who could not see it, and he marveled when he heard somebody speak of doubt.

He knew the reason, though. It was because dust and sin, the world's dirt, darkened people's eyes. He could even understand, himself, how this came to be, for there were girls. He was a good-looking boy, tall and lean and straight, with fine dark russet hair and blue-gray eyes. He had been told more than once that he had the look of an old-time Indian scout. Anyway the girls responded to him. They were always after him. Sometimes one would get him cornered briefly, and these were occasions when he was appalled to hear wicked whispers in his own heart. He knew that he wanted badly to handle their rounded bodies and their soft springing breasts.

But Jud was far above such fleshly things and he answered the wicked whispers with prayer. He had a special place where he prayed, early every morning and every night—a hollow tree like a chimney by the branch at the foot of the hill. There he would be, while the owls tuned up or hooted their last in the gray dawn, down on his knees praying that his heart might be washed and always kept as clean as the Lamb. In a little ritual afterward he would bury his hands in the cold branch pool. There were not any wicked whispers now. There were only owls, and water tinkling and purling around his throbbing wrists and hands.

Prayer was the answer. Or rather, the answer was the grace that prayer called down, without which a man was nothing. "It's a miracle," Salter said, "if a man ain't a hog. Or else a billy goat. For goat and hog is his nature."

Jud listened. Those cold December evenings Salter would have a fire burning on the dirt floor of the shed. There were three walls to break all but a south wind, and half the interior was stacked with folding chairs and the big rolled-up tent and odds and ends connected with his mission. While the smoke drifted and billowed like fog against the tin roof they sat there on chairs or on the ground, the three of them, gazing into the flames. For Salter had another disciple, one of much longer standing than Jud. He was a black man, called Sunk. He was short and walked with a limp and, without lines or creases in his face, looked old. He could not speak. Maybe he could not hear, either, for whether Salter talked or not, or Jud asked a question, it was all the same to the empty look on Sunk's black face. Salter had found him maybe dead in a car wreck a long time ago and had healed him, too, and so had gained a silent helper to labor in God's vineyard.

"Goat was mine," Salter said into the flames. "I couldn't lay eyes on aer a woman but I was lusting in my

12

heart. Old or young, didn't make no difference. And me not even a boy no more. These-here feet was long gone on the down-path. And no rescue." He was looking at his big torn shoes, from which his ankles rose like dusty stalks. His lean head, which was hairless and pale at the crown, was mourning. So was Sunk's head, his hair like black wool touched with frost. Jud remembered how the wind that was threading the brush beyond the shed walls seemed to join in like a sigh. "No help in nature. Don't never count on *it*, son."

Seated there on the ground Jud silently vowed that he never would.

"Help's in the Lord. I wasn't one to pray, but He sent it, for His reasons." Salter spread his scarred hand to the fire. "This-here hand was on a tree. A young beech, it was. Waiting there ready to take hold of a woman was coming to meet me I don't even know if she ever come atall. It was all just one big blast like landing on hell's floor. When I finally could raise up it was burnt bark all over me. This hand laying there looking like a cinder, stinking. And not a cloud. Not one in the sky." He clenched the hand, looking at it. It would not quite make a fist. "It ain't touched a woman that-a-way since. And nevermore will."

The cow eyes shifted and looked at Jud. "Keep your heart pure, son."

Jud vowed that he would, always. He silenced his thoughts of girls by hourly prayers, and he was sure that his hands never would have need of cleansing by God's fire.

Jud wondered if the gift came only by fire, striking sinners down. Then one day it occurred to him that he had been struck down also and burned, although *in*side, with a fire that no mere earthly water could put out. Mightn't

13

the gift be in him too, unrecognized? Coleman shook his head, as he had done more and more often in recent weeks. But Salter also said not. A man who had it would know in his heart. Jud did not know, but he did not know, either, that it was *not* there. Maybe it was there like a seed, growing toward the day when it would bloom out in the sunshine. Jud waited and watched. The better to see what it would be like he persuaded Salter to take him along to a meeting one day in early March.

Because the little truckbed would not hold much except the tent, the folding chairs had to be put inside of and, bound with ropes and baling wire, on top of the house trailer. It had not occurred to Jud before that there would be anything strange in the sight they made on the road, or that stares and open mouths would follow their passage. But this was the way it was. There were even shouts of derision that cut straight to Jud's heart and left him shrinking with pain and humiliation. Now he could see with different eyes the trailer under its clattering burden, swaying along behind them, tilted a little because one wheel was larger than the other. But he saw most of all, because some shouts used them in mockery, the words painted crudely in black on the trailer's battered sides. The largest words said, THE TRUE BIBLE CHURCH OF JESUS CHRIST. Others said, HEAL THEM and BEWARE THE WRATH and JESUS IS COMING. In one town they passed through, cries like "Hi there, Jesus," and "Your church is leaning over" brought scalding tears he could not hold back.

But Salter looked oblivious. From his seat by the window, by glances over the top of Sunk's nodding head, Jud studied the face thrust forward above the steering wheel. There was no sign of pain or anger or of anything but a kind of somber attentiveness to the road ahead. What did

Salter care about their gaping and their jibes. He was not ashamed of Jesus Christ. With the Gift in his hand and the Promise like fine raiment to clothe him, what did he care for the world's contempt. The Bible warned the godly about such mockeries. Jud stiffened his back. When some chairs fell off in a town they were passing through, and Salter, with Jud and Sunk to help, was putting them back on, Jud filled his head with prayers for mercy upon the mocking tongues.

It was sixty miles to Indian Hill, and part of the way, over washboard road, made the trailer dip and swerve and made the steering wheel buck in Salter's hands. But there was no way too rough or too long when the Lord called. Nowadays, Salter said, He most often called from places like this, where the people had been kept free from the poison of infidelity that was spreading all over the world. They were poor people.

The little town was not on a hill at all, but just a high flat place with rocky fields around it. They set up on one of these fields, one so full of limestone shelves that they could barely hammer the tent pegs in. But rock, the Bible said, was the thing to build on. The next night proved it. March wind with sleet came driving out of the north and the tent flapped and billowed, but not one peg got loosened. And the people came, ignoring the cold. They drifted mutely into the tent, one or two at a time, in scrubbed-out denim jumpers and shapeless woolen coats, and sat down on the chairs. Their faces looked empty, and they appeared to gaze only at the light bulb hanging above the table where Salter's Bible lay, swinging in the gusts of wind. Hardly any of them were young people. And some of them came limping into the tent or showed in their faces the wasting of old sicknesses.

But the hymns roused them. They stood and sang

15

about Jesus's Everlasting Arms and Glory Land, lining it out in.one ragged nasal voice that almost silenced the wind. Salter sang loudest of all. With his head tilted back, his voice sounded as if it might have had an invisible dome for resonance not far above his face. But it was only louder than the voice in which he preached, leaning toward the people across his table. He told them about man's nature and God's unceasing miracles, telling his own story and holding up the hand God's fire had burned.

Fifteen or more came up to get healed. They came down the center aisle, some supported by a wife or son or husband. They stood before the table for blessing and for the hand to be laid on. Two were healed right then and there. A thin old woman who looked as if somebody had hit her a stunning blow walked back to her chair without help, and a man lifted up an arm that had been useless for six whole years.

"Raise it up higher," Salter commanded. His hand lay on the man's trembling shoulder. "Right on up to the Lord."

The arm went up, followed by a kind of gasping cry of praise. Jud stood by the rippling canvas wall staring at the man. He held his right hand tensed into a fist and he was almost sure he could feel the power growing there.

2

IT WAS NOT LONG BEFORE JUD HAD A CHANCE TO USE whatever power he had in his hand. The time was spring, when God seemed to be working His miracles at random in the world. The woods were flowering and dappled everywhere with the white flakes of dogwood bloom. The grass made Jud think of a green down on raw winter fields and there were quail whistling in the morning and whippoorwills at night. But Coleman was dying. It was clear: he said so himself. He had been poorly all winter, complaining of pain in his chest and shoulder, and in April the blow struck him down. He lay there very still in his bed, under a calendar picture of Jesus blessing the loaves and fishes, and his breath seemed hardly to come at all. If Jud had the gift, the time was surely now.

One night, while his sister sat asleep in the cane rocking chair, Jud knelt by his father's bed and prayed. Finally, still praying, he put out a tremulous hand and laid it on Coleman's chest. For some moments afterward Jud thought he could feel a new stirring there. He was certain that his father's breathing had changed and he felt awe like a chill from fever plucking the flesh at the back of his neck. But nothing followed. There was only a rise and fall of the chest in a curious retarded rhythm. That stirring had been in his own hand and now this too had stopped. He kept his hand there anyway, feeling how the dim half-moon and the whippoorwills poured sadness in through the window.

Before daylight Jud went for Salter, to fetch the hand God's fire had sanctified. It made no difference, though. Or none except that, when Salter touched him, Coleman opened his eyes and smiled at the corners of his mouth with feeble gratitude. "It ain't His will," Salter said. "The Lord's done called him home." Jud knew how it was. There was no calling back who the Lord had called home. He was still telling himself this when his father died that afternoon, and still telling it when he watched them lower his father's coffin into the ground next to his mother in the little graveyard at Bethel Church.

The farm was sold, bringing just about enough to pay the mortgage. Coleman had an older sister, Ella Parks, who lived in Hallsboro and who, reluctantly, took Jud and his sister to live with her. In the case of the sister it was not for long. She very soon got married and moved away for good to distant Nashville. Jud still had the Lord, but otherwise he felt himself desolate, in an alien world among strangers. Aunt Ella was religious but she was also sickly and self-absorbed. She was a thin woman with a spent light in her eyes and she passed most of the time doctoring herself and lamenting things and lying in real or imagined exhaustion on her bed. As for her husband, Frank, he was not even religious. In fact where religious matters were concerned he was given to scoffing, and he never went to church. Jud was appalled.

Indeed he was a good deal appalled by the whole town. He did not have much reason, actually, not by modern standards. Hallsboro was not nearly so changed as most places. It was a town of about fifty-five hundred people, and there had not been any sudden large increase in population. There was one small stove factory, which was

18

new, but it had not brought any noticeable number of outsiders. To be sure, Hallsboro, like every other place, had felt the modern spirit. But to a considerable extent it still retained the old character of a farming town, with its increase from outside supplied mostly by people from the surrounding county, or counties.

Besides, the town had kept, and still keeps, a good part of its old-time charm. It sits at the foot of hills in a long bend of the Cumberland River. From the river bank a stretch of low bottomland, always in corn, extends up to the railroad embankment which is the west edge of town. Beyond this, between it and the business district in the middle of town, are two streets of old frame country-style houses, a little dilapidated. The road from the river bridge passes among them, running straight into a square that is nearly walled in mostly by dark brick storefronts. At the center of the square, on a lawn shaded by elms and maples, is the courthouse with a cupola and four-faced clock at the top. Almost at the back steps of the court-house the land begins to climb. After only a few hundred feet it becomes the steep side of a big broken-back ridge, and up there are some more old houses but also a good many new ones. There are a couple of churches, most notably the Baptist church, with white steeples that rise above the treetops and seem to dominate the town. Up there on the slope of the ridge you can't hear much from below, and the town, spread out in the green river-bend, looks as tranquil as a picture. You would think that not very much of importance had changed at all. And in fact, as I have implied, Hallsboro is still a little bit outside the mid-twentieth century.

Even so Jud was appalled. Of course he had been down to Hallsboro many times in his life and in the past year or two had often sensed what, to his stainless spirit, was an air of godlessness. But living here, especially in the house with his scoffing uncle, he felt it with much greater acuteness. He saw the churches, all right, Baptist and Methodist and even his own Church of Christ, and he saw that most people attended them, but still his distress was barely diminished. There were so many people, strangers coming and going, spending and making money, gathering on Saturdays by the hundreds to cackle and joke and never even to mention the name of the Lord. And the boys and girls. He had seen boys and girls tease with each other right out in the open before and had seen them, in old topless cars, come speeding by with everything flying, abandoned-looking. But never like this. Salter had warned him about the world. Now he envisioned his old home, and all the Bethel hills, as standing out there far away in a sort of heavenly aura.

As before, the girls pursued him, at school and other places, and he fled. Their interest in him angered the boys, who did not have time anyway for things of the Lord and mocked Jud for his piety. Once he mentioned Salter in the presence of some of the boys at school and discovered that even those few who had heard of him were scornful. "Heal, my ass," one said. "That's his pocketbook he's healing." The pain was all the worse, like a wound in the same place, because this was not the first time he had suffered it. The first wound had come from Uncle Frank. "Boy, you're a bigger fool than you need to be," Uncle Frank said over the glassful of white whiskey he defiantly drank on the front porch every seasonable evening before supper. "Salter ain't, though. Old coot knows a easy living when he sees one."

But there was worse. Worst of all was a boy named Charley Meagher who, though in Jud's class at school, was a year or two older and had come recently to

20

Hallsboro from someplace else. At least this was the impression Jud had, without knowing just how he had got it. Long afterwards, in retrospect, he thought he had derived it from his feeling that there was something strange and also sinister about Meagher. Anyway, from the first Jud feared and hated him. There were plenty of godless boys and mockers among his schoolfellows, but none like Meagher. Compared to him all the rest were innocents, and some such idea was acknowledged by the way the other boys left him alone. It seemed that his isolation was what brought him to fasten on Jud. But his immediate purpose evidently was only to torment Jud.

At school there was no escaping Meagher. On the recess ground, in the hall, in the bathroom, he would find a way to approach and corner Jud. "Tell me all about 'Jesus,'" he would drawl. "Where's he at? Show him to me." Or, "You think that Bible's true just because it's wrote down? It's plenty of Bibles different from that one."

"The Holy Ghost inspired it," Jud would say stoutly, straining not to blink in Meagher's green level gaze.

"Yeah. A ghost."

Or there would be some filth, in a mock whisper. "I know where some good pussy's at. A little 'sin' is just what you need."

More than once he dropped into Jud's pocket little cigarettes wrapped in brown paper, the kind that was the devil's incense, breeding sin. On the way home from school Jud stopped and ground them into the dirt with his heel.

A hundred times Jud planned to raise his fist and smash the crooked grin that had a missing dogtooth at the corner. Meagher was not as tall as he was, and thin and small-boned. But for all Jud's hate, the fist remained at this side. Meagher had cords in his neck. They ap-

21

peared in moments of feeling and tightened and sank with a kind of tremulous rhythm. Under the skin they were raw, Jud thought, and threatened the flesh with their keenness. There was something more besides. It showed in his face and his green eyes whenever he gazed at Jud. It was as if Jud knew, or knew that Meagher knew, of a weapon concealed somewhere in reach of Meagher's lightning hand. There would come a lump of weakness low down in the pit of Jud's belly.

But after school he was free of Meagher. Wish it or not he was free of everybody in this new world, and his only real relationship was the one he kept up secretly with Salter in the world out in the Bethel Hills. Two or three times a month, when his loneliness seemed about to get the best of him, he would leave early and quietly on Saturday morning and walk and hitch-hike the whole distance out to Salter's place and spend the day. The rest of his leisure time he spent closed up in his small room upstairs where in late afternoon, sunshine spilled through the yellow hickory foliage onto his ragged carpet. He got the habit of reading.

He read his Bible, of course, but more and more he read other books too. He began by borrowing them from the small library at school, but he soon discovered that the town had a library that was open three days a week. One book looked like another on the shelf. He chose the titles that struck him, four or five a week, and read or scanned them according to his interest. He got some shocks. They came not only from his seeing the things that people, even women, did in the world, without punishment or any pains of conscience. There were people, unquestionably smart people, who believed terrible things. One book he thought must have been written by the devil, who had guided a human hand. At midsentence he shut the book and hid it away in the drawer as if an eye was watching him. But even shut away the book was there, and in the silence of his room the words, the blasphemies, spoke like evil whispers close to his ear. Until Monday when he could return the book he refused to go near the drawer again.

Just after that, in early December, something else happened. Even at the time, it seemed to him a fateful event, as though all of a sudden, after merely stalking and teasing him all these months and years, the devil had cast a fiery net for his soul. Those evil whispers, first. Then, to advance the design, the innocent voice of his aunt demanding through the door that he go down to Nunn's Mercantile and buy a stewpan to replace the one she had burnt up on the stove. What could have been more innocent-seeming than an afternoon walk through fallen elm and maple leaves down Beulah Street and onto the square and across to Wood Street where the plateglass front of Nunn's made visible inside the counters loaded with tools and kitchenware and garden hose and paint. There was something else in Nunn's, however. He had never been inside but once before, and Mrs. Nunn, if he had seen her at all, had left no kind of impression. He did not notice her this time, either, when he first entered.

He was standing there uncertainly before the profusion of cookers and pots and pans when he suddenly heard her voice. There was the space of two counters between her and him, but he heard it clearly. Though not a loud voice it was distinct and had a throaty vibrant strain. But what struck him was not so much the voice as what it was saying. Later he thought of these words as part of the design, a strand in that net the devil had cast for his soul. Why else had it happened that out of all the day's moments this should have been the one for the words she spoke? "Yes. 'The Lord,'" she said. "Always the 'Lord.' You think He'll pay off that bill for you? I wish sometime you'd show me just one little sign of His famous 'helping hand.'"

"You ought not to talk that way, Lily," a meek reproving voice said. It was Mr. Nunn's voice.

Jud heard a scornful noise, almost like spitting, and then the sound of footsteps. They were hers and she was coming to wait on him. He fastened his eyes on a skillet and heard her turn the end of the counter and stop beside him. "Can I help you?" she said flatly.

She was close and Jud's vision could not help but record an impression of hot tawny eyes and painted lips. And also a pair of round breasts that peered through the taut yellow blouse she wore. He finally mumbled, "A stewpan."

"Like those?"

Her hand seemed to point directly in front of him, but he could see only skillets there. She moved. In leaning across in front of him she brushed against his arm, and her body, or her dark hair, was scented. It felt as if there was heat where she had touched his arm. "Like this one?" she said, holding the pan for his inspection. She was looking into his face.

"Yes ma'm."

"You want it, then?" Her eyes were tawny, drifting with yellow seeds, and her hair was black.

"Yes ma'm."

Following her along the aisle he got, without meaning to, one glimpse of her whole body. And at the cash register his fleeing eyes perversely recorded another thing. There were flaws, tiny pits, in her faintly tinted cheeks—as if small worms had gnawed them.

She was evil. Her eyes were like a wolf's, and little silent coffin worms were at her cheeks in the night. She stalked him in his mind, stealing into his thoughts and into his dreams. To expel her by violence or even by prayer was only to drive her back beyond the light—not far enough. She was still there in the veiling dark, crouching like a shadow-shape with eyes and rotten cheeks.

For most of a week he kept her at bay. But then came the night when, lying there helpless, he felt her creep into his bed. The swimming yellow eyes made him dizzy and she took his strength away. She touched her naked flesh on his and pressed the putrid cheek against his cheek. He waked up in a sort of horrid ecstasy, drowning in despair. A little later, down on his knees on the cold floor, he imagined that a whole lifetime of beseeching heaven would be too short to cleanse this filth from his soul.

But finally he recalled that heaven had infinite mercy. Sleep had betrayed him. Now at night he covered himself only with the bedspread and lay shivering in the frosty dark, huddled up tight and half resisting the swoons of cold black sleep. He kept his mind busy with prayers and, because Nunn's fronted on Wood Street, he took a different route to school. As often as he could he avoided even the square, for it held danger too. Already, since that afternoon, he had met her husband Luther there, a tired-looking man with a limp, who was gray and much older than she and whom Jud stared at with a kind of astonishment. But certain other streets, main streets, were also perilous and even the round-about ways he made himself go were not an assurance. One day he accidentally discovered which was the house she lived in—and also something worse. On the porch posts, like something put there for him by the devil's hand, was a sign that said Room For Rent. So this was still another forbidden street. Along with the other streets he blotted it off the map of the town in his head.

But nothing finally banished her—not even, at last, the coldness of his bed at night. She still hovered in the dark waiting only for the helplessness of sleep to come over him. And guilt was there when she was not.

For more than a month Jud's guilt had been stifling every thought of visiting Salter. How could he face him now, with his heart impure? Then one day late in January—it was his eighteenth birthday—Jud made up his mind. The trip, walking and riding, was almost joyful, like a pilgrimage to where the burden would be lifted from his soul. For Salter understood. He had been this road, himself.

Jud had been too hopeful, though. Outwardly all was the same. The smoke made a drifting yawing cloud against the shed roof and the wind beyond the walls threaded the brush with a sound like whispers. Sunk's black face was unchanged, never would change. It was like listening stone and watched and did not watch from across the fire. Salter sat a little humped, as always, his wrists on his knees and his cow eyes mirroring the flames, as though they watched there something he was hungry for. Jud was sure that he himself also looked the same. The difference was in his heart. It took him an hour to speak.

"You never did feel any . . . hankering to get married, did you, Mr. Salter? "

"It ain't for me, son. The Lord give me my work."

Jud cleared his throat. Above a whisper he said, "And never even a hankering . . . for a woman? "

Salter's burnt hand stirred. A time went by and a draft of air made the smoke cloud against the roof billow. "It ain't a man if he don't feel a hankering. But I made my promise. And I mean to keep it." He turned his hungry eyes on Jud's half-averted face. "You got to do it by prayer, son. It ain't nobody strong enough by his self to stare the devil down."

The words in Jud's throat would not come.

"I was bad that-a-way as aer a man living. It'll burn up your soul, son."

He was still looking at Jud but Jud was looking at the flames. The words had crowded up like a knot in his throat. "What if your prayers don't get answered?" he burst out.

"Then keep apraying. We got the Lord's promise. He don't fail."

Jud waited, but this was to be all. He had not intended the small protesting murmur that finally escaped from his mouth.

"Ain't the Lord's promise enough for you, boy?"

The flames curled in a gust of wind and, as it seemed to Jud, darted upward toward him like the tongue of a lash. Feeling Salter's eyes, Sunk's eyes too, he bowed his head.

God's will was hard and His grace hard to call down. It was too hard. But aghast at his blasphemy Jud crushed this thought and in repentance spent hours that night on his knees on the cold floor.

He had asked too much of his body, however. He waked up at dawn shuddering hard and knew that his old fever had come back. Was it not the Lord's hand burning him clean again? This was what he thought for a time, a whole day maybe, while drifting from swoon to swoon of fire and bitter ice.

Then he was no longer sure. Whatever it was that hovered near his bed was not clear to him and he began to be afraid. He had reason. *She* appeared, finally, with her wolfish eyes and putrid cheeks, and it seemed that he did not have will enough to fight against her insistence. He had no will at all, for her eyes made him dizzy and her flesh, that was like his fever, alternately burned and froze his own. Shuddering he submitted, even to the putrid cheek laid against his. And this was not all. He thought that wicked book was in his drawer again and he could hear it whispering its blasphemies.

Even this was not the worst of it. When she had finished and left him alone and he had summoned the strength at last, he staggered from his bed and across the room to the drawer. There was no book. The whispering was in his mind, his own corrupted heart. Nor was there any praying it out. It tangled itself with his prayers. It was like a whispered chorus that repeated itself again every time he paused for breath. Then he knew he was lost. With nothing to oppose her anymore, embracing him at her will, she was free to suck the last small drop of spirit from his body.

He got well, though, and much more quickly than he had the other time. This alone made him wonder at himself. The sins he was guilty of, guilty in spite of his debilitating sickness, ought to have been enough to carry off his soul and body both to hell. So he told himself, accusing himself of vilest lust and despair. So he told the Lord in long scrupulous prayers. But there was a difference. His prayers seemed to fall short of the fervor they had had before. And even his fears because of this, that his soul was now maybe damned beyond redemption, had blunted teeth. Where was the old sure agony? It was as though he had a dead place in him, where there were only ashes left . . . But all would be restored. He would pray it back again.

He prayed, all right, but except for intervals, an hour

here and there, the old harsh agony did not come back. He pondered and found the reason. It was because he had discovered mercy. That God was infinitely merciful was a fact he had known all his life but a fact that had never had much place in his thinking. Not just once or twice or seven times, but seventy times seven God forgave sinful man. Now Jud embraced this fact. It was enough for a man to do his best and earnestly repent of his failure. So long as he tried and repented. Couldn't he, therefore, without tempting the Lord, follow his natural route down Wood Street on the way to school?

One day he did. And every day after that, going to and coming from school, he passed in front of the plate glass window of Nunn's with his eyes fastened straight ahead. Sometimes a figure standing inside would pull at the tail of his eye, but still his gaze plunged on. Then one day he saw her clearly. He had not looked. He saw her inwardly, as if the sudden thrust of his blood had produced her perfect image, and he hurried on to escape it. Afterwards his steps slowed down but his pulse did not. It pounded on through the afternoon and through dusk and into the night. His prayers were futile, silenced by his blood. It drove him out of the house in the night and finally up the hill to Perry Street where he stood for a long time staring at the dark front of the house where she lived. He could not help it when, later on, she came to his bed. His embraces were as shameless as hers and his ecstasy was that of the wickedest sinner hurtling down to Perdition.

3

IN THE SPRING JUD GOT A JOB AT NUNN'S PART-
time, after school. It was just as if his destiny had
fashioned this chance for him to be close to her, and he
hurried and there by the cash register accepted Luther
Nunn's frugal offer. His job was mostly to clean up and
tote and keep order among the crates and boxes in the
warehouse room in back. There was one other employee,
a little old dried-up clerk named Baker. But he could not
see well and did not pay much attention to Jud anyway.
Neither he nor Luther interfered with Jud's real occupa-
tion—watching Lily Nunn.

She was there most of the time when he was. She
waited on customers some, but usually she was either
tending the cash register or else hidden away in. the
milkglass cubicle of an office back beside the warehouse
door. More often than not she left the office door standing
open. Passing in or out of the warehouse Jud could see
her inside at her desk, her back to him, and if nobody was
looking his way he would pause and for a moment feed
his eyes on the margin of white neck that was visible
under the black hair. If she was not in the store, as sometimes happened, he would think about her in her room in
the house on Perry street. He ached with the thought of
her there, reclining, revealed by her gown, washed in the
glow of dimly violet light that had become the medium of
all his tumid reveries about her.

He was stupid in her presence. A kind of torpor took hold of him and there were times when he felt as if a moment's direct meeting with her tawny eyes might cause him to faint away. He studied the rounds and hollows of flesh beneath her skirt and blouse, the calves of her legs, the changing shades of expression in her face. He noticed how her eyes looked when they were veiled and how her lips looked when they were parted. To the last feature of her body, naked or concealed, he got her shaped in his mind. There, she belonged to him. In the lewdest postures she did his bidding, with lustful eyes and mouth expressing the things he wanted to hear.

She affected him in another way also, a way that was at once a spur to this desire and a comfort to his soul. She was a cynical, sharp-tongued woman whose scorn was specially aroused by evidence of piety. Luther was her most common target. Somehow he had remained a dedicated church member and his combination of piety and slow wit and general feebleness made him, in spite of everything, sometimes incautious in her presence. He would thank the Lord for a small accidental benefit or, to a familiar customer, drop a holy sentiment. Jud would wait for Lily's response. Not always but often enough it would come out-loud, preceded by a tight little grimace at the corners of her mouth. In a dry voice she would take up his words and mock them. And every time, almost, in meek reprimand, Luther would say, "Now, Lily, you oughtn't to talk like that. It's wicked." and she, going about her business, would answer, "Yeah, 'wicked.'"

"Wicked," she seemed to say, meant nothing. What, then, if someone besides Luther, if *Jud*, should take her fancy? Why not in reality, then, those lewd outcries and postures he dreamed about? It was possible. The thought was like a spark of fire in his bowels.

31

Jud's other way of taking this was like a balm on the conscience he was not yet able to ignore, that still in his less guarded moments erupted like a sickness. She strengthened him against his childish self, for what did "wicked" mean? It did not mean anything. It was a word they used for what they feared and hated, and one man's wickedness was another man's good. All along she had known what he knew also now—with his mind, at least.

He had known this for months, since back in the winter when he had retrieved that book, then others like it, from the library and in a kind of stunned amazement read and reread all he could understand. Then he was able to see. It was all hollow, a sham, a thing they believed because they wanted, or feared not to believe. There was no God, no devil. The world went on by its own laws, without any miracles to interfere. Conscience was something they planted in children when the children were too little to know any better, and "sin" was another word like "wicked." But ever after, conscience kept crying "Sin" about every natural thing and was hard, very hard, to stamp out. It was agony sometimes, and terror. A person needed help. He needed it. He swallowed up Lily's mockeries and wished for more.

There came a day—it was summer and he had graduated now, at the top of his class—when Hannah Rice stood at the counter talking with Luther. Hannah was the daughter of the minister at Luther's church, the First Baptist, a plain woman of twenty-eight or so, with a short full body and a very light tow hair. She had a face that looked as if earnestness kept it just a little bit flushed, and a mouth that had, it seemed, one too many teeth in the upper jaw. Because, from a distance, his wife looked on, Luther was restless. But he bore up manfully, nodding and putting in now and again a pious if muted

32

word of his own. The conversation was about suffering. The example was a man named Holly Echols who had learned faith while living with a broken back and the conclusion was that people could profit greatly from suffering.

"It doesn't have to be wasted, you know," Hannah said in a quiet but audible voice. "Because God can bring good even out of the worst evil."

"That's the truth," Luther said bravely, almost as if he did not feel the pressure of Lily's gaze.

The expected, or something like it, happened as soon as Hannah, with a nod and a white smile for Jud, had shut the door behind her. Lily's face wore her version of Hannah's earnestness. She said, "I think we ought to give thanks to the Lord that Holly Echols broke his back."

"Now Lily, don't . . . "

"And pray it won't ever get well, either. He might lose his faith."

"That's wicked, Lily." Luther fumbled with something behind the counter.

"We ought to all pray for a broken back. And to think I've been worrying about stumbling on those steep stairs at home."

Luther moved away and pretended to set right a display of screwdrivers at the end of the counter. Jud was grinning almost openly. He stood not far away with his broom, just beyond the second display counter, and he wished she would turn and see the grin on his face. He waited, holding the grin, and then she did look at him. For a moment she kept on looking. If that was not exactly a grin in answer to Jud's, at least it was an unmistakable expression of complicity. Jud felt as if every bit of his blood had rushed straight to his heart.

That episode had two consequences, one of which did

not seem important at the time. But this was the one that brought Hannah Rice into his life. She had noticed him in the store that day, for the first time, apparently, and afterwards had taken the trouble to find out something about him. Her reasons were purely humane, however he flattered himself. She was, quite genuinely, the kind of woman who never noticed anybody without the thought of whether she could help him or not, either in soul or body. In other words she was, in the thumb-worn phrase the town used about her, an "angel of mercy," and her inquiries told her that Jud was somebody in need of her ministering. For one thing he was an orphan, not much attended to, who seemed lonesome. For another, he did not go to church. For the first months after Jud came to town he had gone regularly to the Hallsboro Church of Christ, but he had done even that timidly and a bit secretly and now for a long time he had not crossed the threshold of any church. This alone was evidence that he needed help. Hannah went into action.

Two days after the episode in the store she sighted Jud on the square and got him penned up against the window of Harley's drugstore. It was late afternoon with not much in the way of distractions he could seize on, so all he could do was stand there nodding and answering the questions she put. They were personal questions but he could tell she already knew most of the answers. If she did not have it before, she ended up with a pretty good brief biography of Jud, lacking only the most important things about him. Of course she welcomed him to her church, the Baptist, explaining that they too stood squarely on the Gospel, and of course he tried to look interested, indicating serious thoughts about attending. For some reason, years afterwards, Jud remembered these moments with special vividness. He often thought that if he had just told her the truth then, straight out to her face, what was to happen would not have happened. But he did not, and she said, in a voice made much softer than before, "We all need Him so much."

Jud nodded, looking solemn, hoping this was the note on which she would leave him. But there was one more thing—a church picnic, on Sunday afternoon. "Please come. You'll meet some fine young people. And make some friends." She added, so that he noticed her unexpectedly grave blue eyes, "Then you won't have to be lonesome anymore."

Jud nodded a last time, mumbling an acceptance. Of course he had no intention to go, and did not, and when she trapped him on the street again a week later he made up a not too weak excuse concerning his aunt.

Hannah was not quite as tall as Jud's shoulder. Her figure, a little wide in the hips and slight-breasted, was neither bad nor quite good enough to catch a man's eye. The one thing striking about her was her tow hair, which was still as bright as a child's, but even this was a self-defeating point. It made people look expectantly at her face and then look away disappointed. Her face was round, with a blunt nose and that look of having maybe one tooth too many—a face not likely to get more than a glance. Her good feature was her eyes, though they were not the kind that people noticed right away. Face to face with her that first afternoon on the square Jud finally noticed them and was vaguely surprised. She was very bright and animated, with too many body movements and peppy smiles, and her eyes made a curious contrast. It was as if they did not participate along with the rest of her, or at least did not in the way expected. Their effect in the end was to obscure the brightness of her gestures.

But this at the time made only a sort of buried impres-

35

sion on Jud. Mainly he was thinking how much she resembled a dozen other holy Sunday school ladies he had known and how much he wanted to get away from her. As a matter of fact he was just then, at the time of that second meeting, on his way to doing something that had been hot in his mind for many days, ever since that moment of silent complicity he had shared with Lily. Already this same afternoon he had discussed it with 'old Luther'—as he always thought of Luther now. Jud did not get along with his aunt and, anyway, since his job at the store had now become full time he had to pay her for his room. Why not the room for rent in Lily's house? Nothing remained but the formality of looking at it before he rented it, and this was what he was on his way to doing when Hannah cornered him. No doubt her interference just then added something to his first feelings · toward her. A little later on, looking back, he was tickled to think that Hannah had been in a way the cause of his move.

The Nunn's house, a little distance up the hill, was one of the older ones, a dull frame house with two stories and a wide front porch. The room for rent was smaller than his former room and had only a hard narrow bed, a chest of drawers, one chair, and a faded picture of Jesus, which Jud took down. But these things were not what disappointed him. The room had an outside entrance. He had expected to use the front door and so, when passing in and out, to find her sometimes alone in the living room or maybe a parlor. The back entrance seemed to dash his hopes.

There was compensation, though, as he soon discovered. The bathroom he was to use was just outside the interior door of his room, at the back end of the hall, and opposite to this door was the kitchen. On his first evening, the first time he opened this door he saw her in there alone and all his feverish hopes were kindled again. He discovered something else. Lily's bedroom was the one upstairs directly above his room and he could hear her tread when she moved about. It was her private room, too. Luther's, Jud soon learned, was across the hall and at the front, and if he ever entered her room when Jud was below, it was without the heavy-footed limp that Jud would have recognized. He was almost sure Luther never did enter it—not while Jud lived there, and not afterwards either, for that matter.

The fact that her room was above Jud's was a consequential discovery in itself. It made not only a fool but a kind of slave out of him. It started the first night, and there was hardly a night for many weeks that did not find him lying there listening intently while she made ready for bed above his ceiling. The better to envision her he would turn off his light. Sometimes there would be a moon casting rays through the maples that grew up close around this corner of the house and he would see her before her window in these rays sliding out of her dress and then, one by one, the soft underthings that hid the last of her nakedness. He would imagine that she went to bed naked and he would watch her get in, lifting the silken sheet, stirring air that carried an odor like a sweet musky incense. Long afterwards, remembering these fantasies made him think of pulp magazines. He would be creeping in the dark up the staircase and along the hall back to her door, and she, rising onto one elbow, would murmur something and slowly lift the sheet to let him in. Or a fantasy would begin at an earlier point—an afternoon in the kitchen when Luther's back was turned, when she leaned close to whisper words of lustful invitation in his

37

ear. It's no great wonder that Jud grew more desperate every day.

In Lily's actual presence, especially in the house, Jud was anything but the bold young lover of his dreams. It did turn out that living there gave him opportunities. After about three days—it was Sunday morning—she saw him in the hall and invited him into the kitchen for coffee. He was all confusion. That first time he even spilled the coffee, and he was sure she could see into his mind, see the reason. Then he felt himself dried up in the scorn of her gaze. His tongue seemed stiff and he could give only fool answers to the simple questions she asked him. He got away as quickly as he could, but that night he was waiting in his room again when the hour came for her to go to bed.

The one that Sunday morning was only the first of their conversations. Whatever she might have suspected about him—and even that soon she probably did suspect the truth—she kept inviting him back. It happened fairly often. Luther was away much or most of the time, and even if Jud did not appear in the hall she was likely to knock at his door and ask him. His confusion grew less, and soon he could at least act in her presence like somebody with good sense. Before long he was fairly at ease, enough at ease to steal secret glances at her body and, for a moment here and there, allow his blood to run with a thought that sprang from some meaningless gesture or movement she made.

In fact all her gestures, at least as his *reason* interpreted them, were innocent of meaning. The only thing she ever did that he was able to construe as possibly by design was wear, on Sunday mornings when Luther was unlikely to appear, a sheer blue dressing robe—which meant that she had on nothing under it but a thin and maybe translucent nightgown. But when she assumed a posture that took his eye, maybe lounging at the table in a way that accented her breast, it was not, he believed, by intention. If he was often aroused by things she talked about, it was his fault. With some exceptions that all came only after a couple of months, her topics had no reference to sexy matters—not for a normal listener. But they did for Jud.

Lily's favorite topic, the one that was almost like an obsession with her, had not been anything unfamiliar to Jud. Here alone in the house with her, though, in this intimacy across the kitchen table when her words were meant only for his ears, it kindled brand-new fire in him. Of course his fear of her sharp eye kept his excitement suppressed for the time, hidden behind a look of gravity. Later, by himself, he would rerun everything in his mind, and the fire would blaze up unchecked. That was *her* voice saying those things. And those things had to apply not only to other people, church people, but also to him and also, just as plainly, to herself. Except her desires, what was there to hold him back?

One Sunday morning was special. Because she wore the robe, Sunday mornings were always special, but this one had an extra quality. It was an unusually moist cool summer and the vegetation in July remained as lush as May. Not far from the kitchen window and the table where they were sitting was a large hydrangea bush thick with soft leaves that looked almost yellow in the flush of sunshine. There was a mockingbird in the bush, singing. Sometimes it would pause a minute but it stayed right there in the bush for a full hour singing with an abandonment that the quiet house echoed like a cavern. This was the church hour. The Baptist church was not far away, and because the doors were open he and Lily

39

heard, in the mockingbird's pauses, strains of a hymn. Then the bird would drown it out again. Abandoned was the word, the feeling.

"Listen to that hymn," Lily said, her head cocked. "I know you know the name of it."

"It's 'Jesus, Lover of My Soul,'" Jud answered in a tone he knew she would approve.

"Yes. Them and their Jesus. And their 'souls,' If they'd shut up and get out of that church building they could hear some real hymns this morning. Like right there in that bush."

As if on call the mockingbird started again, changing songs from moment to moment—a thrush, a wren, a towhee. Below Lily's white throat the robe stood parted as far down as the lacey fringe of her nightdress.

"*There*'s something that knows what there is to sing about. You have to be a bird to get away with a hymn like that around here. Them and their souls. And their 'sins.' Listen to him."

The bird kept on, its song resonant in the still high-ceilinged kitchen.

"Have you got a lot of 'sins,' Jud?" She was looking at him, her eyes swimming with those little motes like yellow dust, and he could not keep the blood from rising to his face.

"I guess they'd say so," he mumbled.

She was still looking at him. "You're blushing. For your sins, like they taught you to."

Jud could not say anything. To cover his muteness he took a sip of coffee.

"My father used to say it was like they had Jesus and the devil crossed up. Everything that's good and natural they put on the devil. That's why this town is divided up between hypocrites and fools, trying to act like they can

40

see what's not there. Looking for a payoff in the sky. There's got to be a reward for cheating themselves out of having any life." She was looking at the bush with the mockingbird again.

Jud wondered vaguely about her father, but he was not in any state of mind to think about the matter. Lily's cheek was turned to him and he thought that the pockmarks there looked bitter but also that they looked sweet and he wanted, as he did every night in his mind, to taste them with his lips and tongue. Why not, one day? Why not soon? He felt his spine melting. In a pause of the bird's song strains of another hymn came through. She caught him with his helpless gaze on her face.

"There they go again. The 'spiritual' life."

Jud had lowered his gaze to his cup.

"Don't let them scare you with their lies, Jud. If you think you've got any sins, forget about them. *They* made them up."

Judd nodded, meaning to say that he *had* forgot his sins. And he had. In her presence he always forgot them, but this time it was completely. They were gone for good, he thought, dispelled and dried up in his heat like that many misty spooks from out of his childhood. Lily's gaze on his throbbing head and that mockingbird's song trilling in his ears told him the final story of what he had now, only now, become. Or so he thought, typically, on that brilliant Sunday morning.

In spite of Jud's opinion at the time, Lily was certainly not a beautiful woman. In fact most people did not consider her even pretty, though she had a slim well-shaped body and fine hair the color of gun metal that she wore just below her ears and, of course, those eyes that burned Jud alive. But it may have been precisely her eyes that, along with her flawed cheeks, damaged her looks in other

41

people's opinion. These made her look tough and too perceptive, lacking any of the milk of female gentleness that most people around Hallsboro liked to find in a woman. Of course there were some of Jud's persuasion too. Once upon a time Luther must have been one of them, though when Jud lived in his house Luther gave no indication of feeling anything but nervousness in her presence. As for Lily's private treatment of him, it would have given support to the viewpoint of those people who did not think her even remotely pretty.

Jud did not think about Luther much, and he was not even very curious as to how Luther and Lily had come to get married. By accident he finally learned the main facts—which, for that matter, were almost all anybody else knew. Lily was not a native of the town. She had moved there with only her father, Charles North, when she was about eleven. For some reason there was skepticism about North's story of where he came from and why, and even about whether that was his real name or not. Some people tried to check up on him, and failed. Justified or not, the skepticism laid a cloud over him that he never did anything to dissipate. As nearly penniless as he was he kept up his aloof, scornful manner, even when he had to eke out a living at an assortment of trivial jobs for which he obviously had no aptitude. He reminded people of a professor, maybe, turned handyman. Finally, all of a sudden, he turned housebuilder, but he was no better at this than he had been at the lesser things. He got badly in debt, to Luther among others, and this was where Lily came in.

She was nearly twenty and still had no prospects, and evidently she was unwilling to leave the town where her father continued to hang on. She had always been under the same cloud with him. Just like him, too, she had that scornful aloofness that kept everybody, even the ones who admired her looks, at arm's length. Curiously Luther was one who did admire her. At thirty-six he had no wife, had never had a girlfriend and must have been nursing secret longings that nobody could have devined. Apparently Lily seemed romantic to him, and also tameable. Unlike her other admirers Luther had leverage, that of her father's debt to him, and when he asked for her he got her. She came without any appearance of unwillingness. After all Luther owned a good hardware store and a good house and besides would allow her to remain close to her father. A year later her father died. Some people expected that this would be the end of her and Luther, too, but it did not turn out that way. She was the same. It was just as if she had dedicated herself to maintaining after her father's death the same cloud and scornful manner that she had shared with him in his lifetime. Out of that cloud, I am sure, came the stroke that left Luther what he was when Jud knew him about his fiftieth year—a lame, tired, and furtively pious old man.

Jud could recall Luther's being present in the house, all right, but not many occasions when he saw him face-to-face there. A couple of times, in quest of his dinner, Luther found Lily and Jud together in the kitchen. Things looked as innocent as always, but if Luther had seen cause for suspicion he would not have dared to risk her anger. And her mockery, which was always there like a lash close to her hand. Even with nothing said to vex her there was danger for him. The fact that he had just come from church might be enough, making her reach for the lash and say, "Didn't Jesus refresh your spirit? I wouldn't think you'd be hungry again already."

"Now Lily, please don't talk like that," he would plead, standing just inside the kitchen door, drooping, clad in his brown ill-fitting Sunday best. His eyes looked like hollows burnt out in his head. Across the table from Jud, the pink nail of one finger poised on the brim of a coffee cup, Lily sat looking steadily at Luther.

"The saints were all there, I suppose. Little Hannah was, I'm sure."

At times like this Jud could almost see why there were some who did not consider her beautiful. Watching Luther shuffle he even felt some condescending pity for him. But not much—not considering this abjectness and all the hypocrisies and little meannesses that Lily had pointed out to him in Luther's "Christian" character.

"Well, you'll just have to wait a little longer for your earthly food," she said finally, dismissing him, making it possible for Jud to drop his neutral mask. For Jud was always on her side, even at times when he thought her pointlessly cruel. After all, these were some more of the kinds of moments that fed and refreshed *his* spirit. Besides, they excited him. Every demonstration of Lily's contempt for Luther was like new hope granted to Jud's passion.

Twice, though secretly, lest *she* should hear, Luther invited Jud to church. Jud was respectful, but afterwards he told Lily, if for no other reason than to hear her laugh. There was special refreshment for him in her laugh. It was low in her throat and gusty and made him feel each time that the last of those old spooks of sin were finally driven out.

Of course they were not. They still assaulted him in the night, and in the day when he was caught off guard. He had to keep coming back to Lily, which only tightened his chains. Now he was not only a slave to his lust for her. She got to be like a sort of fountain that he had to keep coming back to for renewal, to wash his sins away. She was his love and also his salvation. For both reasons he was always listening for the sound of her footsteps in the house.

4

THAT WAS HOW JUD'S FOOLISH SUMMER WENT ON. HE
lived in the vague anticipation of one great day when *it*
would happen, when he would spend in a blaze of passion
on her body not only all his raging lust but also the last of
his stupid guilt. He hardly noticed or thought about other
people, and he talked to almost no one else but Lily. There
was the exception of Hannah Rice, the Angel of Mercy.
She was on his track and occasionally got him cornered
for a friendly or pious chat. But she was the one exception. Even Salter, who still stalked in his mind sometimes
at night, was not much more than a shadow now.

But this mood finally exhausted itself. Nothing had
changed. July passed and August was no different from
July. There were the same almost daily showers of rain
and the same fresh midday hours and luminous rich
foliage of shrubs and trees. The same mockingbird, too,
in that hydrangea bush. Lily was close by but no closer
than before, in reach but not in reach. She would never
be in reach. Final desperation came down on him in a
single night and after that, for days, fastened itself on
every thought he had. The sound of her movements
above his ceiling excited far more pain than desire now,
and he had to go out of the house when her bedtime
came. Even his mirror reflected the difference in him, a
wasting of the flesh under his keen cheekbones.

Lily herself put a kind of answer in his mind. It was far
from the one he wanted, but there did not seem to be any-

thing else possible. She had observed the difference in him and her conclusion, it seemed, was of a kind that probably would have occurred to a lot of other women also. How much more she might have observed, he was left uncertain: she gave him no hint. She did give him more than a hint as to *something* he could do about his problem.

"I don't see why you don't have a girlfriend, Jud. A good-looking young fellow like you."

Jud hid behind his cup of coffee.

"A boy like you needs one."

He managed to say, "I haven't seen any I wanted . . . that I could get."

"You could get any one you wanted."

"Not *any* one," he mumbled. Then his blush came and he wondered if—in fact he hoped—she saw the meaning of it. Of course she must have, but her expression was merely pleasant, interested. Her tawny eyes were always like this, the motes drifting in them.

"Yes you could. They're all available. Even the ones at Luther's church." The shade of a smile came on her lips. "Some of them have practically got a sign out."

"I wouldn't want them."

She looked at him skeptically for a moment, still with that shade of a smile. A shower of rain was pattering on the leaves of shrubbery out the kitchen window. She said quietly, "Not even in the way *I* mean?"

Jud felt his blush again and hot blood in his groin. Her hand, with painted nails, at rest on the oilcloth table top, was in reach if he was to lean just a little forward. A sudden heaviness came down on him. She had not meant, clearly had not meant, to include herself.

She was assessing his face. "I'll bet it's 'sin' that's your trouble."

He shook his head to say no, hoping the reason would

47

be plain in his face. But her manner denied that she saw anything. She changed the subject.

Whether she knew or not, it made no difference. She wanted him to have others, not herself, and all that day Jud had carried the weight of this thought with him everywhere. It made his desperation still worse. Well ahead of the hour for her to go to bed above his room he was out pacing the streets. There *were* other women. If he never could have Lily, then why not one of them?

That night he made himself think of women whom he saw every day and made himself dream about them. If they ended, all of them, by wearing Lily's face, that did not matter. They were there in fact with faces of their own, in real solid flesh that his lust could spend itself on. He made his decision. He remembered, from one of those still-vivid encounters with Charley Meagher, where an easy woman was to be found.

Still it was several days before he went through with it. He had made the discovery that fact was more different from dreams than he had realized. Confronted with the act in the shape of flesh, his brainless conscience rose up and screamed at him as if it had been born all over again. Sometimes Salter came back and stared him down, withering his soul with a glare like Judgment Day. There were even childish lapses when he felt he could not trust the ground not to open at his feet. And there was another thing. Could his blood be even so much as stirred by a body that was not Lily's?

His daily fire soon overcame his conscience, however. The woman's name was Dorcas Poole, called Goldie, no doubt because her hair was all gold except at the roots. She worked at a café on the edge of town and conducted her other business at her home in the country. That evening, from a booth in the stark little café, Jud looked her over carefully. She had some age and some fat, but she was not without the vestiges of a shape and prettiness. When he tried to imagine embracing her, however, it was just as if he had a yielding lifeless object in his arms.

But he went ahead. He had a plan. That would be Lily in his embrace. With lids shut tight he would look down into her passionate eyes and kiss her flawed warm cheeks and then her breasts. So he planned, and it was not until later when he stood waiting in back of the café that his confidence faltered. Standing in the half-light near her car he felt the cold sweat spring.

Then it was too late to run. There was a fence behind him, and Goldie, approaching, her fake gold hair lighted from the windows, could not have missed the shape of him standing there. His plan would never work. She looked at him over the hood of the car. "You waiting for something, honey boy?"

He was helpless.

"Cat got your tongue?"

He saw her starting to grin. He moved his mouth.

"Let me see, now," she said. "Is it something you can pay for?"

The movement of his lips did not mean anything but she took it for assent. "Come on get in the car, then. If you want a little 'ride,'" she said, clearly laughing at him.

She drove him to her house, a small one made of concrete block, on a gravel road at the edge of a pasture half a mile from the highway. A dog, the only other regular occupant of the place, barked, or bayed at them as they turned in. It looked, in the dark, to be an almost black hound and it followed at Jud's heels, still baying, all the way to the door. Goldie turned on a floorlamp, lighting up the grin on her face, lighting up also the cowering figure of Jud in the open doorway. "What's the matter, honey boy? Look like you just swallowed a toad frog or something."

But the thing got accomplished. It was in the cluttered ugly bedroom under a light she would not put out. Her spirit of gross frivolity chilled him even more, and for a long time he did not think he would be able to do it. Shutting his eyes brought nothing but offense to his nostrils. What he saw when he opened them was a shattering jolt to the pearl and alabaster image in his mind. Yet the event finally happened. It was quick, like goats, and afterwards he wished that the dark swoon hovering over his head would come all the way down.

"You ain't but just a moon calf of a boy," she said, not unkindly. "You're pretty to look at, though."

Jud felt emptiness first, and then shame. As he walked home the stars were like gimlet eyes that followed his sweating body through the night. There were other eyes. Somewhere in the dark behind him was Salter. Jud looked over his shoulder many times. Guilt as strong as terror assailed him in his bed and the prayers his lips directed upward fell back like crippled things.

This was how Jud entered his new phase, one even more disordered and foolish than the last. It was as though, after months of lying all but buried, Salter had been resurrected in his mind. For several days at least, the thought of him, a different and terrible Salter with eyes that were not like a cow's anymore, was never far away. At the store or in his room or walking down a street, it made no difference: he had the feeling of being watched. And each of those mornings he woke up with cloudy fragments of a memory that he had been judged and sentenced while he slept. There was no rest, no peace for his tormented soul. He avoided Lily as much as he could and

50

tried to shut her and Goldie both completely out of his mind. In Goldie's case especially it was no use. Thoughts of her, the images of that night, were like toads squatting in every place where his gaze stopped for a moment. Prayers came to his dry lips. Sometimes, like suddenly waking up, he would find himself already deep in an incoherent prayer.

But these days passed. The prayers stopped springing to his lips and the watching eyes stopped watching. Lily's eyes replaced them, and then came the day when he resumed his secret scrutiny of her body. And once or twice on that same day she gave him what he read as a knowing smile. The night of the day that followed, with Lily raging in his blood, he was back at Goldie's café. He would learn to keep his lids shut tight. And Goldie would see he was no moon calf of a boy. He thought he showed her, too, that night. But afterwards the same round of anguish had to be started all over again.

Jud did learn, as the weeks and months passed, to shut his eyes and see, in shapes of pearl and alabaster, Lily's body beneath him. He did not learn how to shut out the sight that always followed: Goldie lying there in folds and creases of stale fat, grinning up at him. But this by itself would have been at least bearable if, in the aftermath, his savage conscience had let him alone. Seen or remembered, the sight each time stiffened him like a lash. The inward cries started again, the eyes appeared. Toward the end of each cycle these throes of conscience would diminish and then die out, but he learned to know that they would return in force. No use to talk back, to argue. Even time and all the repetitions had little strength against these furious seizures.

But the worst of all Jud's moments was yet to come. It came on a Sunday early in December, just when a night of misty rain was closing down. He had been to Goldie's the night before and by now the cycle was far on its downward swing. The knock at his door was like an alarm. Afterwards he thought that he had known at once what the knock announced and that Lily's words through the door had merely confirmed it.

"Who?" Jud said.

"I don't know. He's out front, there."

Of course Lily had not meant the dim, rather shabby living room. Peering through the doorglass Jud could not see anyone on the porch, either, or out beyond, where the rainy twilight seemed to drift among banks of darkness. Yet the man was surely there. Not even the back door seemed to offer any escape from the house and Jud, drawing breath deep into his lungs, went onto the porch and down the steps like somebody certain of an ambush.

Salter was standing under the low branches of a maple tree. There were still leaves on the branches and the shade canceled most details of his figure.

"Needing your help, son. Sunk's down with the pneumony."

"Sunk is?" But the words, Jud thought, had not made a sound.

"Need you to go along with me. Up to Cadenhead."

Jud could not see Salter's eyes. Rain whispered among the branches. "I've got a job," he murmured. "I've got to work."

"This here's the Lord's work."

Brave words approached and faltered at the margin of Jud's mind. "They won't let me off," was all he could manage.

The rain whispered. "Try telling that to the Lord. What you think He'll say?"

Nothing. But Jud's lips could not utter it.

"Him that healed you when you was dying. By this hand."

Jud could see the hand. It was paler than the dark. He did not know where his words came from so suddenly. "I got well, myself." He felt a sensation as if he had stepped out beyond an edge. He was suspended there.

Finally Salter said, "Yourself, huh?" and afterwards let Jud hang there. Salter's veiled eyes were reading him. "You've fell away, ain't you? Fell for woman's flesh."

"I fell away from lies," Jud said, and felt as if these might be the last words he ever would speak.

"Is that the woman?" Salter's head nodded toward the house.

Jud made no answer.

"She's a witch."

"You don't even know her," Jud whispered.

A long time passed, with whispering rain. "It won't never be nothing but hell for you, boy. And no hiding place."

Then he was gone. It seemed as if there was nothing under Jud's feet.

His sleep that night, if he slept, was like one long harrowing nightmare. But at last day did come, slowly defining his windows, with a rainy dawn that was like a feeble reprieve. At the store his face reflected his night, for both Lily and Luther asked him if he was sick. "I'm all right now," he said. It was only Lily's scrutiny he tried to evade. And obviously she saw more than he meant for her to, or the conversation they were to have that night could not have been what it turned out to be.

About eight-thirty she knocked softly at his door. Though the room was cold Jud lay uncovered on his bed, under the lamp, while the wind like a hand rattled his windowpanes. Not one of his arguments but had fallen to

53

powder. His conscience was at the height of its rage and the knocking at his door, soft though it was, startled him like a thunderclap. At first he could not bring himself to open the door.

"I wondered if you were feeling all right," she said. The kitchen behind her was dark and she stood in the faint light from his door only, looking at Jud as she had been looking all day.

"I'm all right now." It seemed that the opened door admitted a draft that had not been in the room before. He began to wonder why she kept standing there. Then he saw. She meant to come in and he had no choice but to step back out of her way. At another time he might have grown weak with excitement. Not now.

She left the door open but she sat down on the chair as if she expected to stay a while. This left the bed for Jud, though he did not sit down yet or, at first, even look at her. Then he saw that she was scanning the room, not him.

"What happened to the picture?"

She meant that picture of Jesus. "It's over there in the corner," he murmured.

"What did you take it down for"

"I just didn't want it there."

"Because you've broken off relations," she said. "Sit down."

He sat, on the bed. There was only the bedlamp, with a metal shade, and her whole head was above the line of shadow. Her eyes did not look to be any color now.

"You haven't completely, though. Have you?"

He could feel the draft from the open door. That or the wind fingering the panes made the window shades stir and sometimes, along their margins, part a little from the windowframes. There were moments when this might

have admitted into the room glimpses from an eye outside.

"Have you"

"I don't know," Jud said, trying to dismiss the question.
His next words simply sprang out of him. "What if all that
stuff was true?"

Lily was still for a moment. "The Jesus stuff, you
mean?"

"Yeah." He was not even ashamed. His suffering soul
made him brave with her. "All that."

"Then I guess both of us would be on the way to hell,
don't you?" He did not look but he knew she was smiling.
All he was conscious of just then, aside from his suffering, was the thought that she must know somehow about
his doings with Goldie. Lily said, "Have you seen any evidence all that's true. There ought to be something besides
just preacher talk."

She waited for him to answer. The windowpanes were
rattling faintly and the shades kept parting from the
frames.

"Like multiplying loaves and fish or something. Or raising up dead people."

Jud was still watching the windowshades. "Some
people can heal the sick."

"Doctors can, sometimes."

"Besides doctors."

"Who?"

His mouth felt dry. "There's a man out in the country
that can. They say he can." Then, "I've seen him do it,"
Jud said.

"Oh, that stuff," Lily said, just lifting one of the hands
that had been lying still on her knees. "You're still such a
kid, Jud. Haven't you ever heard of psychology?"

"Yes," he murmured, vaguely stung.

"It's when people *think* you can heal them. It's in their minds. It happens all the time." She paused. "You're talking about that Salter, aren't you?"

He ought not to have been so taken aback, but it was as if he had heard his most secret thought spoken out loud. He only nodded yes.

"The one that got struck by God's lightning?"

"His hand's all burned."

"Yes. It's making his living for him, too. He's been selling it ever since."

Selling it? Jud listened to the wind outside. It seemed he could hear the whisper as it threaded the field of brush. "He doesn't make money. I've seen where he lives. A little banged-up house trailer. Out in a field. He hasn't got anything. No wife or anything. Not even any company but one old black man that can't talk."

"That's who was here last night? Salter?"

Jud had to nod. "I've been up there." And then, "I *know* him," he said as if expelling something out of his throat.

"I wonder if you do." Lily was faintly smiling again, very still on the chair, her eyes no color in the shadow. "He might not be like you think. He might even have a girl friend. Maybe more than one."

Jud lowered his face. "He wouldn't touch a woman, that way."

"How do you know?"

"I just know."

"Maybe he just *couldn't*. From what I saw of him, nobody would let him."

"He wouldn't, though. Even if they wanted him to."

Lily gave a little gusty laugh. She stood up, standing in shadow down to her waist. "I thought maybe you were growing up, Jud. I think you ought to get out of this town.

56

Maybe then you'd learn to see what hypocrites and liars they all are. Even your holy Salter, I'd bet. Goodnight."

She closed the door behind her, making the window shades swirl in the draft. He sat on the bed for a while, but soon he felt bold enough to get up and lift the shades for a look outside. Of course there was no one there, only the shifting spills of moonlight through the windy branches of the trees.

Lily had left him feeling better in every way. His room seemed less desolately still that night and the wind at the window was not the menace it had been. The same ridiculous cycle had already started on its upward swing once more and, as he had sense enough to know by then, would culminate a couple of nights later in Goldie's bed. There was something more this time, though. Something had been added. It was not even really conscious at first, like a seed back there in the dark of his mind.

But the days passed and the seed grew and one day, still another of those days when his tireless conscience had him on the rack, he saw it begin to define itself. After that he watched it like a secret from himself, examining and weighing it on the sly. There were times when the idea left him aghast. The menacing eyes looked in on it and the blood ran out of his heart. But the cycles, the days of lust that always plunged him back into the days of anguish, never were going to stop. Christmas went by and then came a night two days before New Year's Eve.

"What's the matter, honey boy?" Goldie said.

It was afterwards, in her bed, and the anguish was on him. The doubtful speech he had honed and put off until now was stuck in his mouth. Instead, surprising himself, he said, "I'm thinking about leaving these parts."

"You mean you're going to leave them here for me?" she said with a grin.

Jud was far from thinking this was funny. For once she had the bedsheet drawn decently across her big sagging breasts. "You know what I mean."

"What for? What you going to do for poon-tang without old Goldie around?"

He knew she was still grinning and he kept his gaze on the yellow pasteboard wall just beyond the foot of the bed. It seemed to him that this stark dun-yellow in an unshaded light was exactly the color of his anguish. "I want to get clean away from here." A surge of anger made him add, "Away from all these preachers and stuff."

"When has any preachers bothered you?"

"All that holy stuff. Got everybody tied up in it. It makes me sick."

"Well I don't see how come it bothering you. You don't have to listen to it," she said.

"It just makes me mad. All that crap they pour in you when you're too little to know any better . . . Like, doing it'll burn your soul up."

"Doing what?"

"What we just did."

"Phoo." Goldie had shifted her position against the headboard and Jud had the impression that the sheet had slipped down. He held his part securely across his loins and belly. She said, "I ain't seen a bit of difference in *my* soul. And I reckon I've screwed all the boys and half the men in this part the country. Some of them preachers, too."

"Which preachers?" Jud suddenly said.

"That's a p'fessional secret, honey boy. But I'll tell you one thing. They the hottest ones in the bunch."

Jud hesitated. His throat felt tight. "Virgil Salter's not

one of them." In the seconds that followed it seemed to Jud that he had shouted the words.

"He a preacher?"

"Yeah," Jud murmured.

"Well, I don't recollect him but he might have been one of them. Best part of them sneaks around and gets them a little."

"Not him," Jud said. "He wouldn't touch a woman. Hasn't even got a wife. He doesn't do *any*thing." Jud felt as if something blind suddenly had hold of him.

"He ain't a man, then," Goldie said. "If he's a man he does something. If his juice ain't dried up."

"He's a man, all right. And he doesn't. Anything."

"He just sneaks it someplace."

"I *know*," Jud said. He heard his own voice and lowered it to say, "And he's not dried up, either. When it comes on him, he prays. And the Lord cools him off. It's a miracle. That's what he says."

"Shoot," Goldie said. "Miracle. You know there ain't no such a miracle."

"He's the one says it."

"A gal get her hand in the right place, he'll see what a miracle is." She gave a little braying laugh.

Jud was silent.

"You needn't to doubt it, neither."

Jud was suddenly conscious that her breasts were exposed but this time he did not turn his eyes away. It was not the sight that held him. In a sort of rapt attention he watched his idea spell itself out across her nakedness. His body had got very still. He felt icy with cunning. He said, "You don't know him, though. I don't think even a movie actress could get to him." He looked away from Goldie. "Much less anybody else."

"I don't know about no movie actress," Goldie said with

a little heat, "but I know about men. And preachers is the easiest ones."

"Not him, though." Jud had to compose himself. An uprush of excitement had very nearly made his voice quaver. "The only chance would be a real young pretty girl," he said, looking thoughtful. "*She* might, maybe."

Goldie was looking at him with narrowed blue eyes. "I reckon you think *I* couldn't."

Avoiding her glare, admiring his new-found cunning, Jud picked his words like rare coins out of a heap. "I didn't say you weren't pretty. I just said I bet it'd take a real young girl."

She continued to glare at him. He was almost trembling now.

"Where'd you say he lives at?"

"Out in the sticks. In a house trailer by himself."

"*All* by his self?"

"Yes. Nobody even close around. Nobody comes but just a few people that think he can heal them."

Goldie continued to stare at him for a moment longer.

"How much you want to bet on it, honey boy?"

It was right there, that night in bed with Goldie, that Jud discovered the gift he had for cunning.

5

ON SUNDAY AFTERNOON, NEW YEAR'S EVE, JUD GOT really trapped by the Angel of Mercy. It was the last thing he wanted at any time, but especially just then. Tonight was the night, it was all set with Goldie, and ever since he had waked up that morning his heart had been in his throat. At times he was astonished, then appalled, feeling the blood drain out of his chest. There was no rest for him and this was why he was out walking on a cold day like that, with bitter wind and low scudding gray clouds that kept the earth darkened most of the time.

He had not even been conscious of passing by the Baptist church. But there was Hannah, and she called to him as familiarly and insistently as if they had long been brother and sister in Christian fellowship. She wanted his help because she had the back of her car full of folding chairs. He supposed she also felt that getting him into the church building could be a sort of religious icebreaker.

He helped her carry the chairs, down some steps under the auditorium to a big green-painted concrete-block room where they held Sunday school classes and church parties. They were going to have a party that night, a New Year's Eve party. He also had to help her put the chairs at tables that were set out, while she chattered and skipped around the room on sturdy legs encased in black knee-socks. It looked like a big evening, as he told himself, but he was not in a mood that made it easy to keep up his irony. He could not even summon the force, in the corner kitchen beside the silver urn, among all the pies and cakes, to refuse to sit down for a cup of tea—and this in spite of his sarcastic reflection that coffee of course was too strong for saints. So maybe Hannah's instinct about getting him inside the church building was not completely mistaken. But he thought it was more Hannah herself that, in the circumstances, had the effect on him.

"Why don't you come?" she said, pouring his tea from a pot heavy enough to define the muscles in her round white arm. "I know you'd have fun."

Jud answered, more gruffly than he meant to, that he already had some plans, and this no doubt was what made her chatter slow down and then stop entirely. She sat across from him blowing on her tea in a manner that puffed out her cheeks. It was on purpose, a little comic gesture to fill the interlude of silence. For a minute there was silence, except for the muffled sound of wind from the windows high up in the wall. Then it was as if the sound of the wind had seized her attention also. Jud was made aware of how her eyes looked, dusky, like somebody else's eyes looking at him out of her bright tow-covered head.

"Like the wind's trying to blow the old year away," she finally said. "All the bad things."

Jud mumbled, trying to look impressed with the idea. Why not the good things? But underneath this he was thinking how the wind would be sounding among the brush in the big ridgetop field.

"It's such a lonesome sound, though. I don't much like to listen to it. Do you?"

He shook his head no.

"It makes you think about things passing on. Old lonesome things dying. All worn out. Us too, someday." She looked into her cup, gravely listening. "I guess that's one reason we have to have love in the world, or we couldn't stand thinking about that." She looked up at him and he nodded again. His restlessness was growing. He could barely drink the tea.

Hannah's face brightened a little. "But then you think how everything comes back and grows all over again, all brand new. It's a good time to think about it, New Year's Eve is." She gave him a smile, very white because of all the teeth. "Why don't you try to come tonight. You'd be so welcome." She leaned toward him. "Do. It starts about eight-thirty, right after evening service."

Eight-thirty. He looked up at the windows. Already they were darkening. He felt he could not stand her another second and he had to put down an impulse to bolt out of his chair. He tried to make a joke to himself, and failed. All he made was a mouth, intended as a smile to express his gratitude. It was the mouth he made again two minutes later when he did stand up and, pursued every step by her bright chatter, worked his way to the outside door. "Happy New Year," she said, and then he was outside, feeling in the bitter wind the shape of his still-distorted mouth.

Then it was funny and he almost laughed outloud. He walked in the wind, shivering, and after dark bought some supper that he did not taste. An hour later he set out for Goldie's house.

Goldie was getting more and more restless. Jud had found her at the house still buttoning up after a recent client, with a couple of drinks under her belt, in the best of moods. She had given him her horse laugh and wanted to raise the bet. She had even paused in front of the mirror by the door to give her hair a few ironic touches.

But now their long drive had changed Goldie's mood. Since the Bethel Community where the gravel road left the highway they had passed only one house with lights burning and another in darkness and the flat treeless brush-grown fields stretched away to the distant shoulders of the ridge. The extent of the fields was visible tonight. The overcast had a moon somewhere above it that shed a filtered doubtful light on things. Goldie, driving the car, kept glancing around. "I plumb forgot all about it being Sunday," she said.

"That didn't matter a while ago," Jud said. But he thought of the church and Hannah and then this fact was added to the oppression around his heart. The oppression made him think of bad dreams he had had.

"It don't," Goldie said. "But I never knowed he lived out in any such a nothing place as this."

Clearly she was frightened now. Jud could feel it in his own body, a sort of tremulousness all the way through. Goldie drove more slowly as they went on, but Jud was not impatient.

"It ain't nothing out here," Goldie said.

"It's not much farther."

"It better not be."

But it was still more than a mile, Jud figured. She would balk. In spite of their bet and her stupid vanity she would turn back. What was fifty dollars, either way? It was nothing and she would turn back. The sense of reprieve was like sudden sleep falling on his soul.

Then he saw something, Zion Church, a wan ghost of a building on bare ground back from the road. His pulse took up and the rigor came back to his spine. "Here's the turn-off," he quickly said. "Right there."

They crept into the turn and the headlights swept over an empty field, defined an empty road. "I still don't see nothing," Goldie said. "I don't like it out here."

"It's just a little way down this road." Jud's heart was pounding.

"I don't like it."

"He wouldn't hurt a flea," Jud said, controlling his voice. With an effort he went into his act again. "You wanted to bet and I'm betting you. Money's right here," he said, patting his pocket. He summoned up all his cunning. "I'm even giving you advice, to boot. To have even a chance you got to get in that trailer with him. Tell him you want him to heal you, your belly keeps—"

"I heard you before," she snapped.

"It won't do any good, though."

After a moment she said, with a trace of her old confidence, "You just have that money ready." And the car went on, bumping over the washboard surface.

Jud saw a light. "He's still up," he breathed. "Go on."

There were two squares of yellow light. They could see the tree against the sky. "Stop here," Jud said.

"What for?" But she stopped the car.

"I'll wait out here on the road. You turn in right up there."

"How come you can't stay in the car?"

"I better stay out here." He got out quickly and leaning into the open door said, "He wouldn't hurt a flea." Forcing his tone he added, "He'll just tell you to leave."

He shut the door softly. The car did not move for a few seconds and he could see the dim figure of Goldie sitting motionless at the wheel. The car moved on.

A little way and she turned into the gap through the brush.. In the headlights the trailer, with shed and tree, sprang suddenly out of the dark, like a blow that made Jud's breath stop. For maybe another minute, as stark as a dream, the scene stood sketched against the sky. It vanished. Jud saw the yellow windows again and, now, the trailer door standing open. Next, the lighted doorway lost its shape, darkened, because a figure was blocking it. It stayed that way, no change—and however Jud strained he could not hear any sound. Not until the wind moved, riffling the brush. The door had vanished.

For a long time Jud stood watching, trembling with the cold. It seemed too long, finally, and step by step he moved up to the gap. The yellow windows never winked. The wind came back. He did not think he could endure the strokes of his heart much longer.

The wheel tracks made clean quiet pathways through the dense brush. But his first steps had been as cautious as if the earth might crack beneath them and even afterwards he moved at a rate not much faster than shadows drift. What had started him moving were sounds he thought he had heard. The sounds also had started in his throat a tingling as if laughter was about to come, but this had passed off now. Except for the still windows he was no longer conscious of anything.

A minute later he was conscious of something. He scanned the clearing. He even glanced up at the overcast, as if anything could be hidden behind it. The shack, Sunk's shack, was a blot against the muted horizon. In the lightless door or window, black Sunk could not be seen. No more could Jud, from there, however, and yet he took a backward step and followed it with another. The second step coincided with a distinct noise.

The noise came from the trailer. It came again, a thud, as if a fist had struck a wall, and then a voice, a cry. A violent shadow crossed one window and the cry, whether hers or Salter's, was repeated. Then silence again. The still yellow windows glowed and the wind came threading the brush.

Jud had squatted down on his haunches. His teeth were chattering and the muscles of his thighs, strained in this posture, had long since begun to burn. He did not move, though. When the wind was still the only sounds occurred inside his head. It was like a chamber in which he could hear echoes of that thud and those cries. But at last he got painfully to his feet and, still half crouching, looked out over the tangled crest of the brush.

The trailer door was open. A figure, Salter's, stood silhouetted there, sketched in pale silvery lines against the light behind him. Jud saw, with a start, that he was naked. Some time passed but Salter never stirred. The illusion that he did stir was only the guttering of the lamp when gusts of air came in through the door around him.

Finally Salter moved. He reached and shut the door. The light in the windows went out and the dark stood up like a question in front of Jud's eyes.

At last the stillness reassured him. They were bedded down, and this was success, was it not? His little rush of exultation brought him up from his crouch. After another minute he turned and started walking, quietly for the first few steps, then faster.

On the pale empty road Jud still walked fast, holding tight to his mood of exultation. Though echoes of those cries still persisted in his head, they were soon muffled by the rhythm of his footsteps. He looked behind him only once or twice. At the highway, where lights still burned in a house or two and cars still passed, he felt more than ever a lifting of his spirit. He soon got a ride. In the warmth of the car, watching the harmless fields go by, it seemed as if his chest was full of his heart.

This mood did not last long, however, The sleep he was expecting and that his body was aching for would not come near his bed. Mostly it was those cries that kept him awake and in the first gray dawn he was up and on his way to Goldie's house. He was still there when work time came, pacing around her little yard, while the almost black hound lay watching his every move. Around noon he finally left, walking in the rain.

Jud learned nothing that day. He stood around the square for a long time in the rain, then went to his room and lay on the bed for a couple of hours trying to sleep. Before dusk he was back at Goldie's. From there he went to the café where she worked and spent another hour over cups of coffee. He thought of going back out to the ridge, but he did nothing. Then there was the night to be got through. Toward morning he did fall into a leaden sleep.

The next morning he found out. He heard the rumor first in the store and soon found an excuse to go out onto the square. In spite of the drizzle that kept on falling, there was a crowd on the lawn around the courthouse steps, buzzing, getting larger. Prowling around the fringes listening in he got the story pieced together. And that was not all.

It was at the hour and the cupola clock had just finished striking eleven times. A boy standing on another boy's shoulders against the courthouse wall, with his hands and chin on the window ledge, suddenly jumped down. The crowd stirred. Gooch, the sheriff, in a black hat, stood at the top of the courthouse steps. He gestured

68

at the crowd, waving them back. Behind him in the dim vestibule was a shadow, a shadow with bowed head. Jud quickly turned and retreated. As he crossed the street he saw, down in front of the jail, Goldie's old car parked.

Somehow he made it through the rest of that day at work. He avoided Lily as much as he could and planned his departure for the instant of quitting time. But Lily headed him off on purpose. How she had got rid of Luther Jud did not know, but after the door was locked she had Jud bring some cans of paint out of the warehouse and put them on shelves. She watched him from the cash register. Putting up the cans he made the only sounds in the quiet store.

"You heard the news, I know."

He was standing sideways to her. He nodded and mumbled yes and went on putting the cans up.

"He turned out to be quite a 'healer,' didn't he?"

Jud placed a can carefully on the shelf.

"I guess I really wasn't such a good prophet, though, after all. I never would have thought about anybody killing a woman because he had used her like that. Nobody would have."

Jud tried and failed to say, and then did say, "He didn't mean to."

"Try telling her that."

The can Jud had reached for seemed to heavy to lift. All that night and the next night also Salter must have sat there with her body. "He turned himself in."

"That's not the way I heard it. I heard they caught him out around Bailey's Ford. He was trying to get away . . . There's a Man of God for you." Lily made the cash register ring. "It's plain good riddance, though, for his part. They'll put him where he can't do any more harm. There's no telling how many people he poisoned with his crazy lies." She waited a few seconds. "You're one of them, aren't you?"

Jud could not answer.

"It's the truth, isn't it? He's most of what's the matter with you. Him and his lies."

"I don't know," Jud mumbled.

"You do know. You're one of his victims. But now it's all come back on him. It's exactly the right thing to say he did it to himself."

Jud had finished putting up the paint but his hands still lay on the shelf..

"Can't you see that?"

He looked at it. He knew what she meant to tell him. "There's not just him."

There was a click from the cash register. "That is too bad. But *no*body could have foreseen that . . . At least she went out in a good cause. I only wish she could have got rid of the whole bunch of them while she was at it. Then maybe people could half-way live, around this town." Jud could feel her looking directly at him, her eyes speaking. "But nobody's to blame but him, for that."

After a little Jud took his hands off the shelf.

"I'd forget all about it. Don't you have any friends, from school?"

Jud shook his head.

"Go out and find some." She shut the drawer of the cash register. "Remember it's a brand new year. You haven't even celebrated it yet."

Part TWO

6

LILY'S WORDS THAT EVENING AT THE STORE HAD
been a comfort to Jud. Later on they seemed to be more
than that. Over and over he ran them through his mind
and every repetition made them brighter. At last they
seemed to reach into the darkest corners of his soul,
brightening everything, and he walked through town
that night like somebody in a place unfamiliar to him, a
new place. But he was the one who was new. Passing
familiar faces on the lighted square he imagined that
they did not recognize him and, every time, the thought
increased his feeling of exultation.

In his room he listened to Lily's movements overhead.
He kissed her a hundred times, a hundred different
places on her body, and pressed himself like a flame
against her nakedness. The time would come. That was
how he went to sleep, dissolving into his dreams. Later
that night the wind rose, rattling his windows, and the
room got bitter cold. He waked up groping for his covers.
He did not sleep anymore, and he lay watching while first
dawn smeared the panes with rainy light.

Lily's words were gone. Even when he did hear them
they sounded a long way off, muffled by the clamoring of
his thoughts. The wind at his windows had brought it,
and what he felt, lying there in early morning light, was
fear. Sounds from the wakening house did not dispel it.
Neither did the sun when, for a few minutes, it came out

glistening on the bare silvery limbs of the trees. As he put on his clothes his eyes kept glancing toward the windows. Facing the outside door of his room he had to gather breath before he could put his foolish hand to the doorknob.

At Rogan's café he listened in on some conversations, but nothing to the point was said. It was the same on the square when he paused not far from a little cluster of men talking in front of the shoe store. But he soon got a shock.

The jail stood at the low northeast corner of the square. It was a stone building with two stories and upstairs were two barred windows that looked out almost on a level with where he was standing. The distance, the whole width of the square, was considerable, and he could not really see a head framed in the window to the right. But he thought he did. The gaze he imagined he felt had force enough to set him back on his heels, and at first he could not move out of his tracks. Then he did, hurrying to get the courthouse between him and the window. To reach the store he had to circle and approach from the west side of the square.

That was the route he followed that morning and it was the route he followed every morning for weeks afterwards. This made a kind of sense. Out of sight was out of mind and he reasoned that never to cross Salter's mind, never to start Salter thinking about him, was much the safer thing. Salter's silence had to mean that he did not know. And Goldie was dead. So Jud stuck to his little detour.

This did not help much, though. In those weeks nothing really helped for long. A single moment would rout his assurance and he would feel again as he had felt in his room that first bleak morning. Salter did know. Goldie had cried it out. Or Sunk, without words, had told him.

Those were Sunk's eyes he had felt that night while the wind sifted the brush and Jud stood watching the yellow glow in the trailer windows. After that had come the thud and her outcries, or Salter's. Stillness, the wind again. Salter's hand was on her throat, the burnt hand, tightening like a claw, and her mouth stretched open as if in a silent scream. Then she was dead. She lay on the floor with open mouth, her bloated tongue protruding—all night on the floor and all next day and still another night.

It was not a vision that Jud could keep out of his head for long at a time. And always with it came the thought, like one of God's own certainties, that Salter knew the truth about him. He was up there nursing his knowledge, and waiting—for whatever it was he waited for. Was it only to name Jud publicly? Jud would have been comforted to believe that this was all.

The gossip in town was another thing that kept him always afraid. Somebody's guess (was it a guess?) had come not far from the truth, and this, Jud gathered, was the version accepted everywhere. He heard it in the drugstore once, and more than once on the streets. "She never would of done that on her own. Some joker back of it." Heads nodded, very solemn, and one man spat on the walk. "Worse'n just a joker, though. Meanest trick I ever seen. That's the one ought to go down to the pen for it." They were that close. It seemed as if one little guess more would put Jud's name on their lips.

He heard it again at the store. Puttering over some tools at a near counter he listened while Luther threshed it fine with an old fat man named Dexter. At first Jud thought, and so did Luther, that he was the only one listening to them. This was wrong. Lily was not far away, standing in the door of the little glass-framed office. Jud noticed her finally and once or twice he noticed her looking at him.

75

She meant for him to see this. She certainly meant for him to witness what occurred as soon as Mr. Dexter left the store.

Luther was taken off-guard. When he turned around and saw her, standing out by the main counter now, there was not any way for Jud to miss the sad eloquent grimace that passed across his face. He even bowed his head. Lily, gazing at her fingernails, let a moment go by. "Then who did kill her? If it wasn't Salter?"

"Come on, Lily, let's not—"

"Who? Who was it?"

Luther shook his head. "We've already been over all that, Lily. Let's—"

"But they ought to let Salter go if he didn't do it."

Luther saw Jud and gave him a haggard look—of appeal, Jud thought. But Jud looked away, toward Lily. She stood with her hands flat on the counter.

"We wasn't saying that," Luther said.

"You were saying somebody else *really* did it. Some *bad* person."

Luther was silent. It was clear how Lily's eyes burned him.

"What if somebody did put her up to it? *If* they did. How were they supposed to know he's a wild animal? He's a 'preacher,' isn't he?"

Luther still said nothing.

"A Man of God," Lily said. "So naturally it couldn't be his fault." She paused, gathering indignation. "Where he belongs is in the pen for the rest of his life, he's dangerous . . . But he's a 'holy' man, so they'll just give him a year or two. Then he can come back and 'heal' somebody else."

"Now Lily."

"It's just a tale anyway that somebody put that woman up to it. If they did, though, I hope they've got sense enough not to let all this sniveling bother them. At least they've done us a favor for a year or two," she said and turned abruptly and went back into the office.

This little scene, Jud was sure, had been aimed his way, but it was only the most dramatic of several occasions when she tried to comfort him. Without ever letting the matter come quite out in the open between them she would say, "You think about things too much. Dumb things." Or again, observing him at his grimmest, she would mock his expression with her own and say, "Keep looking the way you're looking and the Angel of Mercy's bound to get after you." Lily asked him a couple of times about friends. Why didn't he look for some? "There's bound to be somebody alive around this town."

But Jud did not look—at least not yet—and he was not comforted. In fact he was not even properly grateful to her, and his response, more and more, was to try and discern what really lay behind Lily's consolations. There was no solid reason for Jud's new feeling about her: the change, starting only a few days after that disastrous night, was in *him*. Not that it drove out his passion for her. Underneath his anxiety and confusion, that survived intact. The difference was that somehow he did not trust her the way he had before. At the worst of times it got into his head that she was not a friend at all, that her friendly gestures were false and meant to entrap him. Entrap him how, he could not imagine, for nothing he thought of made sense. That was his notion, though, like a warning tug at his mind. He began to avoid her when he could. He went less and less often into the kitchen for talks and at work he no longer looked for chances to be alone with her. Now he thought when he found her watching him that her expression was not as it used to be, that her scrutiny was more like that of a spy than a curious friend.

77

A soberer view probably would have explained it as merely her response to the change in him, but he was not in a mood to look soberly at much of anything. So at last he began to be afraid of Lily, too.

This was how it became for him in the middle of the winter. It was a terrible winter. Snow and sleet and rain kept turning into each other and a bitter ragged north wind blew without ever seeming to stop. He learned to hate the wind. It shook his windows and hummed in the bare trees and stiffened the flesh of his lips and nostrils before he could walk a short block from the house. It made the streets desolate, as though it had blown the people away, and sometimes when he came onto the square he imagined that he was the only person left. Except one: Salter watching from his window, biding his time.

He tried not to be in his room when Lily's bedtime came. Nights when he was too early he stopped his ears against the sounds from overhead and tried to block out even the thought of her. He could nearly manage this now. But he could not manage his other thoughts, which came whether he slept or not, as if the recurrent gusts of wind were bringing them back to his mind. They came as dreams sometimes, too vivid for thoughts, and one night he waked up thinking that Goldie lay there dead on the floor beside him. He had to turn on the light, finally. But in the dark again he kept seeing her dead face, that he had never seen. He wondered where she was buried. She had lain three days in the funeral home waiting for some-body. It was an old faceless man from out of the hills.

Jud would leave this town, this whole country. But this thought, repeated a hundred times, always reached the same stumbling conclusion. It was still too soon, was it not? Wouldn't it point the finger at him? Then he would think of himself on the run, pursued, hiding somewhere. But who the pursuer might have been remained always ambiguous to him.

The thought had its consequence, however. It was the reason that sometimes in an idle hour he wandered down to the bus station a block from the square and, browsing among the abandoned magazines, watched the buses pull in and then depart. This was where Hannah caught him again, after all these weeks. But caught is not the right word. He saw her before she saw him, through the door glass, and he could have retreated in time. It was a blind impulse, one he regretted a few minutes later. He did not regret it just then, though, when she looked up from where she was sitting and smiled at him.

It was after nightfall and the ticket agent was gone and they were by themselves in the small waiting room. She was there to wait for a bus, but what was he to say about his presence? He could think of nothing but the truth, or part of it. "I like to come here sometimes and read the magazines."

This made a difference in the way Hannah looked at him. He saw her eyes go sad and the set of her lips change. She answered with just a nod, one that meant "I see," and went on looking thoughtful. It was a moment when he was glad she had come in. He could not think what he was reminded of, but it had to do with the way the gas stove glowed and muttered in the room and with the baffled sound of the wind outside. It had to do with Hannah, also. She wore a dark hat that covered all but a margin of her pale hair, and for just this little time she was somebody out of his past, his childhood. Somehow he expected words that would fall like grace on his soul.

Her words, when they came again, did no such thing. Even so, his mood hung on for a little while and, seated

across from her, he listened with a kind of dim contentment to the story about the aunt she was going to visit.
The stove muttered and he thought how futile the wind
sounded. Her face had brightened. He did not know what
she was smiling at. "You've disappointed me every Sunday," she said. "I've kept on hoping you'd come, though."

All of a sudden he wondered what he was doing here,
apologizing to her, digging for excuses, trapped. His
temper flared and an impudent answer came to mind.
Then he realized how she was looking at him. She was
not only still, sitting there with her small hands folded in
her lap. She was looking at him as if she was saddened by
what she had read in his mind. But what she said was,
"Have you ever gone to visit Mr. Salter"

There was a space when he did not hear anything, not
even the stove. Then he heard the wind, that did not
sound futile now. Ever so faintly the door rattled and cold
drafts touched his ankles. "Why should I?" he mumbled.
Her feet, in galoshes, stood side by side on the mottled
concrete floor.

"Wasn't he an old friend of yours? I heard that."

Heard that? Where? He said, "That was a long time
ago. A *long* time."

This made her quiet again. He could feel the pulse in
his neck.

"Then you weren't still friends anymore . . . when *that*
happened?"

Because he was not sure of his voice Jud shook his
head. This was not enough. He drew a breath and said, "I
haven't seen him in I don't know when. A year, maybe."
Then, "Maybe I saw him once." He was afraid not to add
this. He was also afraid that his face had lost its color.

"I was just wondering," Hannah said.

Wondering what? The thought was like a shout inside his head. But *how* could she suspect him?

"I was just wondering if that hadn't, you know, shocked you? Him doing that, I mean. Because you had thought so much of him. That he was such a Christian."

In his confusion Jud could not seem to get her meaning straight. But she must have misread what his face showed. She must have thought it expressed the very picture of what he had suffered, was still suffering, because her own expression was one of compassion.

"You shouldn't let it, you know," she went on. "We're all so feeble . . . even the best of us. And things happen to us. We have to forgive each other."

He was trying to follow, knowing he still wore the same strained face. She had leaned a little toward him.

"So please forgive him, if you haven't. Think how unhappy he is. My father went to see him. He told me about him. He said he thought maybe the poor man was going to go out of his mind thinking about it."

Jud's thoughts were clearing up and only the shadow of his fear was left.

"I know God's forgiven him. So we should too. It ought not to even be hard when you think about what happened. That woman coming to tempt him. It's almost harder to forgive her, I think. And the person that put her up to it."

Jud must have reacted in some way, moved or changed expression. She took it for a question, because she said, "It looks like there was somebody, you know. The old Negro saw him. Except Mr. Salter thinks it was the devil." Then, looking directly at Jud, "It was *like* the devil—doing that."

Jud realized afterwards that there was nothing whatever personal in the look she had given him. It was just a widening of her eyes, expressing what she felt. But in that moment he read it differently and he could not have felt more helpless if he had been impaled against his chair. It is possible that only the bus, with a sudden roar and wheezing of brakes outside the waiting room, saved him from betraying himself. Except for that, even Hannah must have noticed that something had happened to him. She did not notice. She jumped nervously onto her feet and seizing her bag from the next chair barely paused to flash him a goodbye smile.

Jud was sure that this was the end of what Hannah knew—just what others knew and nothing more. At least he left the station sure of this, walking in the bitter wind, hearing the courthouse clock toll once as he stepped onto the square. There was light enough to see, on the lawn, the bare trees heave in the long blasts and to see, beyond the courthouse, the almost featureless upper wall of the jail. Then he was not so sure. He tried to call back every word she had said, and he pictured again the look she had directed at him. And *his* face—what had it said? Had Hannah's bustling show of haste been the screen for something? He went on to his room unsure and he felt not much surer the next day, or for many days. In imagination he envisioned, through the mask he had thought was Hannah, another Hannah who held him fixed in a shrewd suspicious gaze.

In this mood, just to defy it, Jud almost went to church a few days later. The impulse came suddenly, like all his others at that time. He quickly dressed in what he had for Sunday clothes and shutting his outside door as quietly as he could behind him headed down the block toward the Baptist Church. He never got all the way there. From the sidewalk across the street he saw a woman standing in the shaded porch at the top of the church steps. A dark hat and coat concealed her identify, but it could have been Hannah: she was greeting some people. She might have been still there to greet Jud if he had gone on, and he imagined her eyes turned shrewd, seeing straight through the lie that his presence spoke. Jud changed his mind. He lingered another minute or two watching, while the people kept coming, climbing the steps, letting the sound of the organ flow out when they pushed the big door open.

In spite of his cautious exit Lily had seen him leave the house and seen how he was dressed. He discovered this later, about midafternoon when he came back. He did not hear anything and he had no way of knowing she was in the kitchen. If he had, his new habit of avoiding her would have made him postpone his trip out to the bathroom. Once he had opened the door it was too late to retreat. She sat at the table facing him, her head and upper torso sharply outlined against the rain-gray light of the kitchen window. Though her face was shadowed she clearly was looking straight at him. Without moving, without seeming to move even her lips, she said, "How was church?"

"I don't know," he said. "I wasn't there."

Her head was not much more than a flat silhouette against the window light. She did not believe him. He said, "Ask Luther."

"You looked like that's where you were going."

He just shook his head. He had found he was afraid to explain.

"I thought maybe you were having a change of heart."

"No," he answered. The house was silent. He could not

even hear the rain or wind outside. Something about her moved, or stirred a little, and he realized that there was a smile on her mouth.

"The idler's mind is the Angel's workshop," she said. "You need something to fill up your weekends. And nights."

Jud waited uncertainly.

"I've been trying to get you to look around. There has to be *some* life even in this place. You're not the only 'outlaw,' I'll bet," she said and rose from the table and moved out of his sight beyond the doorway.

Her word was *outlaw*. Long afterwards Jud could still recall with the greatest vividness how that word had lodged itself in his mind. Even at first, though he could not figure why, it seemed to be a matter of crucial importance. Not too much later he did understand why. The word seemed to hold out to him a new and bolder image of himself. The law was not *his*, the word said to him. It was *theirs* and he was *out* of it. Or out if he could evade it. The evasion was all. It was as if his eyes stood open wider than before and he began to see, within that same hour, how much of his fear derived from guilt instead of any actual threat. What threat, if by this time the truth was still not known? And if it came to be known? What in fact could they do to him? . . . There was Salter. But what about him? In jail, with a sure prison term ahead, why was he a threat? Seen in this new light these thoughts had almost the character of a revelation for Jud.

The new light in its fullness did not fall on Jud all at once, all on that Sunday afternoon. But it started then and it led straightway to what was like a next step in the process. He was surprised, and more than surprised, at the swiftness with which he had reached this second step, as if a fate had brought him to it.

Happening as it did, that very Sunday, it certainly was a coincidence. At suppertime in Rogan's Café he came on Charlie Meagher face to face. Indeed, because he was not paying any attention he sat down at a table, his usual table in a remote corner, opposite Meagher. He lifted his eyes and there Meagher was. The fact alone of Meagher's being there was not very curious, maybe, though Jud had not seen or even heard of him for many months. What did strike Jud, and that right away, was Meagher's manner. He not only greeted Jud with a certain cordiality. He talked to him as if Jud was somebody quite different from the Jud he had known at school; or rather, maybe, as if *that* Jud had not in fact existed. The last, Jud believed, was the accurate description. The two boys, Meagher's manner insisted, had been not only close buddies but conspirators together, mocking at the others. Jud finally went along with this. The more they talked, the more he saw as ridiculous his old dread and hatred of Meagher. The green eyes were merely green, with a little tremor when they looked straight at something, and Jud hardly noticed the wire-like tendons in the neck. He thought he understood something now. It was simply that Meagher had spotted him as another lonely one, and all his harassment had been no more than a blundering effort to get across to Jud.

Later, however, Jud somewhat amended his impression of this meeting. He thought that actually it was his own manner that had made the difference. What Meagher saw, almost from the first glance, was what Jud wanted him to see—that this was not the same Jud Rivers, that here was somebody new walking around in Jud's familiar carcass. Lily's word was like magic working in him, in his eyes that had the coolness to weigh and measure Meagher now and in his voice that had acquired a perceptible note of disdain. It was all newborn, all right, but it was enough for Meagher. He stayed until Jud finished eating and walked out of the café behind him. Then, in the gusting half-dark away from the café window, he touched Jud's arm.

"You want to do something?" His voice was too quiet not to have meaning.

"What?" Jud said.

Because of the light he could only imagine the tremor in Meagher's gaze. Out here, standing up, Meagher looked smaller, and somehow wasted.

"It's something you can't talk about around this town." He looked behind him down the empty street. "To nobody."

Jud hesitated. It was a moment when he had almost forgotten. He soon remembered again. "I got a close mouth."

The place was three or four miles up the river and they bounced along in the car on a gravel road that ran at the base of tall rock bluffs. They parked in a thicket behind two other cars, then walked. It was a fishing cabin, the worse for time, perched over the river bank. Jud did not hear anything as they approached. He did not even see any light, because, as he soon discovered, the windows were draped over inside with towsacks. Except for the fire in the small rock fireplace, there was no light anyway, but there were people. Jud was thinking, as he followed Meagher in through the door, how much the people resembled specters with faces turned to look at him in the gloom.

7

ON A SATURDAY NIGHT NEAR THE END OF MARCH JUD
was arrested and put in jail. There were at least a dozen
people at the cabin that night but Jud was the only one
caught. It need not have happened, because the word
somehow had got there just far enough ahead of the
sheriff. He found a fire burning in the rock fireplace and
smoke that was not from wood still drifting on the air, but
the birds had flown. Or all except one had. The sheriff
and his boys were surprised to find Jud seated casually in
front of the fire looking at them, with the little pipe still lit
in his hand.

Jud was stoned, all right, but not really that stoned. It
looked as if he knew exactly what he was doing when,
after they snatched him onto his feet, he cursed them
with everything he had and then, jerking an arm free,
took a perfectly able swing that just grazed Deputy Waller's crooked hook of a nose. He was actually disappointed
that he did not get paid back in kind. All they did was give
him a shaking and drag him out to their car.

In the sheriff's office at the jail he was not much less
defiant. He refused to give any names of his friends (In
fact he did not know the last names of most of them.),
and by his taunts he kept inviting bodily disaster. He
even told the sheriff that he, the sheriff, and his boys
were nothing but a little hick gestapo—a phrase he had
picked up from those same new friends of his. Of course

all this was the hash speaking but it spoke with his tongue: it expressed how he was feeling. Again he was disappointed not to be bleeding when they got through with him.

Just a few minutes after that, however, Jud turned quite sober all of a sudden—if sober is the right word. It was because of where they put him. There was a block of four cells on the second story of the jail and they put him in one of the front ones overlooking the square. They left him without any light on. In the near-darkness he crossed to the window and, as defiant as ever, stood there for some moments looking out. Only then did he feel that something was wrong. It was more than just wrong. His breath stopped and the only thing audible was the successive mounting strokes of his own heart. He turned around slowly, turning his head first and then his body, and facing the dark saw himself standing framed and helpless against the pale window. It was like this while many seconds passed. His final assurance that he was alone in the cell came much more slowly than his panic had. For a while his blood would not acknowledge what he had clearly remembered: that Salter had been moved from here to the prison a month ago.

It was another of Jud's relapses. In spite of everything he had them still, times when his old foolish fears would suddenly come back to afflict him again. They were most like those bad dreams when a person cannot seem to get his eyes open, and this one had seized Jud with particular force. Minutes later he was still hunting for a light switch and, finding none, he finally struck a match. But he blew it out in disgust, with a curse at his stupidity, and made himself go lie down on the cot. Then the last of it went away.

Not that he suffered much nowadays from such relapses. None like this one had happened in a long time and even the usual milder kind came on him less and less often. At the cabin it had never happened. For it to happen he had to be alone, or feel that way, and at the cabin he never felt alone. Jud thought about this in his cold cell all that night. He thought about how they sat there together in the firelight, drawing warmth from each other's bodies, almost as if they were parts of one body with only the one heartbeat. It made no difference that bitter drafts came up through cracks in the floor: he was never too cold. Above him, all of them, the smoke from the lips went drifting on the frosty air, wreathing in the light, and through the languid intervals when no one made a sound they all sat watching it.

That was where Jud had learned best how to see things new. He learned to draw the smoke down deep, though it made his lungs smart, and hold it there and keep on holding it until he felt as if he had parted company with himself. The self that was really Jud went drifting up like the smoke wraiths from his lips, coiling and shifting and changing shape in the air. Then it would seem as if he was able to look down on the heads below and on the bodies sprawled together in the flickering light of the fire. His own body would be among them, his head lying, maybe, on a girl's breast. That down there was Jud. This real self drifting above him was a self without a name.

He had liked to forget that he had a name, that any of them did. Names defined and made a sort of barrier that had to be reached across, and he learned to speak to his friends at the cabin almost as he would speak aloud to himself. Of course he was stuck with many of their names—their first ones, anyway. But these had no more importance than other such facts about them—where they came from and what they did—and he knew almost none of these. He knew that his friends came, nearly all, from other towns and counties and brought the pot and the hash and sat around in front of the fire and smoked with him. They did not even notice that he brought nothing except himself to share.

The towsacks draping the windows sealed out the night. The talk was never loud. There was some singing that was just as quiet, with a guitar maybe, and there were those intervals with the river lapping the bank under the cabin and the flames lisping and boys' and girls' wan faces in the light. The nearly nameless girls did not draw back from the hands laid on them and sometimes there could be heard, at only a little remove, the barely smothered sounds of love. And always there were the smoke wraiths drifting and changing like dreams in the air.

Salter was all but banished from that place. When his image did come back to Jud it was thin like a specter escaped from a world as spectral as itself. It was this way also with Jud's other memories. They all derived from a long time ago, a land of delusion that he did not have to go back to ever again. He would stay here always, now.

That was how Jud felt those nights in the cabin, watching the smoke and the faces. And that was why he behaved as he did the night that Sheriff Gooch and his boys came raging out of that nether world to snatch him back in again. Jud's answer was a flat refusal—refusal at first to believe they were real, and after that, to submit.

It was clear enough afterwards how far Jud had been a fool. He had been a fool that night, and for a couple of days following he was only a little more sensible. His defiance was like something crouched in his throat, hard to hold back when he opened his mouth. This not only made them, the sheriff and his boys, dislike Jud more than ever. It also earned him some unnecessary roughing-up from Waller, his special caretaker, which was not ungratifying to him.

Jud's defiance went farther still. When Mr. Campbell, the preacher from what had been Jud's old Church of Christ up at Bethel, came to see him Jud sat there with his eyes averted, freezing the old man out with monosyllables. He refused to even see Hannah Rice. He smartly said that if there was anbody he didn't want to see more than a preacher, it was a preacher's old-maid daughter. As his lawyer, Barnes, the one appointed to defend him, said, Jud was acting like he was crazy.

But Barnes straightened him out. "Boy," he said, "you know how much that judge can give you for this? Up to *eight*. If I was you I'd make just like young Jesus Christ, starting right now."

Jud looked down at the floor, with something brave ready on his tongue.

"You think about eight years in that place. Put on an act for them, boy. Repent. I reckon you know about repenting. Now's your chance to get some use out of it."

"The bastards wouldn't swallow it," Jud said.

"It's all the chance you've got, now. Mrs. Nunn said tell you that."

Jud looked up at Barnes's birdlike face. "She said that?"

"She thinks it just might work, too—if you do it good. They go specially for that kind of lies. Anyhow you better try it. Think about eight years down there."

Starting right then Jud did think about it—and all the more because Lily's voice kept sounding it in his mind. He thought about it in the night, in the stillness of his cell, and toward morning he had a dream that brought him awake with a jolt. All of a sudden that prison loomed, gaped at him, with grim towering solid walls that could not be got over. Those walls were not a dream. Eight years! Now he could not imagine how the thought had not been real to him before. That was nearly twice as long as the whole span since his childhood, since he was turning fifteen and still the precious child of Jesus singing hymns at the Bethel Church of Christ and spouting Scripture like the fledgling preacher he had been sure he was. It was a lifetime. It was like hell, without any end to it. There was something more, too, a thought that finally had slipped up on him as if from over his shoulder. Salter was down there.

Before the next day was over, the signs of Jud's contrition had already become conspicuous. He astonished Waller by his humility, complying in everything with grave downcast apologetic eyes. And he kept it up. Even alone in his cell, with no audience, he kept it up. At his window that looked out over the square he stood for a while each day exhibiting what he thought of as the image of sorrowful repentance. When he entered the courtroom ten days later he was sure he had brought his act to perfection.

He had started too late, though. Neither the sheriff nor Waller had one good word to say in his behalf. Even Barnes's defense, citing Jud's orphaned uprooted state and the accident of bad companions and society's neglect, sounded rather tired. Judge McCloud did not sound tired. From his high place on the bench he looked down, through black hornrims, without any pity on Jud's repentant head. He said that he had heard enough about dope, that it was ruining our youth, and that he didn't mean to stand for it in this county. He said five years. He did not say eight, but to Jud there was not any real difference. It was still a lifetime. The abyss yawning at his feet did not have any solid bottom to it. And again, in that same oblique retarded way, he envisioned Salter down there.

There was still some hope, however, Barnes told him after the trial. There was a probation hearing still to come. And he told Jud about another hopeful thing. Among those in the courtroom had been Hannah Rice, who had sat watching him with compassionate eyes all the way through the trial.

"See there," Barnes said. "Repenting might could still pay off. She could help you. Mrs. Nunn says she's going to get her up here to see you. So don't quit repenting."

That evening, in hopes of increasing the odds, Jud wrote Hannah Rice a very careful letter.

8

ON SUNDAY, FIVE DAYS LATER, JUD STILL HAD NO word from Hannah Rice. Each day from hour to hour he had been holding himself ready, rehearsing his part as if for a play, with a downcast contrite gaze fixed on the floor. A look of shame, a soul in struggle: that was his part. But Hannah had not appeared and Barnes, too, the evening before, had seemed less than confident.

"She'll show up," he said. "Probably tomorrow. Mrs. Nunn says she will."

"The hearing's Tuesday."

"You were a fool to let that other chance get by."

Last night had been a bad one for Jud, with thoughts about that prison persisting in and out of his sleep in distorted nightmare forms. At times the place was like a maw he was sinking into, leaving the light behind, appalled by the spectral echoes rising to meet him. One sound he kept hearing was a thud, and another was a cry, repeated. He knew that Salter was there below him, waiting in the dark, the hand upraised. He could see the hand sometimes: more than once it waked him up. But even his spells of wakefulness did not bring much comfort. It was no use, lying in the dark, to tell himself that prison was only a place with walls and with cells like this one where he had to spend some years. Even these walls leaned above him like a threat to his breathing.

The day, with yellow sunlight at his barred window,

was better. But if the nightmares were gone, the anxiety was not. It kept him pacing. Six steps from bars to barred window and six steps back. His pauses were all at the window where he stood looking out on the greening courthouse lawn and budding tender leaves like spray on elm and maple trees. Opening the window he rested his forehead against a bar and drew the lucent morning air into his lungs. All of a sudden he tasted the cool of creek hollows on summer days. There was a sound of bees swarming and there, standing under a hackberry and two big hickories, was his old house in the Bethel hills. He was sitting on the porch steps, little Jud, with bare feet and toes that chickens came up to peck, with a Bible in his hands and his father, in the porch rocker, nodding a perfectly round bald head in wonder at this son of his whose voice did not stumble on even the hardest word.

Jud heard a church bell ringing. It was like part of the same memory, just as sudden, and its notes came down almost like stones on his heart. They came from up the incline rising east from the square. He could see, on a naked eminence, encircled by trees and some of the town's older houses, the white front of the Baptist Church. The notes kept falling. His heart hurt him and a thought had stolen into his mind. His only hope was up there.

This thought died out with the bell. In the quiet afterwards he stood scowling. He turned from the window as stiffly as if he had had an audience to confront and started pacing again. His hope was up there, all right. But he had been a fool and now she would not come. He went on pacing, hearing another bell, and later on, another. But the last one was the bell of the clock in the courthouse cupola dropping its dismal iron notes into the Sunday stillness.

He was at the window when church let out, watching the ripple of color along the white façade of the building, and he was there again when one o'clock struck. Just after two a column of direct sunlight entered his window. He was stretched out with his feet extended over the end of the cot that was too short for him, and from under his arm he watched the gradual advance of the light across the floor. At first he did not notice the sound of feet on the iron stairs. When he sat up blinking into the dimness beyond the cell bars he saw only Waller's familiar swollen shape. Hannah, with her pale tow head, was behind him. There was a third person, a man with not much hair, her father.

"Get up, Rivers, you got comp'ny," Waller announced, unlocking the door.

Jud wished he had been watching from his window, because he was conscious of needing time to prepare a face. Not for her, though: he had long since stopped being afraid of Hannah. She was already smiling, starting to chatter, her plain oval face looking as if it was incapable of any judgments but approving ones. He needed the time for her father, whose straight-on gaze might have made it already too late for the face that Jud had meant to put on. The old man's blue eyes were much clearer than hers and had a way of coming to rest, as if for good, on everything they looked at. They were waiting eyes, waiting to be convinced. It seemed to Jud also that the old man had a mouth to match them, that the straight impartial line of the lips in his gaunt face said he was not a man to be taken in. Even the dry hand Jud shook was formidable. Or so Jud thought at the time.

Waller had brought two folding chairs and set them up in the cell before he left. One chair was placed in the sunlight and Hannah sat there with her hands folded over round knees held modestly close together, wearing the kind of subdued outfit—pale blue-gray, this time—that she always wore. Her eyes observed Jud gently. Her father's attention felt like weight and the black snub-nosed shoes under his upright shins stood squarely aligned and trained on Jud.

"I don't guess anybody calls you Judson, do they, son?"

"No sir," Jud said. He was seated on the cot, and however slightly he moved, it creaked a little. "Just Jud." The meekness his role called for would not be hard to keep to.

"Hannah, here, wanted us to have a little talk with you. She's done some inquiring about you."

Jud waited. The Reverend Rice's tone had not been accusing, but except to turn Jud's mind toward his sins, what could this pause be for? Jud let his already bent head droop a little farther.

"Mr. Nunn's got good things to say about you . . . Poor fellow, he can't leave his bed now, you know . . . from that stroke. It looks like he may not be long for this world."

Jud did not know. Lily crossed his mind: even in his anxiety he felt his blood stir. He nodded gravely, moving regretful lips.

After a pause, "You've got a good name up at Bethel, too. Especially with Mr. Campbell." But the Reverend Rice's gaze, Jud thought, did not reflect the compliment. "He said he had a hard time believing this about you. He told Hannah a lot about you. He said he always used to think you were going to become a minister."

This was getting close to accusation. Jud kept his head penitently bowed.

"Was he right about that? Were you really thinking about it?"

"Yes sir," Jud murmured. It was true but it also fit his

act. "I thought about it a whole lot." He added, "All my life, almost. From when my mother died."

There was another pause before the Reverend Rice, in a voice that was nevertheless still mild, said, "It looks like it wasn't enough, though. When temptation came along." One of the snub-toed shoes shifted and moved away from the other. He was gathering up his holy indignation. "You know, son, I'm afraid it's easier to excuse those other young people than it is you. So many of them these days don't seem to know the difference between right and wrong. But you were raised up in the truth, on the Bible." He broke off. . . . to gather breath, Jud thought, glimpsing one of the gaunt hands lifted an inch or two above the knee where it had rested.

The Reverend Rice's hand settled again, and his voice that had seemed about to rise was as level as before. "I hope you're ashamed of what went on out at that cabin. I hope you're more than just ashamed, too. Sin destroys your soul, son. And the Lord's anger's not something a man can afford." He let this sink in for a moment. "Do you think Judge McCloud gave you more than you had coming?"

Jud slowly shook his penitent head. It was part of his act, only that. He liked the thought of himself laughing straight into this preacher's righteous face.

"You honestly don't think so . . . in your heart? It's between you and God, you know."

Honestly. There was the word. Jud felt that he ought to snap his head upright and let the anger glare out of his eyes. Honestly, when every thought stuffed in this preacher's fat brain was a lie. But Jud's anger did not rise up and did not interfere at all with the contrite tone he used. "I know I've got it coming."

He said it just right. There was not anything in the

Reverend's face to tell him this. He saw it in the plain round face of Hannah, whose presence for the last few minutes had not been much more than a shade lying across his consciousness. Her daddy's angel, Jud thought, sitting with her tow hair like a halo in the sunshine, with her small hands folded across her modest knees. She looked at him more gently than ever, and her still, dusk-blue eyes told him that her small warm heart was touched. If she had just come alone: a curse for the Reverend sped across Jud's mind. Even so, she was the one to play to, and he said, "Maybe it's not as much as I've got coming."

A silence followed. Jud did not look up. He wished he had not added that.

"What happened, Jud?"

It was her voice, soft as a birdsong in the quiet, and he could not think how he ought to answer.

"Mr. Campbell was wondering and wondering about it . . . Wasn't it Mr. Salter?"

Jud steadied himself. Feeling the Reverend's eyes he murmured, "I don't know."

"Because you believed in him so much, and then he did what he did?"

Jud fastened his gaze on his hands. He folded his hands, making them tense. Then he nodded. "He was the main thing. But there were a lot of other things, too." This was right. Nearest the truth was best. "Nobody seemed like they meant it much. I heard a lot of things. Learned things I didn't know before. Books I read that said it wasn't true . . . religion and all."

The stillness was beyond what he had expected. It was like the drawn-out echo of something in the empty cells around them, and this seemed to be the reason he added, "Like a lot of people think."

99

The stillness did not go away and Jud moved a little, making his cot creak. If there had been any change in the Reverend's gaze or posture Jud could not tell it. He began to feel uncertain. It seemed curious that the bell-like emptiness of the cell block should take these moments to become audible to him.

"It's hard sometimes, all right." Hannah had leaned toward him to say this, and he saw that there was a glister, a faint mist on her eyes. Suddenly, again, she was somebody out of his past, somebody familiar to him since his childhood. That same maudlin earnestness, the same wrinkle of pious concern in her brow. She was all those Sunday school ladies he remembered with holy tears in their eyes, reflecting on the glories of "our" Jesus. Jud thought of something else. How well he knew where all the strings were, that a cunning hand would know just how to pull. If only she had come alone.

"But there are always hypocrites, Jud. And unbelievers. We can't look just at how it is in the world."

Because of the Reverend, Jud did not risk an answer.

"We have to ask for God's help, though. I hope you've gone back to that."

This required an answer. Watching the snub-toed shoes he murmured, "I've been trying to." Then, "To learn how again." One of the shoes stirred faintly.

"Keep on trying." She had leaned still farther toward him. "*He*'ll help you. You know, there's not any end to His love."

Jud permitted himself a calculated nod.

"Or His justice, either," the Reverend said.

This was delivered, though quietly, like something aimed with care. Jud sat perfectly still.

"A lot of people want to forget what *part* of that means, son. There's punishment the same as reward."

The stillness got loud once more. The air against his face had a vague rawness, as if winter had suddenly stolen back in.

The Reverend moved: he was getting up. In a tone that did not seem any different to Jud, the Reverend said, "There's a chance we might be able to help you, Jud . . . about your probation. Just a chance, of course. Hannah and I want to talk about it a little more, though."

There was the Reverend's hand again, on a boney wrist exposed below the circlet of white shirtcuff and dark coat sleeve. Jud stood eye to eye with him for a second, mumbling thanks and imagined that the eyes were not warm and did not mean the words. But Hannah was smiling at him with a trustfulness he could not mistake. She even pressed his hand lightly when she took it and said, "God bless you, Jud"; and the same smile said goodbye to him from beyond the bars as she and the Reverend passed out of sight.

"Lucky punk." It was Waller, a minute later, at the cell door looking out of his fat beaked face at Jud.

"Why?" Jud said.

Waller slammed the door with a reverberant clang. "'Cause you ain't worth them good people dirtying their hands on, is why."

"Bastard pig," were the words Jud made silently with his lips.

9

JUD'S PROBATION WAS ENTIRELY THE WORK OF HAN-
nah and her father. That their work had not been easy
was made clear enough in the way Judge McCloud spoke
to Jud, looking hard at him through his black hornrim
spectacles. Jud was not even asked to sit down. He stood
a pace away from the judge's desk, his head meekly
bowed, feeling as if he was getting sentenced all over
again. The feeling was not without some basis.

He was not to go to prison—not, that is, as long as he
toed the line. "Just one violation, though . . . " and Judge
McCloud left a heavy pause. "I'll see it's not just *five*
years next time, either." McCloud meant it. He had the
look of a man who, through foolishness, had missed the
opportunity of a lifetime. But what Jud soon realized,
after his moment of secret elation had passed off, was
that in fact he had drawn another kind of sentence. It was
better than prison, all right, but the more he thought
about it, the more depressed he grew. And by the time he
arrived, as free as he was going to be, to pick up his
things at his now-dusty room in the Nunn's house his de-
pression had something queasy about it.

In their backyard the Rices had a garage with a small
servant's room attached. It had been empty a long time
and a little cleaning, plus a few items of old furniture,
was all that was needed. The room had been Hannah's
means—the idea clearly was hers—of persuading an al-

most adamant Judge McCloud who meant to put a stop to this vicious plague of drugs. He would not so much as hear of Jud's running loose, or even on a tether if the tether was to be very long. The little room was Hannah's answer—this, and her and her father's supervision. For what would five years in that prison do to a boy like Jud, who was a good boy and had only been neglected and left to go astray. He needed their kind of help. It was a Christian duty.

This was what Judge McCloud, with something close to a scowl, passed on to Jud. Then he had proceeded to lay on the conditions, conditions that he didn't mean to have a single one of broken. There was to be a nine o'clock curfew. Jud was to drop old friends flat, and every Sunday had better find him sitting in church at eleven. Further, whatever the Rices told him to do, he had better do. For one whole year, at the least, he had better do it, all of it. Jud thought that if this was not imprisonment it was plenty enough like it. There was even one objectionable feature that the other prison did not have. Down there the wardens were not preachers and preachers' old-maid daughters.

After his release that afternoon Jud went, as instructed, straight back to the Nunn's house for his things. He found a nurse there and Luther upstairs, stricken, in his bed—but no Lily. Jud had expected, wanted to see her. Yet, curiously, his disappointment had something ambiguous in it. He had imagined a welcome from her, the months of coldness between them all mended now. So he had come to imagine in his cell, building on the concern she had shown for him. Yet here, after all, was this curious anxious relief at the fact of her absence.

He stopped thinking about it. He stuffed all his things

103

in a cloth bag and set out up the hill, up Beulah Street to the Rices' house. Though the bag was not heavy, he kept stopping to shift it from one shoulder to the other. There were patches of shade under maple trees where he also stopped sometimes. It seemed that the climb was stirring up that queasiness at the pit of his stomach.

Not only the house but the whole yard was invisible behind a tall fence of thick privet hedge. From the gap where the driveway entered, where he stopped again, he saw that the hedge ran all the way around. It made a place apart, a still place. There was vivid shade from frothy-leafed mimosa and hickory trees in the sideyard, but the house, a white clapboard with a long roofed porch screened by ivy, stood all in the afternoon sun. Beyond the house and the trees, down the yard's incline, he could see a large garden full of both shrubs and flowers, with some of the flowers in pink, white and yellow bloom. There was no breeze to stir them. Nothing stirred any-where, in fact, and this seemed to be the reason he kept on standing there in the gap for so long.

When he finally did move he did it under pressure. At least it was what he felt as pressure, imagining that he was being watched from someplace, from behind the porch vines, maybe. Holding his eyes straight ahead, walking gravely, he advanced down the drive. He had come abreast of the house before he saw, past the rear corner, the garage and the little room that was his des-tination. Then he saw Hannah.

Her back was to him. She was standing outside the open door of the room looking at something—a framed picture she held in her hands. For her not to have heard him he must have been walking almost stealthily on the gravel drive and now, still at a little distance from her, he stopped. His effort to clear his throat did not make any sound. He felt as if even the direction of his eyes was being observed from somewhere and he kept his gaze on the back of her head only, vaguely conscious how the sun made a pale nimbus around her hair. This time he cleared his throat with success.

She was not startled. There was only pleasant surprise in the way she turned to him and said, "Well, here you are, Jud," smiling her best and whitest smile. "I was thinking you might like this on your wall." She turned the picture, holding it in such a way that he could look at it too. He could have guessed what it would be. It was another Jesus, this one holding a shepherd's staff and knocking at a gate.

"Thank you," Jud said. "That'd be nice."

She hoped he was going to like his room, she said, and with a smile to summon him on mounted the two steps to the door. He was bound to follow but he stopped at the threshold and from there, conscious of her watching him, made his eyes survey the room. There was a chair and a narrow bed and a table with a gooseneck lamp. A small bureau stood against the rear wall, beside a door that opened into a cubicle of a bathroom. In the side wall at the foot of the bed was the room's single window. It seemed to be practically blinded by the shrubbery out-side, but because she was standing in front of it he could not look to be sure. "I hope you're going to like it all right."

The room was not really too small. Only her presence crowded it so in his mind, as if a single step more would bring him up against her bodily. He felt that queasiness. "It's fine," he said, "It's real nice." He got himself another smile.

She wanted to know where Jud would like to have the picture hung and he pointed to the wall across from the bed. A nail was there already. She took a few moments getting the picture straight enough to suit her and, entirely against his intention, he noticed the curve of her breast under the boy's blue shirt she wore. He snatched his gaze away but it seemed too late. Somehow, he felt, from somewhere, his lapse had been observed.

"I've always liked that one. Jesus knocking at the gate." She stood admiring the picture. "Like at peoples' hearts."

Like at peoples' hearts, Jud thought, or tried to think, also looking at the picture. But what his mind saw, perversely, was the curve of her breast again. The hand in the picture was raised to touch or seize it and Jud felt a blush climbing to his cheeks.

She did not notice. She proceeded to show him things about the room—hooks on the wall for coats and the wicker basket he could use for laundry. She pointed to each one like a gift. Last she showed him how, through the window, even through the heavy shrubs, he could see her flowers out in the garden. Did he like flowers? He said of course that he did and the result was that he had to follow her outside for a close look at them.

It was all garden across the space between Jud's room and the palisade of hedge, with grass walks passing among the brick-bordered flower beds. Large shrubs, camellia and crepe myrtle, made some areas invisible from the house—like the one close under the back hedge where a birdbath and a bench and a couple of chairs stood and where she brought him out at the end of their little tour. He liked this place the best. The leaning hedge made a shelter against half the sky, also, and he felt some release here from the pressure that had been dogging him. His release was not complete. He avoided her with his eyes and looked at her face, only her face, when he was required to do so. If he could have heard a sound of

106

voices beyond the hedge or even of cars passing out on
the street, he might have felt still better. Here, except for
her patter about the flowers, not done with yet, there was
only the drone of bees to fill his head. But soon he was
aware that her voice had stopped. He managed to say,
"You've got a pretty place."

"It's not really ours. It belongs to the church. I was born
here, though, and it seems like ours."

Jud was looking at her feet, in strapped sandals without
socks. When his gaze moved up to her strong white ankles he snatched it away. The pause, full of bees, went on
for a little while.

"I hope you know how welcome you'd be at our
church." She was bending. She carefully picked one of
the tea roses that grew on the pedestal of the birdbath.
"Daddy wants to invite you, too."

"Invite," Jud thought, remembering Judge McCloud.
But his spark of cynicism was only a spark: he smothered
it quickly. He imagined that in this peculiar stillness his
most secret thought was in danger of being recorded
somewhere. "Thank you," was all he dared to say.

10

NOT ONLY WAS HIS JOB AT NUNN'S STILL WAITING
for him. With Luther bedridden there had to be another
full-time clerk, and Lily, in spite of the inconvenience,
had been holding the place for Jud.

"Thank you," he said. He wanted to say more but in the
act of trying to, something surprised him. It was a little
like finding, suddenly there in front of his face, a barrier
like a pane of clear glass, and words already on his lips
fell back and lay silent somewhere close to his heart. He
wanted to but he could not say them.

She was in the little office, at her desk, and had turned
in the chair to look up at Jud where he stood in the
door. Because of the way she looked, with those flecks of
dusty yellow drifting in her eyes, his muteness seemed
all the more strange. Even his pulse seemed to beat with
a kind of restraint. She noticed, too. He saw a shade
cross her eyes. Looking down he said, "Is Luther any better?"

She studied his face. "He's not likely to get any better.
Ever."

Jud's desire flickered, then submerged again. "I'm
sorry," he said.

Old Mr. Baker's voice out in the store was dimly audible. Lily sat with an arm, bare to the shoulder, resting on
the back of the chair and with the bright nail of a
forefinger stroked her lips where they met at one corner.

Jud thought how keen the nail looked, as if it might cut the lips she was slowly stroking.

"How do you think you're going to like living on holy ground?"

"I'm not going to like it," he said.

"Even with an angel to watch over you?"

"If she just wasn't such a homely angel," he said. But somehow the words had come out like a blunder. It was as if somebody standing somewhere out of sight had overheard them, and Jud's impulse was to take back the words. Lily had not stopped watching him.

"I've missed our little chats in the kitchen," she said.

He only murmered, "Me too," and that with hesitation, wondering at himself.

"You could still drop by sometimes."

He nodded, imagining that listener somewhere close. "What if people thought things, though?"

She faintly smiled. "Luther's there. He's always there, now."

Upstairs in his room, Jud thought, and helpless.

"Or you could come after dark, to the back door, if you'd rather."

And his old room across from the kitchen empty. Again there was that presence to check the upsurge of his lust. "I'd like to," he said, avoiding her eyes and thinking he could not risk it the way things were.

He could not risk it. The following days confirmed him in this notion. He had in fact expected to be watched and had been prepared to make appearances every day and carefully play his role before their eyes. But what he actually experienced was a little like being trapped on stage with never any intermission. Try as he would he could not get rid of the feeling that he was constantly, and everywhere, being observed.

At first Jud thought that there was only the Reverend to be wary about. He remembered how the old man had seemed to watch him in the jail cell that afternoon, as if he was trying to see through the mask Jud wore. Jud also remembered how, on the first day when he stood in the driveway entrance between the hedges, in the still after-noon sun, he had felt somebody looking at him. He had thought it was the Reverend, on the porch, watching him through the vines. Just after nightfall the old man had come out to his room. It was to welcome him, the Rev-erend said, and his tone sounded innocent enough. Was Jud settled in all right? Did he need anything? But the old man stood at the foot of the steps while they talked, and the dimness out there made a veil across his face. Jud's face was in the light and clear to the Reverend's eyes and Jud could feel his own expression as if it was something tense and cold laid against his skin.

That was at the very beginning. After a couple of en-counters with the Reverend in full daylight Jud's feeling about him started to subside. After all, the old man's eyes were not so sharp. Even when he looked directly at Jud and his lenses magnified his eyes, Jud was no longer much distressed. As likely as not there would be a smile in the eyes, or a glaze of moisture because a holy thought had crossed his mind. Before long it was not, or not mainly, the Reverend who seemed to be the source of the scrutiny Jud felt. All of a sudden, once again, Hannah was the one he had to be wary about.

Jud remembered exactly the moment when this notion ·got started in his head. It was just a few days after he had moved in, and he was there in the room waiting for the hands of his clock to reach six-thirty. He would go out for his supper then, down to Rogan's and afterwards loaf around the square until his curfew hour of nine. That was the pattern he had established. The interval in his room between quitting time and supper was meant to demonstrate his submission, and his contentment. On that particular evening, whatever contentment he might have been feeling got routed all in a second.

His only window looked out through shrubbery into the garden. There had not been any sound to attract him. He was just walking past the window when he saw something, a vaguely shining something beyond the shrubbery, and stopped to look. It was that moment when the late sun was poised just over the top of the back hedge. Its last direct rays flooded the garden and that bright spot he saw was Hannah's head. It was not far from the shrubbery. She was kneeling beside a flowerbed, but he could see that she was not tending it. She was not only still. She looked as if she had been that way a long time, intently still. Moving a little he saw that her head was cocked, in a listening pose, and that her eyes seemed to be trained on Jud's window. For the second or two before he could step aside, he was sure she was looking at him.

Jud stood out of sight, waiting. He saw the shadow from the back hedge rise up and darken his window and he heard sounds that were those her hands made plucking weeds from the flowerbed. But the sounds were as faint as whispers. They were too faint, and long between, as if she was careful not to make noise that would interfere with her listening. He did not move. He waited a long time, until he heard her quiet footsteps in the grass along the path. He waited longer than that. It was full dusk before he went out and up the driveway past the house.

That was the beginning and it lasted for weeks. Hannah had fooled him. It was a disguise, that bright brainless Sunday school manner she wore, because underneath were eyes that saw the things nobody else could see. Now she was watching. Some careless gesture of his had warned her and now, like this evening, she spied on him from the garden, and maybe from the windows of the house. Maybe from other places, too, when he was least expecting. That same night, as he loafed around the square after supper, he caught himself falling into postures of what he fancied to be conspicuous innocence. Well before nine he was back in his room with two lights burning instead of one to advertise his presence.

This grew worse. It was foolishness, and half the time Jud knew that it was. But the knowledge did not help and even in his room with curtains drawn across the window and door glasses he dressed and undressed with a modesty he never had practiced before. It went farther. There were times when he imagined that nothing, the dark or anything else, quite assured the privacy of his room. At such times his very thoughts did not seem private, and he had no choice but to purge his mind of his old inflaming daydreams about Lily. He thought of his old self, then, of how at such moments he resembled *that* Jud.

In those weeks he really did begin to resemble his old self. It was more than only an act, too, though his need to be always acting a role was at the bottom of it. The thing was that sometimes he almost became what he was acting. It was only "almost," of course, but there really were times when he felt as if his mask was not a mask. Most of these were occasions when he was with Hannah.

It got so that he was with her fairly often. This was his own doing, at least on the first occasion, and the reason was precisely his foolish fear of her. What, he thought, if his fear showed in the way he was always fleeing from her? For two whole days he weighed this thought. Then in the evening when he came in from work, mustering all

112

his boldness he walked out into the garden and offered to help. She looked up smiling, wiping with the back of her wrist a lock of hair from her forehead. "I'd love to have you help me," she said, still smiling, showing him the whiteness of all her teeth. Even so he thought he glimpsed that watchful look in the blue depths of her eyes.

Jud had meant to help her only that one time, just for the effect. But then he could not stop. Each evening's performance seemed somehow faulty, as if he had made a slipup somewhere and must appear again the next evening to mend it. But that was his obsession speaking. He did not think he ever did slip up. Even that first time, after she had forced him out of his intention to keep nearly silent, he found that he knew already most of the lines to go with his role. In a few days he knew them all and he could drop holy sentiments and Bible verses with as much naturalness as if he was still Jesus' own child at the Bethel Church Sunday school. Later on, after the performance, he shuddered with embarrassment at the recollections. But at the time he really almost felt that he meant what he said. In that hour, at least for portions of it, he almost *was* a soul struggling back up the road toward faith.

For that was the part he was still playing, while Hannah listened or led him with a muted question or occasionally delivered herself of a pious though unassuming comment. She never chattered. That was for the public, for strangers only, as he had begun before this to understand. She could even be formidably quiet in a way that now and then intruded and threw a doubt into the middle of his performance. Stopped cold, maybe frozen, he would steal a look at her. There was never any difference. Her hands, working dirt with a trowel or pulling weeds

113

from a bed of zinnias or marigolds, had not paused, and her mild grimaces only reflected the small strain of her efforts. Soon he would go back into his act.

"I think coming to live in town was one of the reasons," Jud would say. "It almost seemed like God wasn't down here. Not like he was up home. The noise and all. And all the people milling around. It was like I couldn't hear his voice anymore, the way I used to. Everything was so quiet up home." And Jud's mind really did go back, hearing how quiet it was with the trees all standing there in the still noon sunlight and the purring chickens and the dryflies for undertone.

"He's here too, though. He's everywhere." Hannah had stopped working. Holding the trowel she had settled back onto her ankles and was looking directly at Jud across the little space of flowerbed. As sometimes happened when he was caught up in his role he did not notice anything more about her eyes than that they were a dusky blue. They looked deeper dusky now because the sun had gone under the hedge and the whole garden was sunk in shadow, a shadow made almost purple here by the big camellia bush.

"Can't you feel Him here?"

There was only the humming of bees, and just then it was as if Jud really could feel Him. His nod of assent was almost genuine.

"I can," she said. "Of course He's everywhere, but it seems like I can feel Him better here. Like at your home. It's always so quiet. You can barely hear a car go by." She looked around her, scanning the garden. "And all the beautiful flowers."

It was a beautiful garden. It was still more so because of its isolation, the way it lay a little sunken in back of the white house and walled in by the dense dark green

114

hedges. There was a maze of green paths among the flowerbeds and shrubs spotted around, and this year, because of the warm wet spring, it looked as though all the flowers were blooming ahead of season. There was nearly every color Jud could think of and shades he had never seen flowers have before. His mood at the time made it easy for him to say, "Sort of like in the Garden of Eden, maybe."

"It is, sort of," she said, looking at him. "I've thought of that, too." Just then he was not even disturbed by the long look she was giving him. She said, "Then it ought to be a good place for you to live, Jud. If you feel that way."

He nodded, lowering his eyes, and made an idle stroke with his trowel in the dirt close to his knee. He had begun to be less comfortable in his mind.

"Have you kept on praying?"

He hesitated. "I think I'm kind of learning how again."

There was maybe a little bit of truth in this, because several times lately Jud had caught himself shaping words that seemed to be addressed to the Lord. Then he thought, no, he had spoken a plain flat lie. And she saw it. What followed was one of those moments when he felt himself stripped naked in front of her eyes, and for fear and shame he could not raise his head. Not, at least, until she said, "Keep on trying. It'll come back," in a tone that reassured him.

In those weeks he had a good many such moments with her. For a little space he would feel sure that he was caught, that it was all over and that the end would be the depths behind those threatening prison walls that he could not stop dreaming about at night. This was what stood behind her in those moments. She might have had the prison keys in her pocket and the choice to use or not to use them, depending on what she saw in Jud. It was no

115

wonder he gave her credit for shrewdness she did not have. .

At his best, though, when he was deepest into the role he was playing, he found Hannah's company really not unpleasant. Sometimes he almost consciously enjoyed their discussions about flowers, about when and where to plant and how to care for them. Now, at the store, he took some pains to pick up facts from seed catalogs and the backs of seed packages, which he brought into their discussions. It was policy, of course, part of his act, but he did take a certain pure pleasure in doing this. It seemed to please her. Though really she knew much more than he did, she always listened intently and sometimes appeared to be honestly impressed. Because of him one day they transplanted a whole big bed of sprouting snapdragons. "They're too near the hedge," Jud said. "Not enough sun. They have to have a lot of sun."

She looked gravely into his eyes. "I hadn't thought of that."

There were other things Jud liked. He liked the scent of the flowers and the cool scent of the earth his trowel turned up. An especially pleasant moment was when the sun went down suddenly behind the hedge. One minute he would feel its weight on the back of his neck, and the next, in its place, the fresh night shadow that lay, when he looked up, like a green veil across the expanse of the garden.

Something else Jud found he liked was to talk about himself. Hannah encouraged him. He had to be careful, of course, but he had experienced enough of those panicky moments to keep him on guard and what he chose from among the facts about himself could not possibly have damaged her notion of him. There were plenty of such facts. He took them mostly from his childhood,

116

about his life on the little farm and his mother's death and his early impassioned dedication to the cross of Jesus. It made a lonesome tale, one that clearly affected Hannah. He could see also that it was gaining him credit with her and soon he saw no reason not to tell her, with appropriate omissions, about his life later on in town and the new kind of lonesomeness he found there. She drew him out, but mostly not by questions. When he paused, she paused too, from her work, and waited for him to go on. He was gaining credit, all right, he knew, but that was not the only thing that moved him. She was the first real listener he had ever known.

Jud had to grant that Hannah was not as ugly as he had first thought. Her eyes, at least when he did not feel that they were prying, were very nice, and when the sun was on her hair making it light up, that was also nice. Her small hands were graceful. They made him think, even when she was plucking weeds out of the dirt, of what a high-born lady's hands would look like. He had never looked, or *really* looked, at her body, but dressed in the jeans and boy's shirt she wore for gardening, it had at least more shape than he had noticed before.

He also had to admit finally that the phony piety she was full of was in her case not all phony. It was just that she was one of them who had it the way some children had it—in their veins like blood—and who, unless something much more dramatic happened to her than already had happened, would have it all her life. It took the form of compassion, mainly, the kind that would keep her tearful about every unhappy thing until the day she died and maybe had a last moment to be amazed when no fire chariot came down after her soul. The curious thing was that, seeing this, he still continued to be afraid of her for a good while longer. Certainly she felt compassion for him

117

and showed it in ways a blind man could not have missed. But he did. Her most open demonstrations of concern simply caused him to put up his guard.

One day she said to him, "I don't think it's good for a person to be that lonesome." He had been talking, glossing a little these days, about his lonesome childhood. Until this moment, while her deft small hands pulled weeds from a tulip bed, Hannah had not said anything. It was that time of day just before the sun went down, and the light was in the threads of loose hair around her head. She had stopped work to say this. Seated back on her ankles, with her soiled hands at rest across her knees, she regarded him steadily. He ought not to have felt uncomfortable. Her look was just a look, to see clearly in his face what he was telling her. He could hear only the bees, and this spot in the garden, concealed by a bush from all the house windows, was one of the spots he liked best.

"Do you?" she added. "I don't think God meant for us to be that way."

"I guess you're right." It was not God's being in it again that kept him on his guard. He could feel how earnestness had knit his brow.

"Things can happen to you when you're too lonesome. You can get to feeling like there's nobody else but you in the whole creation. Even when you know God's there, He can get to seeming a long way off."

"I know," Jud murmured, feeling his expression of grave assent. The expression was wasted, though, he noticed, because she was gazing beyond him. It could not have been far beyond: just in back of him was the camellia bush that shut them off from the house. He repeated, "I know," and saw her eyes come back and settle on her hands.

"Was that the way it was for you, Jud?"

118

He gave a melancholy nod. He was waiting for something pointed and he thought that the moment was due just about now. He did not know why he had the feeling that somebody was standing behind him, behind the bush.

"I have times like that," she said. "When it seems like even prayer doesn't help. Because God's such a long way away and the world's too much for you all by yourself. You feel like just falling into it and letting it have its way with you."

Jud did not even nod this time.

"But you can't, Jud. You can't let yourself. It's what the devil wants, to make us his." She looked up and said, "Christ is the only one that can keep us free. But we've got to ask Him to. And keep on asking."

He nodded, still waiting. But this was to be all. She bent over and started pulling weeds again and left him alone with his tension. For a time he went on thinking that he must have missed the real point, the meaning hidden in her words, and he kept sifting the words in his mind. Of course there was not any other meaning. There never was in the things she said, but it took Jud a while to learn this.

In the meantime his wariness got him more entrapped than need have been. Only a modest amount of confidence would have saved him from at least some of the missions of mercy she pressed him into. The first time, he volunteered. After that she asked him and, hiding behind a cheerful face, with arms full of groceries or old clothes, he followed her into shotgun houses at the edge of town and up slippery paths to cabins at the heads of creek hollows. He repaired a broken window for an abandoned wife and children, and rotten front steps for an old man who could have done it for himself. Not that he much objected to these missions as such. What he objected.to, scornfully, was Hannah's insistence, repeated over and over, that God was the one they were serving. But Jud kept his objections well hidden. He kept them so well hidden that at certain times it almost seemed as if he did not have them anymore.

11

IT WAS THIS WAY BETWEEN HANNAH AND JUD FOR A month or more, on into June. Of course no one will ever know what might have come of it, but probably what happened would have happened anyway in some terms or other. In some way Jud would have caused it to happen.

Two events made the difference. The second was decisive but the first one had prepared Jud for it. Clearly there was a connection between his fear of Salter and of Hannah, and to be rid of the one was at least to diminish the other. So it worked out. When Jud's gnawing fear of Salter went, he found that his feelings about Hannah had changed.

Right at first the news about Salter had the opposite effect on him. He first heard it at Rogan's. The time was the noon hour, with people and traffic passing by, and yet he searched the street like a scout before he moved a step away from the door. Salter was out of prison, pardoned. That was all Jud knew. He did not know when. Afraid to ask he spent the afternoon like that, in fear of what he would see the next time he looked out through the windows of the store. It was Hannah who told him, that evening in the garden, without his having to ask.

"He's back home now. Up there in that little trailer again."

"When did he get out?" Jud said to the ground, holding his breath for the answer.

"A couple of days ago."

Jud felt she was looking at him. "I thought he had two years."

"He's in such bad health. Daddy was one of them that helped get him out." Then, "Why don't you go to see him? He wants to see you."

Jud hesitated. "How do you know?"

"I just do. Because he let you down."

Jud started weeding again and left her with the notion that he was thinking about it.

Jud had a bad night. He locked his door and finally his window and clear on until daylight he lay there listening even in his fits of sleep. Sometimes he thought that the shrubbery outside was stirring against his wall and once he crept to the window and stood for a while. The sounds were not real. All he ever really heard was a dog off in the distance.

But morning was the end of it. Then he did not even know exactly what he had feared. That Salter would come straight to get him, break into his room? In the light of day the idea looked absurd and it still looked that way when the next night came on. He went right off to sleep. Salter free was no more a threat than Salter in prison and, seeing this, Jud was rid of him. He was on the way to being rid of Hannah too, at least in terms of their recent relationship, but this was to take a couple of days.

Then Luther died. It was sudden, in the night, of a second stroke. Baker had the word when Jud got to work that morning and they locked up the store and Baker put up a funeral wreath. Even at the very first, one hot thought came to Jud. He thought of Lily alone in the house and of how, if he had been living in his old room, there would have been only the two of them. But the fire this raised up in him was brief, snuffed out by the memory of these last few months. The fault was his. He was the one who had made the coolness between them, so that now they rarely talked at all except about matters to do with the store. It was true especially in this past month. All his vivid remembrance of what she had said to him—"You could still drop by sometimes"—had made no difference. He never had gone, not once. Was it too late?

The next day Jud got what seemed, maybe, a hint that it was not too late. Luther's funeral was at the old city cemetery, a place full of weathered gravestones and mourning stone figures and cedar trees casting patches of olive shade. Where Jud sat was in the shade, next to Hannah who had collared him at the cemetery gate, in the second row of chairs. Directly in front of him was the coffin under a bank of flowers and, by an act of will, he was keeping his gaze on it. Luther, with his tired face, with his eyes sealed shut forever, was in that coffin. Jud made himself keep thinking about this, feeling Hannah's arm touch him sometimes and hearing the Reverend Rice's voice reciting in the hush the virtues of tired Luther's finished life.

But Jud knew exactly where Lily was. She was seated in the group of Luther's family, a step from one end of the coffin, where his eyes could not for long evade her. However he tried she was there, like something brightly adrift at the rim of his vision. Still he was determined not to look at her, and when the time came for a prayer he shut his eyes. It did not help. As the prayer went on he began to imagine, at last to feel on his shut lids the pressure of

Lily's attention. His eyes came open. Of the heads around her, only hers was not bowed and she was in fact looking steadily at him.

Of this much, at least, Jud remained certain afterwards. She had been looking at him and with a look that was not merely idle. Except for his response, the way his blood betrayed him, he might have had time to be sure of what her look meant. But he wilted like a kid: his gaze fled. He cast a sideways glance to see if Hannah, in spite of her bowed head, noticed. And when he looked back again Lily's eyes were fastened on Hannah instead of him. The Reverend's amen came and put an end to any chance Jud still had. But maybe not his final chance. Not if her look from beside the coffin had been as he remembered it.

What if she was jealous? In his room that night, recalling those moments, the thought came suddenly. It was not only him, it was Hannah too that Lily had looked at—Hannah sitting close beside him. Now Jud's memory seemed to recall a look that was not friendly, that was cold and hostile—a jealous look. Or was his memory playing tricks? The image came and went. But the thought that came back with it each time was like a tongue of flame.

Then the next day seemed to bring him confirmation. It was Sunday and when Jud got back from church there was a note in his room, slipped under the door. It was from Lily. His hands trembled as he held it, read it, read it over again, and all that long afternoon they did not stop trembling. He walked. He walked to the river and back through town and finally to the river bridge and crossed to the other side. At twilight he returned to his room, but not by the usual route. He came through the back hedge, on hands and knees, pausing in the gloom there to scout the garden. In fact he had to wait a while, for Hannah was in the garden. It was nearly full dark before he got into his room. Without any light he washed himself and put on another shirt.

It was a warm night with a little of balmy spring left in the air and the kitchen door of Lily's house stood open. Approaching the door he saw her. She was seated at the table, waiting, and suddenly Jud had to stop. He had to breathe: for a long moment it seemed as if he could not suck air enough into his lungs. It was a moment of near-panic, when he imagined that to get his breath he would have to turn quickly and hurry back to a place where the air was not so charged with heat. He almost did turn back. He took half a backward step before his panic started to subside. Even then he stood a while longer in his tracks watching her, thinking that this was as far as he dare go.

And it was, until she saw him. In the meantime she did not appear to be looking toward the door or toward anything else, either, and her only movement was so obscure that Jud did not notice it at first. The tips of her fingers were on her cheek slowly stroking it. Jud could not see but he pictured the blemishes, recalling from his reveries their texture against his lips. He did not know why, but suddenly, just for the fragment of a second, a chill of revulsion passed over him. It passed and that was all. He saw that he had been noticed. He came forward and at her bidding opened the screen and entered.

Lily wore the dressing robe. Until she got up to get him coffee Jud had not realized this and when, with her back turned, she said something he failed to pick up the words.

"I said, it's been a long time," she repeated quietly.

Though her back was still turned he nodded his stupid head. He managed, "They keep their eyes on me, you know," then saw that this also was inept.

She gave it no answer and until she was seated again did not speak. "There's sugar and cream."

Jud took some moments of refuge in the operation.

"I'm going to make a change," she said. "I've decided to let Mr. Baker go. I haven't got anything else to keep me busy now and I think you and I can take care of things. I'll hire a boy to do what you were doing. If it doesn't work out I can always get another clerk."

"Fire Mr. Baker?" It was all Jud could think of to say. The two of them, he and she? Jud almost dared to look up at her.

"He's never been much account. Luther liked him."

And Luther was gone. It occurred to Jud distantly that he ought to say something about poor Luther, but he did not. He thought how the house was empty except for Lily and him.

"I hope that suits you. Of course you'll get more money."

"You know it suits me," Jud said. Suddenly he added, looking at her, "If it suits you," feeling the pace of his heart increase.

The moment had come. Jud really did expect that this would be it, that the tone he had used would bring it on. The table was not wide and his hand lay on it and he imagined that she would reach out and take it in her own. Nothing of the sort happened. She removed a cigarette from the package on the table and lit it and watched the smoke go up from her lips to the lightbulb inside the yellow shade overhead.

"Not that you've been very attentive to me," Lily said.

Jud cast about him. "I couldn't. I was afraid to. You

126

know. They could send me to prison if they wanted to."

"For coming to see me?"

He hesitated. "I was just scared they might think something . . . that it was funny or something. You know how they are."

"How?"

"You know. Righteous and all."

She continued watching her smoke rise to the light. "Is that why you're afraid of them?"

Jud paused. "I'm afraid of them thinking anything's funny."

"But not of their righteousness?"

He saw what she meant. Maybe he lifted his voice just a shade. "What do I care about their 'righteousness'? I just don't want them to think anything. I just want them to be fooled real good, so they won't watch me anymore."

Her silence went on for a while and Jud was about to repeat himself when she said, "You've sure been working hard at fooling them. All that helping in the garden."

He was surprised. He could not remember telling her about that.

"Doesn't it get kind of tiresome? Every day?"

"Not every day," Jud said. "It gets tiresome, all right, though. I wish I could get out of it now."

"Or maybe you've found a way to liven it up some for you."

Jud really did not know what she meant, not at first—not until, to guide her cigarette ash into the ashtray, she looked down and showed him her expression. In the first instant he felt something like shock. In the next one, remembering yesterday, he felt his blood again. She was jealous. Wanting a clearer sign he said, "What do you mean?"

"I was just wondering. All that time in the garden with

her. It's pretty private back there, isn't it?"

She *was* jealous: her small grin had a forced look. Drawing a tight breath Jud said, "I wouldn't have her if I could. I never even thought about it. Not even once."

"Are you sure?" She looked up at the light and Jud felt as good as certain that her mockery was put on.

"I couldn't be any surer," he said. "She's the last one I can think of. God, no."

A wreath of smoke went drifting and coiling up from Lily's mouth. "She's really not all that bad. Especially from the neck down. Didn't you ever even take a good look at her?"

"I don't want to look at her." But there she stood in his mind's eye, with legs and hips and not unshapely breasts. He shut her out with a sort of violence. "I don't want *her*," he said, watching Lily's face. But there was no change.

"Even if you had a chance?"

"Not *any* way," he said. "Besides, there never will be a chance. For me or anybody else. Not unless she could get somebody to marry her."

"Phooey," Lily said.

Once again Jud was vaguely shocked. It was not *just* her tone. He did not know exactly what it was he wanted to say.

"Is it because she's so holy?"

Lily's gaze was direct. Jud fumbled a little. "'Righteous,' I mean. You know. All the Jesus stuff."

"You think that would stop her? All that phony stuff . . . that's not even real?"

"She thinks it's real, though. That's what would stop her. Thinking it."

Lily put out her cigarette in the ashtray, carefully,

tamping among the dead ashes. "It's what would stop *you*, anyway, I expect."

Jud shook his head no. He could not think of anything else to do or of anything else to say, though he felt as if there was something he ought to say. He also felt, suddenly, how all the exciting promise was gone from the empty house. Not only was it gone. He saw that Lily's new posture meant it was time he was going, too. Then she said it, though not harshly, and took up the package of cigarettes. There was nothing for him to do but rise from the table, where his cup of coffee stood untouched.

But there was a moment yet to come. Jud moved slowly and his slow hand on the screen had not yet pushed it open. Then he saw that she was behind him, close to him, so close that turning around would have caused him to brush against her. The strength went out of his arm.

"When are you going to grow up, Jud?"

It was not much more than a murmur, like her voice in his dreams about her. It was just as if he was dreaming now and he saw, aslant over his shoulder, the white flesh where the lapels of her robe met above her breast. Her face appeared, looming up, her body touched his arm. For one brief second her lips were on his cheek. Jud could not remember the interval after that, for it seemed only the next second when he found himself in the dark backyard facing a door that was shut.

Part THREE

12

IT HAD BEEN A WET SPRING AND WHEN, ALONG IN June, the showers suddenly stopped, the effect was visible almost right away. In a week the grass had started to turn brown. By July there was a drought. The sun became a brassy smear in the noon sky and foliage drooped and from a little distance the heat looked like water shimmering over the town pavements.

But Jud was not in a state of mind to notice the weather much. When he did notice he thought of it as appropriate, as if the drought had been designed only to reflect the way he felt. There were times, whole hours, when he burned, feeling a dusty, almost painful dryness in his throat. A sort of limpness would follow, a sort of drooping that was like the way those tree leaves hung in the afternoon. Two weeks of this, then three. He had intervals now when he was certain there would be no end to it.

It all went back to that kiss. That night in his room, and every night, he had felt it touch his cheek again, the preface to his fiery wasting dreams. But it did not touch him only in the privacy of his room. It might happen anywhere, on a crowded sidewalk or alone with a crusty old farmer he was waiting on at the store. All of a sudden the hot shape of her kiss would bloom in his cheek and his lust would surge again. There was no place where he was free of such moments, but least of all in Lily's presence.

There was much more of her presence now. Mr. Baker

was gone—with ill-will and resentful last glances directed partly at Jud—and the new boy, Riley, was in and out of the store. There were not always customers, and there was closing time and after, when he and Lily were completely by themselves. This was the special time. The stillness brought them together and every word she spoke was for Jud's ears. Their bodies were often close together, too. Passing along behind the main counter they were liable to brush against each other, or, both of them busy at some task, they might find themselves standing where their elbows nearly touched. In those first few days Jud was always waiting. More than once he had shut his eyes and waited. He had had such a physical sense of her nearness that, for an instant, feeling the kiss grow suddenly hot in his cheek, he imagined her lips approaching to give it again.

This, or anything like it, was not to be, however, though the realization took him a while. For days he waited, thinking that each one of those moments when she came close to him and stopped was a moment of preparation for something. He thought he even had new reasons to think so. For one thing, he thought she looked different since Luther's death, and better. It seemed that she kept her hair more scrupulously combed, giving it a glossier darkness than before. He had supposed he was familiar with all her clothes, but now some of them looked new—blouses in the yellow or green that were her favorites and now and then a skirt he had never seen. The difference went still farther, or deeper. Her face had more color, even more flesh, Jud thought, and he was certain of a new, more vivid life in her eyes. And he let himself believe that it was for him.

There was something else he misread. Hardly a day went by when she did not ask him, in words that varied more or less, the same question, or questions."How is the garden doing? "

"Getting pretty dry," he would say. "Not much to do but run the sprinklers."

"After dark, I guess."

"That's the best time to water things . . . after dark," Jud said, thinking that she was jealous, trying to make her so.

"Does she really need your help, to run sprinklers? "

"You have to move them around sometimes." From the corner of his eye he was watching Lily. Busy at a task she did not look at him when she spoke.

"What do you do the other times? "

"Oh, talk. She likes to talk."

"About spiritual things, of course? "

"Mighty spiritual," he said, thinking that although this was true it sounded exactly right.

"I see." Then, maybe pushing the cash drawer shut, "That's what an angel *would* talk about, isn't it? But I wonder *you* don't get bored."

It would end like this, or something like this, and Jud would be left imagining that the time had nearly come. One day, one day soon, she would break. It would come in that interval after they locked the door and he, with his eyes fallen shut, would feel her touch him and feel her kiss renewed on his flaming cheek. Then he would turn to her.

But the days kept passing and it was always the same. The interval after closing time was soon routine like the rest, concluding with Jud's little tour to check the warehouse doors. When he came back into the store she was always gone. Out on the sidewalk where six o'clock felt as hot as noon, he turned and locked the front door again and made his way up the square. It was an empty hour, no breeze, no traffic much. The courthouse clock might strike as he crossed the lawn. A few old men still kept their places, looking blank, as if their long day of idleness on the benches under the drooping foliage had drained the last of their energy. Jud passed and walked to Rogan's. It was coming dusk when he headed for his room.

The weather had changed Jud's evening routine. Hannah would be out in the twilight, already sprinkling but still expecting him to join her; or if she was late finishing her work in the house, she would come and call to him through his window. Despite his increasingly cynical attitude toward her, he felt that he did not have any choice. He had to go out and "help" her, which meant, mostly, sitting there with her on the stone step at the top of the garden until he could reasonably plead bedtime. At least it was dark. When one of her phrases vexed or, as sometimes happened now, enraged him, it did not matter if he scowled or lifted his brow in irony or shaped a silent obscenity with his lips. At least these nighttime sessions had this much to redeem them.

Otherwise these hours with Hannah were worse than the daytime ones had been. Then, she had had weeds and flower diseases and all such problems to distract her, but here at night her spirit had only the competition of a couple of water sprinklers that had to be moved once in a while. She had not only the idle intervals but also the stars and the moon to inspire her. The result was inevitable.

"They're like eyes, aren't they?" she said, her face uplifted, as usual. "Thousands and thousands of bright eyes watching the world. And shedding light on it. Looking down on us wherever we are and wherever we go, all our lives. Like they were God's eyes that we can't ever get

136

away from, no matter what we do. Because they'll always be there."

How about when it's cloudy? Jud thought. He was not laughing. Later on he would be able to laugh, but not now, and the fact added to his vexation. His foolish anger took hold, again. Letting his face express it in the dark, he thought how all her glorious stars together did not shed even enough light to make his grimaces visible.

"Daddy always says," she continued, "that all creation's like one big book of lessons for us. Because it's all God's handiwork and teaches us about Him. All things are made for our instruction, the Bible says. I always thought the stars were the best instruction of all. Just look at them, Jud. And some people doubt miracles. When every one of them is a miracle."

Jud had already looked and his only response was a mumble of assent. No danger that she would notice. She was still gazing up and the vague light her face caught from the stars suggested an expression of more than commonly dumb complacency. Miracles. From somewhere a voice came into his mind and he thought, What if I was to put a hand on her, on her thigh? That would be a miracle to make her look down instead of up and to wipe that expression off her face. Between them was barely a foot of the wide stone step where her thigh, with her hand beside it, rested. Her thigh had no real shape in the dark, but Jud found himself staring at it. When he really became aware of this, he also became aware of something else. In the stillness, contained within the high black palisade of hedge, the ragged wheezing of the water sprinklers went on. But what he mainly heard, off in the distance, was a dog barking. He had heard the dog before at night, and yet, somehow, for the space of a few heartbeats, it set the skin at the back of his neck tingling.

That was when he got up from the step and went to move the sprinklers.

That was a curious moment. Later, in his room, Jud heard the dog again and it was just a dog, like any other, and he put the matter out of his thoughts. He did not want to examine it. He did not want to know what in fact was already there as a dark intimation at the back of his mind and so he labored to keep it dark, deceiving himself.

But self-deception is never perfect, and the inkling Jud's mind could not shut out moved him to redouble his cynicism about Hannah. This was his substitute for the whole truth. It was the proof of what Lily required in him and his almost daily accounts, delivered in that private time after they closed the store, became a kind of running testimonial to Jud's manhood. For this was what he was proving to Lily now, by his cynicism, remembering her words that night when she had kissed him. This was what she was waiting to see in him.

That, for the time, was what Jud persuaded himself to believe and it fed his cynicism. And as his cynicism increased, so, as it happened, did the occasions for it. The day came when Hannah even invited him to supper and sat him down to eat in the Presence Itself of the Reverend Rice. After that, it was once every week or so, like it or not. Hannah would intercept him in the morning and when suppertime came, there he would be with his back to the west windows that overlooked the garden, facing across the table an old sideboard that had on it a load of still older-looking silver and china vessels. Hannah would be seated at the table end to Jud's right and the Reverend at the other end, presiding. Behind the Reverend was an arched doorway into a shadowy hall where a clock ticked heavily in intervals of quiet. Jud's first time, when his cynical detachment had not yet put him completely at his ease, those intervals with that ticking disturbed. him. He imagined something ominous nearby, with the clock's deliberate strokes to measure its approach. But the feeling did not last long and after that he rarely heard the clock.

Except for Jud's enforced attendance at Sunday morning church service, where the Reverend was always up in the pulpit, he had not seen much of the old man. Otherwise Jud would not have retained anything at all of his original impression. He wondered at that impression now. Instead of sharp the Reverend's eyes were rather faded, a pale cloudy blue that his lenses magnified, and his mouth that Jud had thought straight and unbending was often tremulous with emotion. This was particularly so when the subject was spiritual things. The least occasion reminded him of Jesus or love or the soul's salvation and such thoughts, before they could produce a single word, would already have set his lips stirring. Even when he looked at Jud with a question in his eyes, it was not the kind of look to make Jud wary.

Anyway the Reverend looked much more often at Hannah. Obviously he doted on her and was glad to have somebody besides himself at the table once in a while to admire her qualities. To her embarrassment he would sometimes point them out. "Daughter," he said once, "I wish you could see your hair right now." As on each of these evenings the room was full of the sunset, brightening her hair. "It looks just like God's grace on it. And I've not got much doubt it is God's grace on it."

"Now Daddy," she said, displeased, lifting a small bite to her mouth. She was quiet at these meals, always listening, and sometimes Jud could feel her observing him. This was nothing new, though. He had felt it many times in the garden.

"She's a good girl, Jud," the Reverend said, bringing Jud in now. "And it shows in her. The fruit of the spirit. It shines out." Once again he had forgotten about his food. He sat with his thin hand resting on the edge of the table, his fork inverted and pointed toward Hannah. She was looking at her plate, embarrassed. Jud nodded discretely, humble in such a presence.

"That's the best way we've got to see God's grace—in people like Hannah. We can see it in their deeds and we can see it in their faces. You can't miss it if you look. There's people that want to deny it, because they've got none of it themselves, but in their heart they know better. It's the Spirit made manifest."

"Eat your supper, Daddy," Hannah said.

There was a pause and, for no special reason that Jud could see, it was one of those when he could hear the clock in the hallway ticking. Then the sound was gone. Jud's silent mockery had replaced it in his head and moments later his humble voice was asking a question about the mystery of grace.

Questions like this fitted Jud's act and he showed up on each occasion with at least one already prepared. He would choose an interval of quiet and, with hesitation, say, "Do you think men can *earn* God's grace, just by being good?" All he had to do then was sit there, forgetting to eat, with his eyes humbly aslant on the Reverend's eager face. Jud knew the answers already, the whole rigamarole, and sometimes he would even think of a Bible verse of his own to interject. "Like when Paul says, 'Through grace and not of yourselves'?" he would murmur, catching the Reverend's, and maybe Hannah's, glance of benign approval. It was all so easy, so natural. There was even leeway to stand back from himself and admire his performance, and to think how amused Lily would be to witness it.

Of course he always rendered up those accounts in detail to Lily. She rewarded him by smiling at his wit and, by her questions, showed him how interested she was. Jud was surprised at some of the questions. She wanted to know even what it was like inside the Rices' house, what kind of furnishings and decorations they had, right down to the china and silver vessels on the sideboard Jud faced across the dinner table. He described things as best he could. He supposed her curiousity had something to do with getting the whole picture, the better to relish his increasingly witty accounts.

But all this proving of Jud's new manhood got him nowhere, either, that he could tell. He was no closer to Lily. It was like being stuck at dead center, or like beating wings that never lifted anything. The only change of any kind was *around* him, in the drought, which got worse day by day. August came in hotter than July, and idle farmers, standing under awnings around the square or trees on the burnt-up courthouse lawn, declared that not in fifty years had there been a drought like this one. It was easy for Jud to believe them. In the steady breathless blast of heat off the town pavements, when the midday light set even the near horizons shimmering, it was not hard to believe that there never had been such a drought before. It might even be the final drought, making tinder for the promised fiery end of the world.

13

JUD COULD NOT SLEEP MUCH AND HIS INTERVALS OF
sleep were full of dreams. Then one night, as he lay on his
bed in the hot dark, half in and half out of sleep, his
dreams were suddenly different. Fragments of scenes
from out of his life kept crossing and crossing his mind.
There he was, going somewhere, little Jud with bare feet
on a red dusty road. He was singing a hymn at church,
his voice drowned in the unison of all the voices around
him. It was first daystreak over the ridge to the east and
shrill roosters proclaimed the coming miracle of the sun.
He saw his hands in the hollow-branch. They were as
white as ghost hands under the water, and the movements of his lips were prayers sent up for virtue, for
purity.

But the dream that really waked him stood all alone.
Night wind came cold and humming, threading the
banks of brush to left and right. There in the channel between them he crouched and shivered and watched two
windows like yellow eyes that never blinked in the gusts.
A cry, then another, and suddenly, as hot as if the air was
burning his naked skin, he lay awake on his bed. He sat
up to breathe and sat there afterwards wondering where
the man had buried Goldie.

There was no more sleep for Jud. By force he lay very
still on the bed but his muscles seemed to writhe. Once

he thought he heard a hand fingering his doorknob. Then it was at his window and then it was no special place at all. It was not real. Neither was his guilt. An accident. Wicked, devil—what did those words mean? They did not mean anything: they were scare words, Salter's words. They were the reason poor old Goldie was lying somewhere in a grave.

These thoughts did not settle Jud's restlessness. After a while he got up and stood naked in the dark. The bushes at his window stirred faintly, but the cause was a night breeze: he felt it pass across his body. Finally he lifted the shade from the doorglass. The house lights were all out, had long been out, and there was nothing to see in the wan starlit yard. Dropping the shade he reached for his clothes and dressed himself in the dark.

Jud let himself out through the window, replacing the screen. Then he crouched for a long time in the bushes watching, while the night breeze came again and stirred the leaves around him and the flowers out in the garden. He heard the dog barking.

Three or four cautious steps brought him to the rear corner of the building, and another dozen quicker ones into the blackness under the leaning hedge. He looked out over the garden. Of course there was no one there, although for a moment he had the illusion of a head limned in the starlight. Creeping on hands and knees between the trunks he could not help but rustle the hedge. When he stood upright in somebody's deep backyard, it seemed as if he had got there by a sort of magic.

Jud thought he knew where the place was. He kept to backyards all the way down the incline and, through alleys, skirted the lighted square. There were no people out and he had to wait for only one car to go by on the River

Road. He crossed and stepped onto the railroad embankment just as the courthouse clock behind him was striking midnight. He walked at the foot of the embankment on the far side where there was a path and nothing but a field of corn all the way across to the river. He was no longer walking fast. He was no longer even sure that he wanted to keep on.

Still a stride from the crest of the embankment he stopped. He knew, though he had never been here before, that this was the right place, because the house stood next to the lumberyard across the fence to his left. That lighted window in the back of the house, then, had to be Meagher's. Even so, Jud kept standing on the embankment, thinking now that he had changed his mind, that after all he did not want to see Meagher. He would retrace his steps, passing back along the railroad and through the alleys and dim backyards and under the black hedge into the garden once more, like a film running backwards. Settling down on his bed again in the torrid dream-filled dark.

Something moved. Jud located it next to the paling fence below the embankment: a dog, dark in color. He thought it looked up at him before it moved again and vanished through a hole in the fence. Descending Jud found that the fence lacked a paling and he ducked through under the beam and stood up in a weed-filled backyard. It was a stone's throw to the lighted window. His feet were on a path that led directly toward it.

Afterwards, after one quick glance through the window, he would turn back. He did not know what moved him. He only knew that he wanted a look into the room, at Meagher off-guard, and that his own stealthy feet on the path were bringing him up the slight incline to the

144

window. But the path led to a door. The window was several paces away through weeds along the wall. Jud found that his eyes just cleared the ledge.

His first glance brought him surprise that amounted to a kind of shock. He was looking into a perfectly bare though lighted room, without a bed or chair or carpet, without even so much as a calendar on the cracked plaster walls. Some scraps of paper on the floor—that was it. The light, though dim, gave a stark quality to the empty room.

But Jud was wrong. A change of position showed him, with a second surprise, the sagging end of a bed. There were two bare feet heels-down on the mattress. Moving farther he could see the rest of Meagher and after that Jud stood with cheek against the windowledge staring at him.

Obviously the figure propped up on the bed, naked but for undershorts, was Meagher—Meagher smoking. The face, even with eyelids shut, and the black lanky hair against the headboard, were unmistakably Meagher's. Jud's trouble, his feeling at once of uncertainty and revulsion, could only have been because of Meagher's nakedness, his body that Jud had never seen except in shirt and trousers. It was a scrawny body, with a pinched look almost like that of starvation, but this much could have been partly divined through his clothes. The thing that struck Jud was its color, or lack of color. The sallow tint of Meagher's face and neck and of his arm and hand holding the cigarette was no warning of what his clothes had concealed. The flesh was too white, a toadbelly white, as if the arms and head had been fastened onto a different species of body.

That was the way it seemed in that minute or two while

Jud stood watching. Later he recognized that the quality of the light, whose source was a yellowish hanging bulb invisible from the window, had merely tricked his vision; but this was not for a while yet. Just now he observed, suddenly, that Meagher's eyes not only had opened but were looking directly at him. He drew back too late. The next instant he saw a moving shadow on the wall and heard the thump of Meagher's feet on the floor. It was too late even to escape. There peering out at him was Meagher's face and then Jud heard his voice through the glass. "Wait a minute."

It was a minute, maybe two or three, before Jud heard the click of the doorlatch. Meagher was dressed. "Come on in," he said quietly.

There was a chair and a small table, as well as the bed, but nothing else, not even an object on the table. The one discolored lightbulb hung on a cord between bed and door. In the opposite wall was another door that looked to be sealed shut. Jud took it all in, avoiding Meagher's eyes. The room was unexpectedly cool, with a slightly fetid odor.

"What you doing?" Meagher said. "I don't like getting spied on."

"I wasn't sure you lived here. I couldn't see you at first."

Meagher was looking him over. The place was not only cool, it was as soundless as a cave. Jud wished he had simply fled. He could not even remember what he had wanted with Meagher.

Meagher got back on the bed and propped himself on the dirty pillow against the headboard. "Have a seat."

Jud did, on the one chair. "Just for a couple of minutes." He could not look back at Meagher. He observed,

146

aslant, that Meagher had taken time to put even his socks on.

"Bible class let out late?"

Jud tried for an amused grin. Plainly the bulb's discolored light was what had tricked his eyes, because his own hands now looked pale.

"I know you ain't already got tired of the spiritual life, have you?"

Jud hung on to the grin.

"Must be something eating you. Maybe you came to save *my* soul."

"Not hardly."

After a moment, "What did you come for?" Meagher said.

"To visit."

"Took you a long time." Meagher, very still on the bed, kept looking intently at him.

"I had to be careful," Jud said. "Till I got them sure of me."

For a little while they said nothing. Finally Meagher reached and opened the drawer in the little table beside his bed. He took out an ashtray with three or four gray-colored cigarettes lying in it. "One of these here ought to taste good to you about now. Bring you back to life again. Like old Lazarus." He held one out to Jud, and then a match.

Jud did not want to and yet he lit it at once. Drawing the bitter smoke down deep he suddenly knew how much he had not wanted to. His belly told him. Nausea surged up, burning his chest and throat, and he sat there with his eyes blank, bent forward and propped on his own knees. But the joint still dangled between his two limp fingers.

"God a'mighty," Meagher said. "You *was* getting purified. Just hang on a minute."

Smoke from the dangling joint drifted up across Jud's gaze, purling somehow like words that made no sound.

"Try it again now."

Jud's hand came up, but slowly, pausing on the way. The smoke burned his lungs again, then stopped burning, and the faint new wave of dizziness in his head was not from nausea.

In time Meagher had another joint already lit for him. It came to him floating in the grip of insubstantial fingers. The room was adrift around them, in curling yellowish tides of light that carried away and returned the sound of their voices. Sometimes, to hear them, Jud had to wait for words he had just now spoken, and many words that he saw shaped on Meagher's lips seemed to reach him from over one of his own shoulders or out of the air above. Some words, some of his own, got lost completely and at last he actually grew uncertain as to which ones he had spoken and which ones only thought. Yet his mind seemed perfectly clear. He was thinking that if objects around him looked insubstantial, shifting and changing their shapes, it was because they were this way in fact. What he saw was what they were, and a man too was what he thought he was. This was the meaning of the words that were falling right now like seeds into his mind.

"Your trouble is *you*. I noticed it a long time back. You're stuck with yourself, man. Like he's got hold of you too tight to shake."

Jud waited. Meagher was wise.

"That kid self, I mean. You've got to shuck him. You might fool you, but you can't fool a woman like that one. She wants a man."

"I could show her I'm one, if she'd let me."

Meagher shook his head.

"But I *could*," Jud said. "She won't give me a chance."

"You got a chance. Takes nerve, though."

Meagher had stopped looking at him. He had even stopped smoking and he sat with his head leaned back, at his ease, still but also adrift in the tides of yellowish light. Then Jud thought he looked like a corpse floating. A time passed.

"I've got nerve," Jud said. "I showed her I have."

"Not enough."

Without looking at him Jud finally said. "What would be enough?"

"Come on. You ain't that dumb. You know what kind of a woman your lady love is. She's sitting there waiting to see if you got it in you."

Something took hold of Jud then. It was like rage and not like rage. It was like something on his back that he had to throw off. "She couldn't *really* mean what you mean . . . not if she likes me. That's crazy."

After a moment, "You don't know much about women, do you? Ones like her, anyhow. That'd be a little tickling for her. More ways than one."

"You're crazy," Jud said, his voice rising.

"Why?"

Hannah stood in Jud's mind, the sun on her head. "Because that couldn't be done, for one thing."

"Couldn't, huh?"

"Not to her. Nobody could. You don't know her."

Meagher rolled over onto his elbow to look at Jud. He had a little grin that exposed the missing dogtooth. "You mean she ain't got a ass like other gals? . . . Or is it just too holy for you?" It was seeing his own pun that caused his grin to widen. Then, "You got a look on your face just

149

like a little Sunday school boy. Looking at somebody's said something 'wicked.'"

"It's because you're crazy." Jud's voice had upset the quiet.

"Come on," Meagher said, rising a little higher on his elbow. "That ain't why. It's because it'd be so wicked, is why. Just like the old devil his self."

Jud stared at him, hating him. "It's because I *couldn't*. Even if I wanted to." The muteness that came in the wake of his voice was as if he had now astonished the quiet room.

Still grinning, Meagher turned onto his back again. He lit the joint he had been holding and let the smoke drift up from his lips, purling in the light. "I reckon you couldn't. But it's you, not her. Don't tell me. I know about that kind of a aging gal, loving Jesus to keep her juice from drying up. Wishing He'd hurry up and get here in the flesh. She'd take anything come handy. Already loving up to *you* and don't even know it. You're halfway there right now. Just try giving her thigh a little squeeze. Do a gal a favor."

"What do you know about her?" Jud's tongue felt thick. That hot slow something down in his throat was pure rage gathering.

"Enough," Meagher said, watching his smoke. "Only trouble in it is you." His gaze came back to Jud. "Can't stand the thought, can you? Look at you. You ain't come two good steps from where you started out."

Then Meagher laughed. Or rather he chuckled, a low extended chuckle from his throat that seemed to raise up echoes all around the room—Meagher laughing from everywhere at once.

Jud stood up. He saw himself stand up and saw his hand rise and throw the burnt-out joint at Meagher, hard, missing, hitting the wall behind him. "You dirty son of a bitch."

Still grinning Meagher said, "I ain't any dirtier than what you are."

But Jud was already halfway to the door. Then he was there and out, leaving it wide open, hearing Meagher's diminishing laughter back in the room behind him.

14

IF THERE WAS ANY INTERVAL WHEN JUD DID COME close to turning back, it was in the aftermath of that visit. He left there loathing Meagher, walking fast, as a person would hurry to put a distance between himself and disease. For that was about the way he felt—as if he needed, and quickly, to get where the air was clean.

But no place on Jud's way seemed far enough, not until he had reached the hedge in back of the garden and crept on hands and knees between the trunks and stood up straight in the black shade. The air seemed right again, but something else did not. He did not know what it was, and he stood for a long time listening, searching the starlit garden for sign of a human shape or movement among the shrubs and flowers. There was no one. At least there was no one except him, standing nearly invisible under the hedge, a shadow newly risen from out of the black hedge trunks. He had a curious moment. He saw himself there, and more, saw himself with a taste of that loathing that had followed him all the way from Meagher's place.

The moment was brief, gone as soon as Jud stepped out of his tracks. What loathing remained was for Meagher and this stayed with him long after he went to bed. Something even spilled over from it, taking the form of an ugly dream about Lily, Lily with putrescent wormy cheeks. He waked up shuddering, because his lips had touched one of her cheeks, and after that, clear on until day, an obsessive notion would not let go of him. Daylight did not quite dispel it, either. As groundless as it was he kept being harassed by the thought of Lily and Meagher darkly conspiring together.

That mood did not last long, however. Half a day and just one of those intervals when Lily stood so close that her arm touched against him were all that was needed to purge it clean from his mind. His cheek was tingling for her lips again and the chance that he might yet turn back was not a chance any longer. Or rather, if he did have a chance it depended completely on Hannah.

But it was like fate, both Jud's and Hannah's, that launched itself the very night that followed that August day. This, the choice of moments, was one thing that made it seem so much like fate at work. Until then there was still one big restraint on Jud. His conviction that Hannah would be quite unapproachable *that* way remained almost unshaken by Meagher's words. He imagined her face if he were to touch her, and maybe an outcry, and maybe even consequences compared to which these would be nothing. So there was at least his fear to restrain him. But this depended on Hannah's keeping her distance, her same sisterly way with him, and suddenly, that night, when Meagher's mockeries were not a full day old yet in his mind, it was different. Or, which came to the same thing, Jud thought it was different.

He did not know what had given Hannah the idea. At first he thought it was some bit of gossip that had reached her and happened to lodge a certain way in her head. A little later he decided that the idea was her own, one that she had been stewing over for a good while, maybe. And now the oppression of the hot night and her withered garden sprang it. Something in the tone of things was his first warning.

They had set the water sprinklers going and, barely settled down beside her at his end of the warm stone step, Jud began to notice. He was not accustomed to silence at the start. Their silences were for later on, for reflection on the spiritual thoughts they had uttered. This one had no preface. He noticed that she had not looked up, either, though the stars, if hazy, were their old steadfast selves. There was something heavy on her mind. And presently, as if in preparation, the crickets had attuned themselves to fit her silent mood. Jud found himself listening for the dog, but he did not hear it.

"Jud." She was not looking at him. The palest sheen of starlight defined the lowered posture of her head. Something was coming.

"You think of me as a friend, don't you?"

"Sure," he mumbled.

She hesitated. "Can I talk to you about something . . . personal?" Her voice was so low that there was no margin for hearing, and this time he was not as quick to say, "Sure." Then he had to wait another while, watching her pale hands clasped together across her knees.

"It's about Mrs. Nunn."

She was giving him time to answer. Adjusting his voice he said, "What about her?"

"I don't want to sound . . . mean. Or gossipy."

He waited. Already his anger was gathering—but anger mixed with a certain queasiness.

"She's not a good woman, Jud. I'm sure of it." Hannah's voice was still no more than audible, the voice to utter a melancholy secret. "I've known her a long time. Please don't think it's because I hate her or something."

154

Yes, Jud thought. Not a "good" woman. There was not much, just a taint, of that queasiness left in his anger. He said guardedly, "I only just work for her. She always treated me all right, though."

Then there was nothing but the slow wheeze of the sprinklers.

"I don't trust her, Jud."

Jud did not know what to do but keep silent.

"I wish I knew how to say it. I don't even know why I'm so sure of it, but I am. I've been thinking. About things she's done for you. Like firing Mr. Baker, after all these years, for you to take his place. And all those—"

"She just thought I had a better head than Baker," Jud said faintly. But Hannah went on.

"And all those times she keeps you late. Is it just for work, Jud? Or does she talk to you about things?"

"Just business stuff," he said, his queasiness rising. How *could* Hannah know anything? "Inventory and stuff. That's all. There's lots of things—"

One of Hannah's hands touched his arm, resting there for a moment. "I don't mean something bad, that you do. Please don't think that. I'm thinking about her influencing you. Because you're young. And she's . . . she's a godless woman."

Hannah had removed her hand, but only to place it on the step so that it lay touching his hand. This was when something else gave a first faint stir in Jud's mind.

"She'd like to make you that way too. Or anybody she could. Poor Mr. Nunn could have told you that. Only he never would have, the kind of man he was. I know she hated him. She hates everybody that's not like her. I almost think he died just to get away from her." Hannah paused. She was looking at Jud, for he could see, aslant, her dim night-blotted face and pale hair in the starlight.

155

"I can't help but think of one of those people the devil uses," she said, " . . . to ruin souls."

Jud could not say, "Bunk!" or even, "Why? How do you know?" He could only sit waiting, hearing in a silence otherwise perfect the sprinklers like a sound of troubled breath. He did not know why his scorn did not rise up and sieze him, make him bold, make him laugh.

"Please don't think it's because I hate her. That it's just something personal. Because it's not."

But it was, Jud thought, clenching his teeth. Of course it was. Pious hypocrite. The thought he had had a minute ago stirred in his head again.

"Please don't stay there, Jud. Get another job. Daddy'll help you . . . Will you think about it?"

He was busy with that other thought. He said carefully, "But I don't see any reason to. Mrs. Nunn doesn't bother me any." He waited. He had to wait a good while.

"Are you sure?"

Jud realized that she was trying in spite of the dark to search his face. He let her go on searching until he thought it was time to say, "I don't see why not. I guess I don't even know what you mean."

Very softly Hannah said, "That you're young. And still not sure about things. And she's older." After a pause, "I don't think you can believe she's what she is—a wicked person. For years I didn't either. I tried not to."

Yes, "wicked." There was the word, the good old Bible word.

"They say the wicked are the lonesomest people there are. That's why they try to make other people be like them. That's what I'm trying to say, Jud. If you'd believe me."

Still waiting Jud mumbled obscurely. Wicked Lily. Also wicked Jud, if Hannah but knew.

156

"Will you think about it . . . about quitting? We'll help you get a job."

Jud started. It was because Hannah had laid her hand on his.

"We look for so much from you. We think the Lord's got his eye on you for something good in the world."

And there lay her holy hand on his wicked one. It not only lay there: it had closed on his, and with tension enough so that he could feel her pulse working. Not working for Jesus, though, Jud thought, remembering Meagher's words. It was for him, Jud. And the cause behind it was wicked Lily, whom Jud must drop. Hypocrite. He felt something around his heart soar up. With cunning he said, "I don't know. I'll have to think about it." Then, still more cunningly, he said, "We ought to move the sprinklers."

Her hand was slow to let go of his. As he stood up, the first to do so, he could tell that she was still trying to search his face.

It was a big discovery. She was, he thought, not only jealous. She was also a hypocrite, like the rest of them, disguising her secret letch for him in the need to save his soul from Lily's clutches. That was how he read it. In a matter of minutes the ground had shifted for him and his first hours of bloated confidence did not allow him even to see any problem but the choice of proper tactics. Go slow, he thought—that was the first thing. Not all at once. Keep cool and watch and let the moments ripen one at a time. And Lily, the wicked Lily, was his weapon. As Jud thought about this that night he smiled in the dark and wished that he could tell it to Lily.

Jud's confidence was still with him the next morning and this did tell Lily something. He could see her appraising him, a new question in her yellow eyes. Finally she said, "You look like you just swallowed a canary."

"Nothing like that," he said, grinning, wishing that she could see how coldly, like a bright new blade, his mind was working.

Later this confidence deserted him, or seemed to, as if it could not survive the glare of a whole hot August day. By evening that blade of his had lost its bright edge, and when, that night, Hannah called him out of his room he felt like a man in the wake of a foolish dream. Things were as they had been before—the same hazy stars for her to marvel at and the sprinklers softly wheezing in the half-transparent dark. No hand was laid on his, no mention of last night: it had not happened. Yet he experienced one perverse moment when it *had* happened and sweat not caused by the heat of the night stood out on his skin. He imagined that he had made a move, had touched her, and that her startled wounded face stared at him through the gloom. What had he done? That was the way he felt, and more than that. He thought that other eyes had seen him, watching him from the garden. He was safely back in his room again before he could get this notion out of his head.

But late in the night Jud dreamed of Lily. The words he heard, though in Meagher's voice, came as if by magic from her lips. He waked up feeling as if he had skipped a day, and after that his lapses did not amount to much.

15

JUST HOW IT HAPPENED, IN EVERY SINGLE DETAIL, was to remain in Jud's memory with all the vividness of a thing accomplished only minutes before. But the vividness, even in the immediate aftermath of the event itself, was of a curious kind. He remembered everything, but not quite in the way a participant does. He was half like an outsider looking in on himself, supposing that that likeness of him was not really him. It remained this way in his thoughts and it was this way then, right after and also during the event. *That* could not happen. All along, deep in his soul, he had known that really it never could happen. Yet it did, and one of the persons involved was him. The other one was Hannah.

The way things fell out for him, like ducks in a row, had something to do with Jud's curious feeling about it all. Suddenly there had been no Reverend Rice to look out of windows or to spook their privacy just by the fact of his presence in the house. "Daddy's gone to a Bible conference," Hannah said to him. "For two whole weeks. I'm going to miss him." The house behind them was not only empty, it was dark. The better that way to see the stars, and every night she left it dark when she came out to the garden. It made a difference, too. The stars gave even less light than Jud had thought and the stealthiest spy in the world could not have got in range to see them.

That was one thing. Another was the way Hannah handed him his chances, as if she was leading his thoughts on purpose to where her weakness lay. On the first night, too, and early, just minutes after they had sat down on the step. The slow way she sidled into the matter of Lily warned Jud and he thought again about the fact that no one was there in the house behind them.

"I'm afraid you don't like me bringing it up again," she said.

"I don't mind," he answered dimly. That was all. His manner caused her to squirm a little and for a moment he feared she was going to drop the subject.

"I know it's your business. And maybe you think I . . . But I know things about her, Jud."

He was silent, sullen.

"She has ways that . . . fool people."

Looking at the stars Jud let her fumble.

At last she said, "I don't want her to fool you." Then, "Mislead you," she added, as if this were to make it clearer. "She's so much older than you are. You don't realize . . . "

He looked at the ground, sullen. His confidence was growing apace.

"She's the kind that would use herself," Hannah murmured, " . . . to blind a young man." There was more to come. He could tell she was choosing, rejecting words. As if she was speaking to somebody else she said, "Her charms, I mean. The kind she's got."

Jud was doing it right. He saw this clearly now and did not make a sound, waiting. It was a long wait, into which, under the sound of the sprinklers, tingling cricket voices intruded. He heard that faraway dog again.

"You must know what I mean, Jud. You do, don't you? "

With his head bowed he let his silence say yes for him.

160

And this was also right. He knew. He did not even need to see her troubled face in the dark.

Jud did not relent, either—not that night. He sat and felt his silence working, speaking in a way that no words could have done. When she fell silent too, he left her, early, with only the weakest plea that he was tired.

Everything he did was right. The knowledge was there like a gift when the moments came, and at times he felt like somebody traveling an old familiar route. His adroitness surprised him. It was as if he had skills he had forgotten about, that came back new and fresh when the moments called for them. All his life he had heard talk about the mysteries of a woman's soul. What mysteries? Given the key handed to him, he could see that what looked like mysteries was merely part of a not very complicated clockworks.

Jud did not know, then, why he had the feeling, like a dark stream running at a level below that of his confidence, that there was no possible chance of success, that every move he made in this direction was in some odd way unreal. Because the feeling had not only been wrong. It had barely fazed a confidence that each new night added something to.

What seemed like the biggest leap so far came on the night when he held her hand for the first time. He had had the chance before, but this was the right chance. He had learned to recognize which of her silences held the thoughts that she did not want just yet to risk repeating, and this silence was one of those. At the same time her hand lay next to his. It was just as if the moment had been prepared for him, even down to the words he would say and the posture his body would take. For one long moment he hesitated, obscurely aghast at himself. Then he put his hand on hers.

161

"I don't want to like her." He said it just above a whisper.

There was not any response. Her hand lay still and he could not be sure that the pulse he felt was not his own. His astonishment at himself was already fading. There was other cause for astonishment in the fact that words to follow these, exactly the words, were taking shape on his lips. "I wish I never had gone to work there."

Her hand did not move. Nothing about her moved, though he was sure she was looking at him. The sound of the sprinklers went on and, much more faintly, the crickets. Slowly, as if it only reflected the grip of suffering on his heart, he tightened his hand, and waited. He felt an answer. It was her other hand, which settled on the back of his and pressed.

Jud's strategy worked like magic. He had only to be slow and watchful, calculating the displays of struggle passing in his soul. The best of his moments were the gloomy intervals when he sat speechless, with bowed head, holding her hand as if here only was the strength that could lift him out of the devil's clutch. Though he had to will it, himself, of course. If only he could muster the strength to will it. She understood. She knew how a boy, a lonely boy, could fall into the snare of such a woman—an evil woman, with evil fleshly charms. This, that she could not say with words, was what her hand said to him. It was warm and small, a little rough with calluses, and sometimes in the way it gripped his hand he thought he could feel something more than desire for just his soul's salvation. In the end, something told him, this would turn out to be the strongest magic of all.

No doubt Jud was partly right: to make it finally possible there must have been at least some of this involved

162

in Hannah's submission. But to Jud, by then, this had become the real, the whole magic. The night when at last, sinking with despair, he leaned and put his head on her shoulder, he felt the little shock of blood in her neck. The hand that later came to rest on his cheek was not quite steady and her voice murmuring, "Poor Jud," in his ear had a kind of tightness he was sure he recognized. He even heard the beat of her heart, thinking that the dog in the distance was barking in lament for virtue's fall.

This was not to happen quite yet, however. There were two days left to her, on one of which, for unexplained reasons, she did not show up when the evening hour came. For a little while Jud's confidence lapsed again. Seated on the doorstep to his room, waiting in vain by now, he saw the whole thing as like a dream that never, never could happen. But his confidence soon came back. It told him why she had not appeared that night, and he went to sleep with the illusion of hearing, even from this distance, the quick heavy stroking of her heart.

The next night was the one. As it seemed to him later, he had known this all day long and it must have been, as he went about his work at the store, that the knowledge was somehow mirrored in his face. He thought that Lily's eyes followed him even more than they were accustomed to do and once or twice he actually turned aside for fear she would read the whole thing in his face. It was not time yet. Tomorrow would be the time.

This thought about tomorrow not only excited Jud for the moment. It kept him excited clear on into the evening and furnished, really, all the lust he could summon up for Hannah. At least this was true at the start. It seemed that Hannah's body alone would not be enough to lift his sluggish blood—not even when she lay open and given up to him, with her hair unfolded on the grass like a pale nest for her head. Jud had to shut his eyes, thinking of Lily. Then his blood rose up.

After that Jud had no need for any thought at all. The woman beneath him, whose breath came faintly shrill between her teeth, whose arms held fiercely to his neck and would not let go when he was spent, did not even have a name. Not, at least, until she lay motionless under him and his eyelids came open. Then he knew her name. The soft breast where his head rested and the heart that went on stroking against his cheek were part of Hannah Rice.

It was not true. In Jud's moment of first shock this was his instinct—to deny the truth of what had so unmistakably taken place. It was not possible, and to see himself roll free of her and to watch her sit up slowly and with slow hands arrange the clothes that he had put awry, was more like a dream than a dream could be. Then she was all finished. She was back on the step beside him, silent the way she often was, while the sprinklers went on and the dry tingling sound of crickets in the grass and flowers. On her head, as always, lay the sheen of light from her steadfast hazy stars. It had not happened.

The stillness was not broken again until she got up and putting a hand ever so briefly on his shoulder went into the house. He heard the door drawn shut, the latch click. It was true, of course, and the hot little body under his and those shrill breaths and thumping heartbeats had in fact been Hannah's—the saintly Hannah. Then that was holy fire. For a week, by those displays of struggle with his conscience, he had been stoking holy fire. He felt a smile come on his lips. Here was holiness stripped of its fraud. And wicked Lily was wicked for wanting what a

Christian saint had wanted. Jud could feel his smile in the dark. It was an interval of perfect lucidness, without a trace of the odd distortion that soon would impose itself again on his memory of the event.

In fact by the time Jud got back to his room this lucidness was already gone. It was hot in the room, breathless. There was sweat like dew on his face and neck and he took off his shirt and stood in the dark by the open window. Not a leaf stirred in the shrubbery outside. Through breaks like peepholes in the foliage he could see out there the featureless shadows that were the garden lying under the stars. She had never said a word, not one. But he was wrong: she had said someting. It was right after he kissed her and her face lay in the hollow of his neck so that he could feel her breath and feel her lips move. She had barely whispered, as if to herself, "Poor Jud." And that was when, or rather was just before, he got his one real glimpse of her face. She had drawn back a little and it was as if a sudden increment of light showed him her eyes for a moment. It was just for a moment. It was also the preface to his final attack, which had met no serious resistance.

Nothing stirred, not even the crickets now. He thought of her shrill breaths, but the stillness, as if it had the effect of distance, simply swallowed the sound of them. It was all fast becoming this way, his mind's eye observing the scenes of a half-incredible dumb show. When the faraway dog started again he thought at first that the sound was reassuring, that it offered a point of focus for his mind. This did not last long. Instead the remote barking, as if it came from a different world, only distracted him more. He began to hate the dog and made vague plans to go out and find it and kill it. The dog was the last and the only thing he heard as he fell asleep. But by now he was not really thinking about the dog. His last dissolving thought that night was about some shadowy person in the garden, some one who had been hiding there the whole time since dark.

Part FOUR

16

JUD REMEMBERED THE SPELLS OF FEVER HE HAD had when he was younger, and he wondered if that fever could be about to come back. The way he felt much of the time reminded him of those spells—a way of feeling remote and shut out from himself, watching himself performing actions that failed to quite make sense. Sometimes he thought that the drought, which went on unbroken in September, which might yet end by returning the world to dust, was calling his fever back. The noon heat was like an affliction poured down from the sun.

There was an air-conditioner now in one of the high windows in the north wall, and this kept a fragile coolness alive in that part of the store. Jud lingered there when he could, feeling remote, his eyes most often on Lily whenever she was not looking his way. She never sought this cool spot. Usually, when she was not in the little office or out among the counters with a customer, she was standing or sitting near the cash register, a place as hot as any in the store. Jud tried to remember when he had seen her with sweat on her face or blouse or with any indication that she was hot. But there was no such time. Watching from his distance he often thought that instead of hot she looked cool, or even cold, as if the touch of her skin would come as a shock to his fingers. Then a little shiver would scurry up his back.

This kind of feeling about her was something new, but

the explanation seemed clear. It was simply that between Lily and him nothing had changed, nothing whatever. Yet she knew, and had known since that first morning after it happened. She knew because he had told her, though not with words. He had told her with his eyes and with a little smirk that was on his mouth and with what must have been a new flush of expectation in his face. He saw her understand it, too. He saw the flicker when her eyes looked into his and, less certainly, the ghost of his own smirk stir on her lips. But that was all. After that the day had been like any other at the store.

By the end of that day Jud thought he knew that nothing would come of it—nothing, that is, where Lily was concerned. Yet he went right on, in a way that later reminded him of a person acting in his sleep. What he did appeared to make sense. His head always seemed perfectly clear at the time and he convinced himself that he was not only gaining ground with Lily but also proving yet again the hypocrisy of Hannah and all her kind. He was that cool, keeping to plan, ready with his precautions when the moment came. It had become easy for him now, as if Hannah had been a ripe peach hanging by to be picked when he wanted it. He had only to work, with small refinements, the same careful strategy as before. "Save me," his gloomy silences kept saying, and before too long little Hannah would be persuaded all over again. Then, at the crucial stage, she would be Lily in his arms, Lily's thighs yielding the way for him to enter her body. There had now been three such times. But there could have been more if he had wanted.

Jud's second score—there on the step and the house still empty and dark behind them—seemed in his memory almost like a rerun. The third time there were some differences. The Reverend was back home and so it could not happen on the step. Under the hedge by the birdbath, sheltered even from God's watchful stars, was the bench, and luring her there was no big problem. The bench was good enough. But if the place was changed and the Reverend's presence in the house added a little spice of danger, these differences did not come to much. Another difference made more of an impression.

After the second time Hannah had not said anything at all. She sat up close against him and held his hand as if she did not mean to let go of it, but not a sound escaped her. This last time she had done the same way, for a while, and when she finally moved Jud supposed that she was moving to rise. Instead she leaned and put her head in the hollow of his shoulder and, as wordless as before, left it there. She said something at last, but so much later that by then Jud's body ached from the rigid posture he had to keep. There was too much heat where her head touched him and the yellow glow in the one house window visible to him seemed to flicker faintly. She said, "Do you think you could ever learn to love me, Jud?"

He had to respond in some way. He did it by putting a hand lightly on her head, on soft fine hair that was barely even pale in the darkness under the hedge. Her head did not stir. It was too hot against his chest and he did not know whether he could go on breathing if she did not move it soon. Even when she left him—exactly like the other times, in silence—it seemed that he could not get back the breath he needed.

In these mid-September days Jud often felt as if there was not air enough. The thought of suffocation would become a vague threat standing by, and at the store he would hold up his face to the air-conditioner for the cool breeze it gave. Every morning early when he got up, when the day was still pale enough to raise illusions, he

171

would go outside expectantly and look up at the sky. Sometimes he would imagine that the sky was overcast and that he could make out on the western horizon the dim shapes of thunderheads. The rain was coming, torrents of it, and sweet fresh rain-filled air to wash the taste of dust out of his throat. But his moments of joy were brief. After he gazed for a while, always there was nothing on the horizon. By nine o'clock the sky had turned to brass and the sun to a relentless molten eye.

Now he spent his best hours at Meagher's place, alone. One night late, in a mood of desperation, he had got up out of bed and, passing under the hedge, made his stealthy way to Meagher's room. Meagher was not there, but the light, the one discolored bulb, was burning. Also the door stood partly open, and Jud went in and sat down on the chair to wait for him. Meagher did not come. He did not come the next night, either, or any of the nights that followed, and Jud could never see the least sign that he had been there in the day. So Meagher was gone. But this suited Jud. The place was like a refuge, remote and cooler than other places, and there was Meagher's pot for him to smoke. Jud had found his cache. It was buried in the mattress, plenty of it, and almost every night for an hour or two he would sit propped on the bed where Meagher had sat and draw the smoke down deep and watch it rise coiling from his lips in the yellow-tinted light. The weight went out of his body. Remoteness grew around him like a veil and drifting with the smoke he watched the antic scenes of his life take shape and dissolve again. They came and went and were not real. Even that Jud on the bed down there was like a thought in his mind. Once he stayed the whole night long and could not believe the brightness at the windows.

But the feeling of peace he took away with him never lasted very long. It was like stepping back into time, but a time that did not lead anywhere or make anything change. Lily still followed him with her eyes, but this was so much a part of things that it had grown meaningless by now. He did his work, came and went, wishing sometimes that that old fever would go ahead and strike him. It seemed to hover but did not strike. Restlessness kept him awake in his bed and the hours of sleep that did come made him think of swoons.

There was one thing that had changed, though—his hour with Hannah in the evenings. Jud still went out and sat with her for a while on the garden step, but the experience had a different character. The smallest difference was that they did not run the sprinklers anymore. There was no use anymore, she said. Also there was not enough water now. But the big difference was in Hannah. There were no more rhapsodies about the stars, no more of her tiresome moral reflections. She was nearly always silent, moreso each evening, and she sat there beside him in a way that did not ask or even expect him to say anything. She had only one mute request, signaled each time by her hand lightly touching him somewhere. She wanted him to take her hand and hold it. He always did, until he could gracefully let go, feeling the tough small calluses and the passiveness that, because of these, seemed the greater. He knew she was saying he could have her if he wanted, all of her he wanted. But if he ever had wanted her, he did not anymore, and he sat, while the crickets chirped from the dying flower beds and that far-off dog barked sometimes, waiting for the moment when he could let go of her hand. Especially here of late this had been true. There were times now when even so little a thing seemed full of risk for him. It was as though hovering somewhere close was a dark dismaying consequence that had better not be provoked.

This vaguely ominous feeling was all Jud ever had to prepare him, because what in fact happened was the one consequence that he had never paused to think about. It was too simple, maybe, or unfitting, like an underhanded affront to his dignity. Besides he had been careful, coolly taking precautions he thought were sure. So at first, just as if the words had got stopped at a point still remote from the center of his brain, he could not quite take in what Hannah said to him. When he did clearly understand her his next thought was that she was lying. He almost said this. Finally he did say, "You just *think* that, though."

"I'm afraid it's true."

Jud was holding her hand at the time and after a minute he was conscious of it lying in his like a severed part uncannily alive. Yet he could not seem to let go of it. "That's not like *knowing*."

"I've been thinking so for a while. I'm sure of it now."

Her profile, bowed a little, was defined in the dim light. Suddenly he saw her face the way it had looked last night at the supper table, and the Reverend saying, "Don't you feel good, daughter? You don't look very well." Jud had glanced and seen in her pallor and drawn cheeks the evidence of some little illness or, possibly, remorse. He saw it differently this time. He heard her say again, though only inside his head, "I'm sure of it now." and felt in his the stillness of the hand he could not let go. His mind groped for something, anything. Where the thoughts should have been was a dry chirping of crickets and the faraway sound that seemed as though it had been with

174

him constantly for a long time. That dog. He felt a sort of cold panic spreading along his blood.

It was, or seemed to be, much later when she took her hand away. But the panic did not let go and Jud watched her sidelong, tensely, imagining that somehow her next move would come like an alarm. He saw her look upward, catching a little starlight in her face, then down again at the featureless garden. Then she did startle him, but only by getting to her feet. "Good night," she whispered. He heard her steps on the porch and the doorlatch like a nerve plucked inside his head.

This set him in motion. Except to his room he did not know where he was going, but once inside he walked straight to the window. His pause lasted a few seconds. In a moment he was out and under the hedge and he came up walking fast toward Lily's house.

The house was dark, every window. At the back door Jud raised his fist to knock, then did not. To carry all the way upstairs it would have to be loud and the stillness of the neighborhood made him think of heads bent to listen. He stood beneath her window, but that attentive silence stopped his tongue. He tried pebbles, hitting the wall up there and then the screen.

"Who's there?"

Her voice seemed not only loud but tense, making him jump. He tried once in vain before he answered, "It's me." Then, "Can I talk to you?"

For a while there was nothing. When she spoke again her subdued voice was the familiar one. "Wait a minute."

Jud stood at the back door waiting. The light in Lily's window now and the memory of her subdued familiar voice had made him somewhat calmer, and at last the thought that she was taking a long time made another

175

difference. Was it to fix her hair that she was so slow, or to paint her lips? He thought how the house was empty except for her, for them, and suddenly his reason for being here seemed less substantial than it had before. The kitchen light came on. He saw her, in the dressing gown, her hair combed and her lips freshly painted. Regarding him through the glass she opened the door. "What's the matter, Jud?"

She stood holding the door half open, standing in the gap, blocking it. Then "*Is* something the matter?"

He had to call it back to mind. Even then it seemed half ghostly at first, while he gathered the words to say, "I need some advice."

"Are you in trouble?" With the light directly behind her, her expression was not clear.

"Yes."

"Well? What kind of trouble?"

He could not tell for sure, but he had the notion that she was looking at him with a certain new intensity of interest. She said, "Is it girl trouble?"

"Yes," he whispered.

Finally she stepped back and held the door for him to enter. When Jud turned around she was already standing with her back to the shut door, facing the light, and he saw that he was not mistaken. There was a glitter in her eyes. She said, "Not little Hannah, surely?"

He nodded yes. It did not seem real, and his eyes stopped for a moment where the margins of her robe met, a point where the hollow between her breasts began.

"You *are* a bad boy," she said. "And all this time I thought you two were tending the garden. But that's not what you were tending to, was it?" Suddenly she moved. She moved as if to approach him, so that he missed the

176

breath he had started to draw. But she only passed close by and went over to the stove, where she set the coffee pot on a burner, After that she appeared to forget what she had meant to do. Her gaze was on the wall in back of the stove and Jud could not see the expression on her face. A minute passed like this, an empty kind of minute.

"Are you sure she's pregnant?"

The word was somehow a surprise. It was an ugly surprise, an ugly sound, and Jud fancied he could hear its echo returning from the empty house behind him. Everything came back. It was like weight, a cold heavy object settling down on his heart. Finally he answered, "She says she is. She says she knows it."

"A lot of girls have said that."

"*She* wouldn't," he murmured. "If it wasn't true."

There was silence, flat silence. Jud said, "They could make me marry her. Or send me to prison if they wanted to. That judge would love to."

"Why don't you marry her?"

Lily's voice merely asked it, without irony. She was still gazing at the wall but at a point higher up, as if she had found something interesting there. Jud felt like sinking down on the chair close by. "You know I wouldn't do that. I'd rather go to prison."

"Would you really?"

"Yes."

There was another wait. He heard Lily draw a breath just before she spoke. "Why don't you talk her into getting rid of it, then?"

It took him a while to understand what Lily meant. When he did, the thought was not exactly a shock to him, yet his voice came out a little too loud, saying, "She wouldn't do that."

"She did something else," Lily said, still gazing up at the wall. "That you used to think she wouldn't do."

He said, "She wouldn't do this, though."

"Try her. Look at what's going to happen if she doesn't."

Jud looked, seeing himself through bars in that dark prison.

"Think about where it would leave Daddy. That would really be something. With the church and all. She can't very well hide it, you know."

Jud thought of the Reverend's face at the table, then of Hannah's at the other end, bowed. A haggard look. "She still wouldn't," he finally said. For it was true.

Lily stopped looking at the wall. She turned her head and looked at Jud. "And even that's just part of it. There's keeping you out of prison, too."

"I'm not all that much to her," he murmured.

"She gave up being a saint, for you. She even put herself in danger of hell fire," Lily said, her irony barely evident.

"That was just . . . You know." He said boldly, "She just wanted it. That's really why. That's all." The glitter he saw again in Lily's eyes did not stir his blood this time.

"More than once, too, wasn't it?"

He nodded. He had stopped looking at her.

"She'd do anything you asked her to." Lily paused. "She'd call it 'love,' though."

Jud shook his head no, avoiding Lily's eyes. "It wouldn't be any use."

"Give her a try. It's not even any big thing anymore. There are lots of places. I'll find out for you." She was waiting for Jud to look up at her, but he refused. There was nothing, not a sound from the empty house. Then she said, "Because I wouldn't want to lose you, Jud. Not now."

Her tone seemed to reach him before the words did. It was as if she had been standing close and whispering, breathing the words into his ear. But this was followed by another, different kind of sound. He saw her feet move, coming toward him. She only passed him by, though, and he heard the latch click as her hand turned the door knob. "Goodnight," she said.

When the light went out in her window upstairs Jud was still there in the dark backyard recalling the sound of her voice.

17

BUT A FLAT NO WOULD BE HANNAH'S ANSWER. A
final no, made clearer in her eyes, her face, than any word
could ever make it. Jud tried to envision her face as it
would look, with wide startled eyes assessing him and
mouth that could not find expression for this. And then,
what? Wasn't this the one thing bound to strain her
sweating Christian soul too far? He could not risk it.

So all the next day, telling himself this, he fled from
Lily. Or he tried to. There were not enough customers or
new excuses to keep him always at a distance from her.
Even when there was half the store between them Jud
could tell that she was often watching him, even pausing
at her work to watch. Then, his blood rising, he would
think what she had said, had murmured to him last
night. "I wouldn't want to lose you, Jud." Today she wore
a blouse she had never worn before, tawny like her eyes
and silky sheer and tense where it spanned from point to
point of her breasts. Its touch would have been like
touching flesh. Jud tried not to look, not even with his
mind's eye.

There was a period in the afternoon when she was absent from the store, and in that time all the force of Jud's
thoughts about Hannah came back and seized him. A flat
and final no would be the answer. Nor could he risk it.
But later, nearly at the end of the day, Lily came back too,

in person. Then it was as before. It was worse, for closing time had come and soon there were the two of them alone.

"I found out for you."

Jud stood with his back to her, pointlessly arranging tools on a counter. Her voice made him start a little. "Found out what?"

She did not answer. He had to turn around, finally, and he saw that she was holding a piece of paper. It was for him. He had to step forward and take it.

"I expect you could find one closer than that, though."

It was an address, written in her neat angular script. He made it a refuge for his eyes and kept them there, conscious how close she was standing and how his heart had begun to sound.

"You know you've got to do something."

He could see her feet, in strap sandals, her painted toe-nails honed and sharp-looking. Above the drone of the air-conditioner that cooled nothing where they stood, he could hear only his heart.

"Ask her tonight."

"She won't do it," he murmured. "She—"

"She'll do it."

One of Lily's feet stirred and moved a little closer to him. Very softly, almost whispering, she said, "I meant what I told you last night."

Jud's sudden languor was like a weight that stopped him from lifting his eyes. Even his arms felt too heavy, or he might have dared to raise a hand and reach out toward her. But now her feet moved with decision. Looking up he saw her walking away toward the door, and he watched her go out and pass out of sight beyond the plate glass window.

181

Later, moving as slowly as if there was need for quiet, he turned off the air-conditioner and then the lights. Except up front the store was all in shadow, but the street outside to a point midway across lay in a glare of dusty sunset light. This was why Jud did not see him at first. Beyond midpoint the street was a dusky shoal, and the figure was no clearer than other objects on the far side. Darkly clothed and black in the face it was less clear, and only Jud's long heavy pause inside the door caused him finally to notice. It was like a jolt. For maybe a whole minute it left Jud standing helpless in the certainty that Sunk both saw and knew him and now was only waiting for the door to open.

Jud drew back and, safely hidden in the shadows, also waited. He thought there had been no change in Sunk's posture. When the stream of sunlight paled, then all of a sudden went out, Jud could see him standing etched against the brick wall over there, still watching, as if he had taken his place for the night. Jud moved slowly backwards. He turned and went into the warehouse and out through the alley door. Later, when Sunk had left, he would come back and lock the front door.

He did come back but it was much later. It had been dark a long time, and he approached like a scout, avoiding places where the light was brightest and waiting at the corner until he was sure. He even went and stood where Sunk had been standing and watched the dark door where his own face had appeared. At eight, when the courthouse clock was striking, he finally crossed the street. Then, as he took out his keys, he got another shock, shock enough to make him drop the keys. He had it solved in an instant. That in the doorglass was only his own ghostly face looking back at him. Even so he did not want to see it again, and picking up the keys from the sidewalk he kept his gaze trained on his nervous hand while he locked the door.

It was close to nine when he started for his room. By now, he thought, she might not be still waiting, seated on the garden step, waiting for him to come out and sit beside her. She never called to him anymore. She merely took her place and left it to him, who would know she was out there, to come or not to come. Of course he always did come, feeling that he had to. But not tonight. Tonight it was nine o'clock when he turned into the driveway and walking off the edge of the gravel where his feet would make no noise cautiously approached.

At the point where Jud could see past the corner of the house he stopped. It took a moment to make certain, but there Hannah was, still waiting. He did not move. After a minute he even crouched down, determined to wait her out no matter how long. It was a while. There were times when he thought maybe he was mistaken about her presence, because he would see her and then not see her, as if she came and went like a firefly's light. Yet there was no light, not from the house. There was no moon or stars either, he noticed now, and then he saw the reason. The whole sky was overcast. Behind the clouds there was lightning and this was why her figure kept blooming out of the dark. Rain, he thought: that was what the clouds might mean. If it *could* rain anymore.

She was standing up. He saw her in one of those sustained flickers of lightning, and he almost thought she was standing so as to look at him where he was crouched. The lightning went out. When it came again she was gone and, hearing the door close, Jud stood upright. In his room, just to signal his presence he turned on the light for a couple of minutes, but he stood with a hand on the switch ready in case he heard her footsteps or her call. Afterwards in the dark he went on waiting, breathing air that seemed hard to breathe, watching through his window the pale fits of lightning out in the garden. Once he thought he saw Hannah, but this illusion did not come back. Then he thought he saw Sunk. The figure was like a part of one of the shrubs out there, all hidden but one shoulder and the head and the blackness that was the face. To be rid of it Jud had to stand staring a long time and wait for a fit of lightning brighter than the others. Being rid of it did not help, though. He tried to hear wind rising and first drops of rain. He heard nothing. The silent lightning flickered on and off, and what he felt was like the restlessness of fever that set his muscles writhing. He endured this for a minute or two. On one impulse he unlatched the screen and stepped through the window and made his way through the hedge.

It was cool in Meagher's room. Or maybe it was only the pot, that set him at a distance from the sweaty self lying propped on the bed in the yellow light. He smoked and smoked and drifted from sleep to sleep, and once when he waked up Meagher was present, seated on the chair where Jud had sat. Jud was not surprised. In fact it was soon clear to him that they had been talking for a good while already, and any surprise or discomfort he experienced had all passed off by now. What Jud was saying, in this first of his lucid moments, he had said before, and so was his denial a repetition. He shook his head. "No," he said, "that's *not* the reason. *She*'s the reason."

"*You're* the reason. Same old thing. Trying to hide it behind a lie to yourself. Even now when you ain't got any choice."

Jud shook his head, but tiredly, having done it too many times.

"Come on, man. It's about time, ain't it?"

184

Seated in Jud's own posture on the chair, elbows on his knees, Meagher grinned at him, mocking him. Jud turned his face aside. He shut his eyes and drifted away and when he opened them next Meagher was gone. Jud was still there in the room alone when daylight came at the windows.

He thought that this with Meagher might have been a dream, but if so it did not matter. The dream, then, was decisive. Not that Jud realized this at once. That whole day at the store, in fact, was almost like a copy of yesterday, full of the little dodges and flights he designed to keep him at a distance from Lily. The same argument gave his mind no rest, and the same fierce sunlight at the windows said that last night's hope for rain was gone. The only real difference came at the end of the day. Peering through the bright doorglass into dusk across the street he could see that there was nobody waiting for him.

When, in his room that night, Jud finally realized that he did mean to do it, the moment was almost upon him. There was no time to think how, with what words, and he nearly stepped back from the door where he was standing. But she did not appear, not yet. There was light from a hazy half-moon and he could see the stone step that led down into the garden. He could not hear the crickets. What could he say in that quiet?

Jud's watchfulness must have lapsed for a few moments, because when he saw her she was already seated on the step. The surprise left him doubtful at first, wondering if his imagination had conjured her up. Even when her image persisted and he brought himself to open the screen and go out, there was still the lingering shade of a doubt in his mind. Even approaching her did not dispel it. She was looking away from him and she could not have been sitting any stiller in a dream of his. Maybe, though, this curious doubtfulness he felt was all that gave him the courage, after a long pause, to sit down on the step beside her. Then the feeling went away. It was because he could hear the crickets and see when her eyelids blinked.

He tried to say something, anything but he did not make a sound. Neither did she. She gazed down into the garden and her hands, far from seeking his, lay on her lap like stones. Like stones, he thought, and cold, cold to him. He felt a stirring of panic. She had confessed it, had told it all to her father: this was the explanation of her coldness. The panic subsided. Jud did not think so anymore and then he was able to say, in a whisper, "Are you still sure?"

"Yes."

This was all she was going to say and her cold hands stayed there on her lap. His panic came back. He could not think where to go from here and finally, with a motion that was too much like a lunge, he reached and took one of her hands. It was like something small and dead. To warm it he closed it in both of his and kept on holding it that way, feeling only the throb of his own pulse. But he was rewarded. He felt her hand come slowly back to life, with a pulse of its own and one slight movement that was like a word softly spoken. Real words followed. "Poor Jud," she murmured.

His tongue suddenly loosened and he said, "What are you going to do?"

"I don't know."

Suddenly he could feel, still there in his pocket like something hot against his thigh, the address that Lily had given him. He said, "I've been thinking." His voice had

186

meant to go on from there, but this was as far as he got.

"What were you thinking?"

Now he noticed that her hand felt like something trapped and not at rest between his. The cause of this, he realized, was her pulse and he did not know how this told him, after a while, that whatever he asked of her she would do. He was certain. He said, "You've got to do something."

But the rest would not come through his teeth and he sat there mute for so long that her hand went limp again. Finally she withdrew it and he saw that she was about to get up. Still he could not say it. He could not say anything, and if she, standing up now, had not lingered a moment too long it might not have happened at all, ever. But the moment was long enough for Jud's panic to start again. "Wait," he said.

She waited, and her waiting seemed like a threat, a last chance offered to him. "What are you going to do?"

"I still don't know."

Even these words seemed like a threat. "I've got an idea," he said, feeling as if he had thrown himself from a height. She moved and sat down again, and waited.

"They do operations. Doctors do. It's not even against the law anymore. There are places you can go." He did not look at her. He heard his voice plunging on. "It's not even any big thing anymore. You could go away on a trip to visit somebody. You could be back in a week or two and it'd be all over with. I . . . I could find out a place. Nobody would know." His voice ran out and was gone in a stillness that made it hard to believe he had just now said those words. He thought that the crickets had stopped.

As quiet as her voice was, it startled him. "I couldn't ever do that." She stood up.

"Look what's going to happen if you don't."

187

"I know. I'm sorry."

Then she was gone and it was strange. What he felt in the moments afterward was anything but panic. He drew a deep slow breath, and then another, for it felt as if something had now, and for good, let go its grip on his chest. He got up without weight and started toward his room. But these moments were a deception that was nearly spent already.

For three evenings after that Hannah did not appear. In fact, though Jud was always watching, he got no glimpse of her at any time, anywhere. He saw the Reverend once, from a distance, imagining that the old man walked in a different way, more slowly, as if turning a grave and painful matter in his head. And the second day, on the square, Jud saw Judge McCloud. The judge was already looking at him when Jud saw him, and Jud walked past him in a blind certainty that the judge followed him with hostile glaring eyes.

"Stop worrying," Lily said. "She just needs time to think about it. She'll do it."

He shook his head. "She said she never would."

"Wait and see. I know her. Just wait."

On each occasion Jud shook his head, hiding his face, because she never would. Just wait. That was what his whole life had become, a waiting, a suspension without any end to it. There was prison, but even that no longer seemed like an end. He had had a dream about it. His cell became a tomb and then a coffin where the lack of breath did not put a stop to his life.

But after those three days had passed, this thing came to an end. Jud had finished his evening hour of futile watching. He saw the house lights go out and then he turned his own lamp off. As always, for a margin of safety, he waited a little while. It was barely long enough: another minute and he would have been out the window and under the hedge and gone. He never heard her. She stood at his door with the same kind of apparitional suddenness that had surprised him three nights ago when he saw her out on the step. But this time he was too startled to move. When she spoke he did not hear what she said.

He was about to step to the door when she forestalled him. Opening the screen she came inside, allowing it to close quietly behind her. That was where she stopped, standing silhouetted against the light. Facing her from darkness that must have made him practically invisible he began to have a curious feeling. It was a feeling as if he was somebody different from himself—a stranger; maybe a dangerous one.

"I want you to find one of those places for me."

It was an eerie feeling. It was like and yet not like those dreaming drifting hours apart from himself in Meagher's lighted room. Here in the dark he felt apart in body as well as mind, as if the familiar shape of him stood defined in a cold new skin. With a new voice, even, that said faintly, "You're going to do it, then?"

"Yes."

After a while he said, "All right."

"Can you find out soon?" Her dark head, outlined as by a silver pencil, did not move.

"Yes . . . Wait a minute." This strange cool body of his moved with unexpected authority in the dark and retrieved the slip of paper from the second drawer of the chest. But a sudden pause fell. He might have been left standing in the aftermath of a quite audible protest that his own voice had made. He had this paper in his hand and for just a second or two he did not know what he was doing with it. Somebody might have put it there. Then

189

his head cleared and looking at Hannah, feeling the paper between his rigid fingers, he said, "Maybe you ought not to."

"I've made up my mind."

In the dark where he stood she could not see the paper or know that he was holding it.

"Please don't worry." When Jud still did not move she said, "I would have thought of it, myself, after a while."

He had to take a couple of steps and he did, finally, holding out the paper that was whiter than his hand. "It's an address."

She touched his fingers when she took it and afterwards she held her head bent as if she were reading it in the dark. She said nothing. Neither did he, even when she turned and with a goodbye whisper quietly left.

18

FOR MOST OF A WEEK, UP UNTIL THE NIGHT HANNAH left, Jud did not see her again. He did not see her up close, that is. She was absent from church that Sunday, and the times when he did get a glimpse of her she was standing at the back hall window featureless and still against the light. Not that he wanted to see her. What he wanted was that the thing be over with, completed, and all his anxiety now came of the thought that she might change her mind. His two or three glimpses of her told him nothing.

"It's bound to take a few days. Arrangements and all," Lily said. "She's got the old man to fool, too."

Lily was not as confident as she sounded, though. Every morning early, arranging a little cushion of privacy around them, she asked Jud the same question. "Any new signs?" She watched his lips say no and he could see a shadow cross her yellow eyes. She was nervous, like him, and her sure voice saying, "She'll do it, though. Just wait a little longer." could not disguise the fact.

But if these moments fed Jud's anxiety more than others did, the real cause was not Lily's doubts. It was what he saw behind the doubts. He saw that she was waiting with him, the two of them with one head turning the same restless thought. It had never been this way before, their heads together like this. That was why for Jud these moments were so much like sworn promises, making his cheek where her lips had touched kindle as though a flame had come too close. But promises depended. What was the good of these promises if Hannah changed her mind?

But she did not change her mind, and the next Monday evening brought this much to an end. Rounding the corner onto the square he ran, almost literally, into the Reverend. The old man had come looking for him, and Jud in his confusion could not think of any way to refuse the invitation. A little farewell supper, kind of, the Reverend said. She was going away tonight to visit some kin. And get her some rest. "I've been mighty worried about her," he said.

The courthouse clock, with hands right at six, made a small diversion for Jud's eyes.

"Mighty worried. But the doctor says she's just run down, just needs a good rest." The clock began to strike and the Reverend said, "You go ahead on. I'll be along, directly."

So there Jud was, half an hour later, tensely seated in his place across from the big sideboard. The white table was already served with food, but Hannah's place was empty. He did not know what the Reverend had been saying, at some length, but he noticed when the voice stopped. He could tell that the Reverend was listening now, wondering why no sounds came from the kitchen and why the swinging door stayed shut. The clock ticked on. On the sideboard the silver things had a dusty tarnished look and the Reverend's rimless spectacles were like stained mirrors over his eyes. But he was watching the door, not Jud.

She must have been standing just beyond the door, because there was no preface of footsteps when it opened. She had a plate of biscuits that she carried as if it needed

192

balancing, and she placed it on the table in front of Jud. He watched her small hands uncertainly let go of it.

"I didn't mean for you to fix all this much, daugher. Right when you're busy getting ready."

"I'm all finished," she murmured.

With her head already bowed she took her seat, reminding Jud that now there would be an interval of release. He hoped it would be long, and it was. Gazing into his empty plate he sent his thoughts away, to Lily, and tried to keep them there. But the Reverend intruded. His prayer voice, that Jud was so well practiced in shutting out, kept slipping in between Jud and his thoughts, and dropping things. Some of these things fell with a little jolt that left them standing alone afterwards. Hannah's name was one, repeated several times, with blessings tied to it. There was Jud's own name, also blessed, followed by that of Jesus who was looking down from up There and defending them from evil. Suddenly there was the biggest jolt of all. Jud saw, with the detail of a mirror-image, his own self seated here at the table, bowed. Pious Jud. It was as though he could hear, in the room with the stark yellow light, Meagher laughing at him.

After that it was different. When the prayer stopped he was not afraid to hold his head up or to look straight back at the invisible eyes behind the spectacle lenses. He could look at Hannah too—or could have if she had been willing to lift her face. When a long silence fell he even spoke to her. "What time are you leaving?"

"Ten-thirty." She did not look up.

"Do you have a long ride?"

"To Virginia."

"It's her mother's people," the Reverend said. "It's not far from the ocean, ought not to be so hot there. She can get some rest. That's what she needs: a couple of weeks

193

of good rest." The sunset light in the room had lost its color and the Reverend's eyes through the lenses were visible again. They were looking gently at Hannah. "She's always too busy. Always about some work of mercy, helping somebody out or making them happy. She doesn't know a thing but to give and keep on giving. It's the gift of love she's got, Jud," he said, turning to Jud.

The laughter seemed a long way off but Jud could hear it. His nod in reply to the Reverend's gaze lacked nothing for earnestness. The gaze was not pointed, anyway. What it expressed was a sort of lingering astonishment at the marvel he had just now given utterance to. A fitting astonishment, Jud thought, nodding again, while the far-off laughter sounded with irony.

"God's special gift," the Reverend went on. "The only one that's any real account. Finally all the rest of His gifts just ride on that one. You see that when you get old and see how even good things dry up on you. That's when you see what the world's like without it. Just a torment of wanting things that don't ever satisfy you. Till it burns you up, finally. Unless you got what my Hannah's got. Love of God and man and everything else too—alive and not alive. She's the kind—"

"Hush, Daddy."

This, though it was not exactly loud, startled Jud a little. When he looked she was sitting exactly as before, with her head bent over her plate, and he decided that her voice had surprised him only by its unexpectedness. It had surprised the Reverend too, apparently, because the stillness now had in it nothing at all but the ticking of the hall clock.

"Eat your supper, Daddy."

A slow smile came on the Reverend's lips. He cornered

194

some beans and got them on his fork. He said softly, "It's the truth, anyhow," and started eating.

Jud had felt a little more than just surprise. But the rest was only his dim sense of alarm that she might be about to reveal something. This was all, however, and now the moment of danger, if it had been such, had gone by. Hannah's posture assured him of this, and so did the Reverend's tiresome if now intermittent reflections. Jud felt almost as if he was looking back from a safe place on a thing already done, watching the final minutes pass and at the door his affectionate goodbye in the muted last of the daylight. The thought began to excite him.

It did not all go quite this smoothly. The telephone rang and instead of Hannah it was the Reverend who got up. Jud could hear his voice, though remotely, and that between spells when only the clock was there to be heard ticking in the dusky hall. Hannah might have been debating whether or not to go on with the food still uneaten on her plate. At last he had to speak. "Did you find a place close to there? In Virginia?"

She shook her head. Then she looked up, suddenly, directly at him and he thought it was only the flat diminished light from the windows that put this starkness between her face and him. There had been no such haggard look before, when the light was good.

"No," she said. "It's the place you gave me. I'm going there first."

He fumbled. "Won't they wonder when you don't come . . . in Virignia?"

"I told them I wouldn't be there for a few more days." After a while, just breathing it, she said, "Please don't worry."

There was the clock and presently a space of time filled

with the Reverend's distant voice. The room grew much darker, the gloom sifting in from the hall, and without knowing exactly what it would turn out to be, Jud started to say something. Later he thought it had been something about the operation's being no big thing anymore, but he never had a chance to find out. She got up from the table just then. She did not got into the kitchen but around the table opposite him and into the dark hall. He remembered that on the way out she spoke. He did not really hear what she said and he did not know whether he had made any kind of an answer, but that was the only goodbye there was.

This was not the last time he saw her, however. He wanted to actually see her leave and when the car went out of the garage a little after ten he was ready. Almost directly across the street from the bus station was a narrow alley and he was there, standing back in the dark, well before the bus arrived. Hannah and her father waited outside, their figures distinct against the station window, the suitcase on the pavement between them. The Reverend was surely talking to her, but even in the quiet when no cars passed by Jud could not hear a voice. He never saw Hannah move out of her tracks or move any way at all until the bus, thundering, turned the corner off the square. Her face and hair looked stark white for a second in the beams of the headlights and then she was out of view behind the bus.

He got a glimpse of her through the bus window, but it was as if he could not be really sure until the bus pulled away and he saw the Reverend standing alone, following with his eyes, and no suitcase on the pavement anymore. The Reverend stood motionless, and so did Jud, until the sound of the bus also had died away in the night. That was the moment when all the blood came leaping to Jud's heart.

The brief interlude that followed that moment was another one that remained vividly set apart in his memory. If a mood can be like a place, this was how it was. It was like a place he had finally got to, after a world of sweat and agony, where nothing whatever was left to oppose or even disquiet him. If it was like a place, it was *his* place, completely and without dispute, the way his hands and feet were his. Though surely on a different scale, successful conquerors must feel, in the aftermath, something like what Jud felt then.

At the least, what he felt was that kind of transforming exhilaration. He was conscious of the dangers involved in being abroad after his curfew hour, but it did not seem to matter. He was safe. It was as though he could will that the Reverend, leaving the garage, not look into his room, or that any person he met on the street would be one who did not know him. In fact, for a block or two after he left the alley he walked without the least effort at concealment. He even crossed a corner of the square and he did meet somebody. The result was what he expected. The man, a stranger, did not so much as glance at him. A little prudence came over him after that and he turned into an alley and then, seeing that the alley would only exit on another street, into a backyard. Even so, his mood was not much altered. Passing from yard to yard, all strange to him, he still had the sense of walking on ground that belonged to him alone. He did not see a lighted window, much less any person. No dog barked at him. He slipped through fences of privet and vine as if he knew ahead of time where all the little passages were.

He was walking much faster, hurrying, when he came face-on to a high board fence. It was a jolt, though he had not touched the fence, and made him think where his blood was hurrying him at such an accelerated pace. He felt like running at it, crashing through the boards. As it was, he stepped back and made a running leap to hurtle the fence on his hands. But the fence was too high. His knee hit the top and he fell to the ground head-first, hard, on the other side.

It was a familiar place. This was what he was thinking before he discovered that instead of sitting upright he was lying full-length with the side of his face on the rough ground. When he did sit up he was not so sure about the place. He sat in a deep fenced-in backyard looking at a tall house some distance away and at a bent dishevelled tree that broke the horizon to his right. He could not hear a sound. Then he thought that maybe this was a place where he had not been for many, many years but had sometimes dreamed about. Or had he only dreamed it out of nothing? This was the way it seemed to him now, unreal. Real places had sounds of some kind—at least of crickets in the grass.

He did hear a sound. It was the sound of breathing, fast breathing, and before he located the source he recognized the panting of a dog. The dog was not twenty feet away in the fence corner, maybe chained, sitting there. It was fairly large and without color in the dark, though it seemed in the cavity of its mouth to have a black tongue. The dog had not barked at him. It just kept sitting there, panting, neither friendly nor unfriendly, watching him. Still he began to be afraid of it and to make plans for his retreat. The fence was close. He got his feet under him. Standing up he almost fell and, leaning against the fence, he looked to see if the dog had moved. The earth moved, heaving like a dark sea, but the dog just sat there riding on it. Jud struggled over the fence.

After that he felt lost, in a strange country, and he knew he wandered for a while before he found the way again. He kept being afraid that the dog was following him and this was why he never stopped to let his head get clear. Not until he came onto the street where Lily's house was. There, in her dark frontyard, he leaned against a tree and rested. Soon his head got clearer. There was no dog following him and he knew again why his heart was pacing so.

It was exactly as if Lily had been waiting for him. The kitchen light, even this late, was still burning, but this was not the main reason for Jud's impression. She was there too quickly, like a robed apparition stepping suddenly from the dark hall, looking straight at him. Though his hand was lifted to the doorglass he did not think that he had even knocked yet, much less waited the two or three minutes that he had counted on. Or so it seemed, and he was not ready. When she opened the door he had to hold to the jamb. He also had to draw a long breath, as though his strutted heart had crowded all the air from his lungs. Then he managed. "She's gone. On the bus, a while ago."

"Nobody with her?"

"No. I watched her leave. She's supposed to be going to visit some kin."

Then there was silence and he realized that Lily was not looking at him. Her gaze was on him but not her attention and he said, "So I'm out of it, you see." But this made no difference. He made his voice louder to say, "So I came to tell you."

Then he felt her attention, though it was slow in coming, like a recognition that took a moment or two. "What happened to your face?"

Raising a hand he felt the blood clotted on his temple and cheek. "I fell down," he said. "It's nothing much." But he was holding to the door jamb.

"Come on in."

She sat him down at the table and afterwards just stood there over him as if lost in contemplation of the wound on his temple. Finally her hand settled on his head and tilted it. He grew dizzy, but not from the tilting. "You're pale," she said. "You'd better lie down somewhere."

Then it was his arm she touched, lifting him and walking him across the hall to his old room and to the bed. For a little while she was gone and he lay in the dark with his heart beating, listening to the distant sounds she made. It was his heart that made him dizzy. He thought he recognized those sounds, from overhead. She was taking off her clothes. Then her footsteps again, close by, and she was standing over him in the dark. She was naked. He lifted both his arms.

The light came on. She was standing over him but she was not naked. She looked down at him, at his arms, and then he could see the expression on her face. It was a cold moment, stopping his heart. His arms came down and lay at his sides stiffly and he shut his eyes to be rid of her expression. Yet her voice, when it came, was the same measured voice. "Turn your head over."

He lay with his face to the wall, eyes shut, and there was a wet cloth and pain at his temple, flashes of pain.

"I told you, didn't I?"

He had a second of blankness. The cloth hurt, burned his temple.

"I know her. They're all just like her."

Her hand was too rough and her voice, filtered through his pain, seemed remote and different. "Liars." He heard her breathing. "You see, now, don't you, Jud? Tell me something she wouldn't do." It was as if her hand meant to punish him, and one touch, like a blade, almost made him cry out.

She stopped. There was a click, followed by a smell of antiseptic. The smell grew strong and the wet gobbet she pressed into his temple burned him again. Then it burned like a coal of fire. He bore it in silence.

"Tell me. What wouldn't she do?"

"I don't know," he breathed. It was not the pain anymore, it was the smell, crowding his nostrils, taking his breath away. The room seemed airless and nausea grew in the pit of his stomach.

"There's not anything," she said, her voice remote and in some way distorted. "I've known her all my life. I've known all of them."

His nausea grew. When she took the wet gobbet away he opened his eyes to the mottled yellow wall, without shadows. There was no air. "I need to go outside."

"Just rest a while. You'll feel better."

Then he thought her voice had grown soft and his mind gave a sort of leap. But there was no answer in his blood, only his nausea rising. It seemed as if she stood poised above him as tall as a tree, the rank smell making him sicker. "I need some air."

She walked away and he heard her raise a window. But she came back and stood over him again, hovering.

"Just stay there. I'll wake you before day."

The light went out and she was gone. After a moment he sat up to get breath and for another while he thought he would end by vomiting on the floor at his feet. But the nausea receded. He lay down again and almost at once felt sleep descending on him. It was not complete when it came. It was more like a muffling of his senses and he seemed still able to perceive things, though as if through a thickness of cloth. On and on he kept hearing, or thought he did, movements of Lily in the room above— Lily undressing. He also thought, later, that she came back into his room and stood hovering over him for a long time. It seemed he had to fight for breath, while his heart kept laboring to pump the stiffened blood through his body. But that was surely a dream. When it happened another time he knew that it was, because he waked up and saw, in first gray light from the windows, that he was alone. Yet the panic was still there. Quickly, staggering a little, he let himself through the outside door and fled.

19

IT WAS TWO DAYS BEFORE JUD WENT BACK TO WORK.
The first day he kept to his room, sleeping and trying to
sleep, telling himself that he was sick. It did seem as if he
was sick. His old fever, hovering all this time, had come
down on him at last. Or was the trouble something his
accident had caused—a delicate organ in his head that
last night's fall had dislodged? The effect was like that.
So, in spite of the suffocating heat, he stayed there on
his bed.

But that was the first day. After this it was no use to tell
himself that he felt worse, or different, on his feet. He
was not sick, and had not been, and the reason for his
absence from work had to be looked at now. But he did
not look at it squarely. He only saw that he was tired of
Nunn's, too tired—tired of Lily, even, at last. He would
find another job.

This was what Jud kept thinking all day. He wandered
the streets for hours without a purpose and ate something
at noon and wandered some more. He walked clear out of
town finally and went to a place he knew on the river and
after a while sat down on the bank. The river was low. All
the way across to the other bank, a bluff, it was like a
great still pool, brackish-looking and without sound. He
sat for maybe an hour and never saw anybody, not one
soul. Everything was so still, for so long, that he finally

shook his head to get it clear. Later he shook it again and that was when he noticed.

The feeling was with him still as he walked back into town, and it refused to be displaced by sounds and movements in the streets. At the corner of the square he stopped. It seemed to be the kind of afflication that one slight jolt might remedy. The effect was a certain sense of distance from everything around him, as if even vivid close-up things were far beyond his reach. And he beyond theirs, as well—like being a figure barely reflected in the eyes that turned his way. Almost like a shadow. It was a curious feeling, and lonesome, the lonesomest feeling he had ever had. For a moment he actually thought about making some kind of a small spectacle of himself, just to draw the attention of passers-by.

It amazed him how the feeling persisted, even after he had moved on, deliberately, to another spot, crossing Mill Street to get there and speaking once in his clearest voice when old Mr. Calder limped past. He stood right on the sidewalk in the late sun's slanting glare and watched the people and cars and trucks go by and looked at the dusty trees on the courthouse lawn and the old men settled on the shaded benches. All was the same, nothing different, not so much as one new shape or patch of color in the scene. And yet . . . Lonesomeness closed in like pain around his heart.

It let up after a while and seemed to be nearly gone when, at dusk, he stood suddenly face to face with the Reverend. The meeting was anything but intentional on Jud's part. The Reverend ought to have been indoors at this hour and not, as now, standing by the garden step where Jud could not see him until he stepped past the house corner. The nod and smile came right at him. If throughout that whole evening Jud experienced any moment of real release it was this one. But it was only the briefest of intermissions.

While the Reverend stood talking to him the twilight gathered, little by little obscuring his face and obscuring Jud in his eyes. It was like distance growing between them. The old man was standing not ten feet away and his voice, talking about Hannah, could not have been any clearer. "She's doing a little sight-seeing first," he said, "before she goes on to her aunt's house. Lots to see up there . . . historical things." Jud heard him perfectly, the full resonance of his voice, and he answered him when he had to. So *distant*, maybe, to describe how Jud felt, was not quite the word. But *lonesome* was.

Later that night he went to Meagher's place. Right at first the stillness in the room, the immobility of the stark discolored plaster walls and gauzy light, was a comfort to him, like a refuge. But he reached into the hole under the mattress and found nothing. Meagher? Jud's eyes pointlessly searched the room. He lay down on the bed finally, stretched out, and tried to make his mind as blank as the ceiling above his face.

When he dozed, Lily came, standing or bending over him, and he forced his eyes open. Then he realized, without alarm, that there was somebody in the room and that it was Meagher. He knew before he looked that Meagher was seated in the chair. "I guess you took the rest of it, didn't you?" Jud said.

"It's mine, man."

Jud did not even look to catch his expression. "I thought you had left for good, this time."

"I like to come back once in a while, keep my hand in. Get the news. Man, you know you can't quit."

"Quit?" Jud said. This almost roused him.

"Your lady love. You said you were. Just while ago."

The memory was a blank. What had he been saying in his sleep?

"It's too dangerous."

Jud stared up at the ceiling. "What do you mean?"

"You try and you'll find out. You better keep courting her, man. You've went too far."

Jud looked at him. Meagher's bright gaze trembled slightly and his lips were parted, showing the dull crowns of his teeth. It was mockery. Jud hated his face and to keep from showing it he turned his own away. He even shut his eyes.

Finally Meagher said, "You can use my room, though."

Jud heard him get up. He did not look and he did not hear any other sound until the door bumped faintly shut. It was so faint that when he looked and saw it standing shut he scanned the room to make sure Meagher was gone. His eyes would not close again. A while later when he left he already knew that he would go back to work.

In fact he was already at the store when Lily arrived in the morning, already busy placing new boxes of light-bulbs in a rack, and his greeting was a sort of blind nod that took in nothing except the color of her greenish yellow blouse. Before she said anything she went into the little office and came back and opened the cash register. She waited another minute, until Riley, whistling, went into the warehouse again. Jud was still arranging the lightbulbs.

"Do you feel all right now?"

"I'm fine," he said, keeping busy. It seemed that he could not risk exposing his whole face to her. "I still had a headache yesterday."

She said nothing and he remembered yesterday. She might have seen him, or Riley might have. He waited. He had no more lightbulbs to put in the rack. From the warehouse Riley's whistling was faintly audible.

"Any news?"

He did not risk playing dumb. He shook his head. "No. Not yet." He picked up the big pasteboard carton and took it into the warehouse and when he came back two customers were waiting.

But his new feeling about Lily did not get its real start until later. In fact before it became anything like clear to him he was in his bed in the dark that night, suddenly made wide awake by the dream he had just then dreamed. It was not the same dream, because this time he could see her face as she stood over him, see it in detail. He saw her eyes and her cheeks with the little pits where the worms had been feeding. His dread, or terror, waked him up and afterwards he lay there remembering the things of the preceding day that had led him as by so many half-blind steps up to this moment.

One thing was the way she had watched him. Just to feel her watching him was nothing new: he was almost used to it. But he was not used to this. The gaze that had followed him so much of the time looked as if it meant to burn right through to his brain and pluck out his thoughts in spite of him. It made him think of a conjurer's eyes. He kept his back turned to her when he could.

There were other things. Mr. Black the mailman always left the mail on a shelf just inside the front door, and it might be an hour, it might be closing time, before Lily would happen by and pick it up. Not today. She went right for it and taking each letter looked carefully at it. Even so there would have been little in this to strike Jud if nothing had preceded it. But he recalled the look she gave him when Mr. Black came in. She had looked to see what Jud was going to do.

Later, watching in that intent way, she asked him whether he thought the Reverend had heard anything, and at closing time, as soon as the door locked, she said, "Do you think you'll hear from her?"

Jud shook his head no. He did not want to look at Lily.

"I think you will."

He walked over and turned off the air conditioner, making the stillness perfect.

"I'd like to know, when you do. I just want to be sure."

"What else would she go off for?" he said faintly.

"I just want to be sure she didn't lose her nerve." Lily waited a moment. "Don't you?"

"Yes," he said, but so faintly that he thought maybe he should say it again louder. He did not. He saw a shred of paper on the floor and bent to pick it up.

"Or do you?"

Her question hung there in the stillness between them. Like a threat, he suddenly thought. "Yes. Why wouldn't I?" But he could not look squarely into her face and he was not sure what she meant by the pause that followed.

"Then you'll tell me?"

"I will if I hear. I don't think I'll hear."

He still could not look right at her face, yet he got, in the final moment before she turned away from him, a clear image of what it was like. The expression was familiar. He realized that it was like the one on her face the other night when he had so stupidly lifted his arms to her. It was not only cold. There was irony, but there was something else stronger than irony. Now he saw it and he thought he knew what it meant—though not until up in the night when this dream waked him out of his sleep.

Jud did not sleep any more that night. The more he thought, the more he was sure why Lily wanted to know. She wanted to be certain about it before she spread the news. For that was what she meant to do. And meant to do it in spite of the cost to Jud. It would all come out, *they* would know who, and Lily did not care. For that was contempt, or worse, he had seen in her face. He kept seeing it, though sometimes, later on, there were other faces also. The Reverend's was one, and Judge McCloud's. When dawn came on Jud was pacing the room, feeling vaguely sick and light in his head.

To intercept any letter that might have come, he was there when the post office opened at eight o'clock. There was not any letter. He was late to work and seeing the question in Lily's eyes he thought how to make use of it, the question *and* his lateness. "I went by the post office," he said. "In case there was a letter. If one got sent to me at home I wouldn't get it till tonight." He tried to look straight at her. He tried to look and not look. "There wasn't one, though." His gaze had stopped on one of her pitted cheeks and he turned away. Already he felt that she did not believe him. Her answer, the briefest of nods, confirmed him in his feeling.

That nod led into a day Jud would not forget. In one respect it was like the day before, because Lily kept the same intent searching gaze on him. But in its effect it was not the same. The skin at the back of his neck would tingle and he would see her as in his dream last night, ugly, with pitted wormy rotten cheeks and eyes too icy hot to look into. He kept trying to shake this vision out. When a moment offered he stole a hurried look at her real face, her eyes and her flawed cheeks that his lips had touched in all those burning reveries. But this real image would not stay fixed in his mind. The distortion soon crept back again and also that sensation like feathers grazing the skin across the back of his neck.

He tried, he tried desperately, to hide his feelings, to seem at ease with her, but it was no use. Every attempt was like a small disaster, ending in a silence deeper than the one before had been. Toward closing time he made one last reckless effort. He brought up the letter again. "Maybe in the morning," he said. "If I *am* going to hear."

"You'll hear." She did not lift her eyes from the ledger page.

"I'll tell you if I do."

"All right."

Then silence. His lips made a single movement as if about to speak. He was staring at her, at her cheek, and perceiving this he snatched his gaze away. He heard her pen scratch, then stop, and then the ledger shut. His lips started to move again. Without a word she turned and walked away along the counter and disappeared into her little office. That evening he was left alone when it was time to lock up.

Jud did not go to his room at once. He went up onto the courthouse lawn and stood for a while near one of the benches. There was an old man on the bench, his hat pulled down against the rays of the setting copper sun. Finally Jud said something to him and he raised his head and looked Jud's way with rheumy sun-blinded eyes. He did not see Jud and he did not answer. Jud left him alone.

The letter lay propped against the lamp on the table by his bed. Jud did not see it at first and when he did it struck him like something hurled straight into his face. There was a long space when he felt as if his heart had stopped. But he approached it finally, leaning first for a look before he touched it. Then, because the address was

210

typed, he had a moment of hope and this was what gave him the strength to reach and pick up the letter. It was sealed tight. There was no place even for his fingernail under the flap. He went quickly and shut the door.

He stood in failing light from the window, taking a long time to get the flap unsealed. The letter was not typed and the handwriting, though large, was pale, as if it had been done in ink that was almost water. He had to turn sideways to the window.

Dear Jud,

It's all over with. It happened yesterday and did not take but a little while. It did not hurt. It must have been tiny. I don't know what they did with it but it must have been very tiny. They say I am all right. So don't worry. I am going on to my aunt's home now. I would like it if you said a prayer for me. And one for it.

Hannah

The heat in the room was too much and Jud had to open the door. He thought of burning the letter. He did nothing. It was all over with. The time for his supper had come and he got as far as the threshold and looked out in the twilight at the house windows and up the driveway. It was as hot outside as in, he thought now, and he was not hungry yet and he was tired. He was tireder than he had known. To wait for dark he sat down on the floor against the wall, shutting his eyes, the letter still in his hand. It was over with. He decided that he had been wrong about Lily, scaring himself, *making* her cold to him. He would go to her now and tell her and things would be no different from before. He went on sitting there with his eyes shut.

It was not yet quite dark when he got up off the floor. The letter was still in his hand. He thought of hiding, then of burning it, but he ended by folding it up small and

211

thrusting it deep in his pocket. Somewhere on his way he would stop and burn it, some hidden place. It was Lily's house he was going to and he opened the screen and stepped out.

There was no light in any of the house windows. There should have been light by now and this was what made him, after a few quiet steps, pause to scan the yard. His eyes fell with a little shock on the figure off to his right, the Reverend's figure. Jud thought of retreating into his room, but he did not, even when he made out that the old man was not looking toward him. There was something wrong about the Reverend, something more than the fact that he was seated on the garden step where he had no business to be. It was the way he was seated, as if he had been struck and injured and now could stay upright only by virtue of the prop his extended arm made. The thought that he had actually suffered a stroke went briefly through Jud's mind.

With his eyes still on the Reverend Jud finally took a backward step. That one step was all he ever took. His plan to retreat had somehow slipped out of his mind and when it returned the Reverend had already lifted his head a little, enough to put Jud in his line of vision. Now Jud got another impression. He thought the Reverend looked like a blind man who would not know whether Jud stayed where he was or quietly retreated. This was not true. Suddenly the Reverend said, "Jud."

It was all he said and he still looked like a blind man. He might have said it that way in his sleep—not an acknowledgment or a summons either, just a name falling from his mouth. Later, though, he repeated it. After all it was a summons, and there was nothing Jud could do but draw a breath and lift his feet and move closer to him.

212

Not too close, only to where an azalea made a knee-high barrier. Looked at by blind eyes Jud still had to wait a long time. Then:

"She's dead, Jud."

THOSE WORDS, THE WAY THE REVEREND'S VOICE HAD sounded them, had something like the quality of a cry heard at night from a long way off. That was the way they still sounded in Jud's head, even after two or three hours and other voices and people had intervened. The first people, three men from the church, had arrived almost in the wake of that moment, with headlights of a car scattering the dark and muted kindly voices and shapes bending to urge and help the Reverend onto his feet. They did not speak to Jud. He thought that they did not even see him, as if he had been a shadow standing there behind the low barrier of azaleas. That was what he wanted, though, and for fear of drawing notice he did not move. He watched them support the Reverend into the house and heard the silence come back and those words like a nightcry.

Soon the house was all lighted—at every window, it seemed—and other cars and people began to appear. Jud drew back farther into the dark, to the door of his room finally, watching. Listening, too, for the whole yard, even deep in the garden, seemed to have come alive with the murmur of kindly voices and these obscured the night cry he kept hearing. He must have stood there not less than two full hours.

He learned the facts, though, later on, by stealing up

close to where some men stood talking just outside the back door. The facts were not much. A truck. Looking the other way she had stepped off the curb in front of it. A broken neck. In Richmond, to see the sights, before she went on to her aunt's house. This was all, and not enough—not to make it real. But the old man's cry was real, and so was all the light and the murmur of voices.

After another hour, maybe, all but one of the cars in the driveway had left, and soon the lights, in every window, went out. Then, while minutes went by, there was not a sound. Jud was afraid, himself, of making a noise and when he started he set his feet down ever so carefully, moving toward the hedge. Ducking he crawled with the secrecy of an animal between the trunks. Without being clear in his head about anything he knew he was on his way to Lily's house and he followed the dark backyards downhill and crossed a street and followed some more backyards. But he knew the route perfectly. When the tall fence appeared he expected it and, remembering, turned to follow it around. For some reason, maybe to listen for the dog beyond the fence, he paused. This was when it came over him, like something tracking him all the way that had needed just this moment to catch up. Such a feeling of wretchedness had seized him that the strength went out of his body, leaving only the fence to hold him upright. He leaned against it, head and shoulder. He thought he could hear the dog panting in the empty dark beyond. When finally his strength came back he went on. There was some purpose driving him.

But he did not know what his purpose was, even when he approached the door and saw Lily, in the robe, seated over a book at the kitchen table. She noticed him at once, with the kind of bored expression he had seen her turn on Luther so many times. Then her face changed. She got up rather quickly and came to open the door.

"Have you heard something?"

He nodded.

"Well?"

Jud found that he could not answer. Somehow he could not get clear in his head what he had come to tell her.

"Are you sick again or something?"

"No," he managed.

She was looking at him as she had done all day and yesterday. "You'd better come sit down."

He came in but he did not sit down, not at first. He stood looking at the chair meant for him.

"Did you hear something, or not?"

Jud drew a breath. "She's dead." Then he sat down. Somewhere in the back of his mind he knew that this was not the main thing he had come to tell her.

"How, dead? Is that the truth?"

He nodded his head yes. It was as if he was telling a lie.

"How do you know?"

He lifted a hand, pointing with his thumb over his shoulder. "The Reverend. A lot of people came."

"He told you that?"

"Yes." She had not sat down. Now he saw her hands, with polished gleaming nails, holding the back of a chair. "Just a while ago," he said. "I listened to them talking about it."

Some time passed and then he saw her fingers move, straighten, stretch themselves. "Then it's all out."

She had drawled the word *all*, and this, after a moment, was the thing that focused Jud's mind. He lifted his eyes. She was looking out over his head as if her gaze was intent on something at a distance. The naked bulb hung not

216

much higher than her face and shown directly into her eyes and on her parted lips. He stared at her, reading her face, unable to speak the words on his tongue. She moved before he could. She walked across to the window and stood as if watching that same distant spectacle through the night-blinded pane. She stood very straight, in a way that made the dressing robe lie close to the lines of her body. This was why Jud could see when she took a long slow breath. Suddenly he found that he could speak his words, and they were loud. "It wasn't at any hospital. Or any place like that."

"What?" she said, dimly, without turning her head.

"It was on a street, in Richmond. She was run over."

Lily turned around. He quickly recited the rest of it, what little there was to tell, hearing his voice die away at the end. She kept looking at him. But now it was a different look, one that he knew he could not go on meeting eye for eye. Yet it seemed that he *had* to, just as if there had been the danger that she might suddenly spring at him bodily. It was a fear like something cold down in his viscera.

"Was it after or before? The abortion, I mean?"

He remembered the letter in his pocket, against his thigh. That was what had brought him here. He drew a breath. "I don't know," he said. When she continued looking at him he added, "I didn't hear anything about that."

She stood at the window a little longer, never taking her eyes off him. She moved to the table, very slowly, and sat down on the other side. She was facing him almost directly. "Are you sure?"

He nodded yes. But he should have said it out loud. He needed to swallow.

"I want to know," she said. "I want to *know* it happened."

217

He lowered his head and swallowed. "But she's dead. It doesn't matter now."

"I'm sorry she's dead. But I want to know, anyhow."

Jud kept his head down. "What for?"

He waited and never dared to look up. It was just as if the house had been an empty drum. He could hear her breathing.

"It doesn't need to affect you. There are plenty of other men; she went a lot of places by herself. And you're just a boy."

Finally he said, "You are going to tell it, then?"

"After I make sure. You know how they hate me."

He got just a glimpse of her eyes. It was enough.

"I want them to know the truth about their 'angel.' That'll be some 'truth' for them."

It was an effort to clear his mind that made him in fact, without intending, shake his head. He noticed that this had an effect on Lily. In some way she moved, maybe with her head.

"Is it just your skin you're worried about? Or is it the blame?" She waited and when Jud did not, could not, answer she said, "Well, the blame for this will be mine. So you won't have to feel 'guilty.' Not about this." Again she waited and then said, "You haven't told me everything you know."

He roused himself. "I have, though." But the words came out so feeble and hoarse that he knew they were wasted.

"You're lying. You're a lousy liar. I think you heard from her."

He could only shake his head. Without looking he could see her eyes. They were the eyes in his dream, smoldering as no human ones could do. It was a feeling of helplessness. Jud shook his head in vain.

"Didn't you?"

He did not know how, caught up as he was in that limp bloodless moment, he summoned the force to answer as he did. He thought it was the letter in his pocket. All of a sudden, in the very sweat of envisioning it there, he recovered some part of what he had felt in the twilight at the window of his room. But it was enough, or almost so. "But I didn't," he said, even lifting his face when he said it. And he saw the doubt come into her expression. It did not stay long, however.

"I think you did," she said. And then, "You know what, Jud?"

It was like waiting for something to fall on him.

"You know, I used to have all kinds of hopes for you. I had the notion I could set you free. But you didn't have it in you. Nothing but a lot of boyish lust. For all the things you've done, you're still just Little Jud. Except now you're Little Jud with his 'soul' damned."

He still waited.

"Maybe his body, too," she said. "No reason I shouldn't tell the whole truth. That's right where you belong, in the prison. Because that's where you'll be when the truth gets around. And don't think it won't get around." Then she said, "Look at me."

Then he did and it was as if that something about to fall had already fallen and hit him.

"I don't need you. I have to get proof, because it's me against an angel, but I know how to. And don't think I won't. And don't think I won't see it gets up on a signboard for all the Jesus-loving hypocrites to look at the rest of their filthy little lives . . . Whatever it takes."

But he heard her voice only as from a distance. Her

face was what he was thinking about, staring at in amazement, imagining his stiff lips pressed to one of those odious cheeks.

"Now go back to your holy ground," she said, standing up. "You've still got a few days left."

Part FIVE

21

SOME OF THE THINGS THAT HAPPENED IN THE FOL-
lowing days never did become perfectly clear to Jud. Yet
it was not that his memories lacked vividness. On the
contrary. The trouble was that they had about them the
atmosphere of a dream, a bad dream that went on too
long, and things that happened had a look as if in reality
they did not happen. This may even have been true of
some of them, literally speaking. His fever was there as
an explanation.

The fever that had been hovering all those weeks came
down on him that very night—right after he left Lily's
house, in fact. It was not the same as before, when he
was younger, striking him down and keeping him there.
This time, the hours when he was too sick to get out of
bed were relatively few, but on the other hand there were
hardly any times when the fever seemed to let go of him
completely. Much of the time it affected him just about as
in those minutes when he noticed it first, while he was on
his way home that night. His head felt overstuffed, yet
weightless, as if the stuff was air, and details of the yards
he passed through appeared at the same time vague and
also clear. Once or twice he got mixed up, uncertain
where he was headed. There were moments when he felt
as conscious of himself as if the objects he passed by had
eyes to watch him with. Flashes of light kept coming, as
if the eyes, suddenly popped open, observed him passing

in the glare of their own illumination. He was almost back to his room before he realized that this light was from the sky, was lightning in the clouds.

He remembered well how, in those lightning flashes, the garden looked when he crept from under the hedge—the leaning criss-crossed flower stalks as if a pencil had scored them against a ground of shuddering white. Afterwards the image was left recorded behind his eyes and, in his room, whenever the lightning flickered on the walls, he saw it once again. It did not help to shut his lids. The lightning might have been inside his head, flickering over a burnt-out garden there. This went on all night.

There were not any of those nights without the same dry lightning. At sunset the clouds would gather, clotting into a low gray pall across the sky, and at dark the lightning would start up. Beginning then, it seemed that everything he saw, both real and imagined things, came to him in these stark fits, hurtling out of the dark and lingering for a moment in suspension. Afterwards blindness came down once more, and often a little stroke of panic terror. Invisible fear was at his throat like something with a mouth and in his mind he cried out for the lightning to flash again. Even his visions of Lily's face, like a bloodless parchment mask before his eyes, were not such seizures as those moments were.

The days, though different, were not much better. In some way they were like hollow places between the nights, low sunken places where the only sounds came filtered from above. At least for the quiet he soon discovered the reason. The Reverend was gone, the house was locked. There was nobody. There was Jud, here at the still center of things, gazing out at the blasted garden

224

and hedges that seemed to creep like the slow circling rim of a wheel across his field of vision. He left the place only once in those two days—on the first morning. He thought it was to be for good, because he changed his clothes and took his checkbook out of the drawer. But he came back, almost straight back, glancing neither to right or left of him. He had bought some fruit. He ate a little of it and lay down on his bed in the hot room, to wait.

His head got clearer later on and he knew what he was waiting for. There were two things. One was the Reverend, who would come back—and Hannah's body with him. In a coffin, that real hands would lift and carry into the silent house. The other thing, standing behind it, like part of it all, was Lily. He envisioned her about to speak, her lips parting. His mind shut down. Sometimes he got up and went outside and stood for a few minutes in the shade of the garage. The garden lay in the sun, in shimmering light, slowly drifting. He saw the clouds come up at sunset and gather into a clotted flickering dome.

That was the night when Meagher came—or one of the nights: Jud was never entirely sure. Meagher was already in the room when Jud saw him first by the lightning, and when he saw him again Meagher was seated on the foot of the bed. His face kept flaring out of the dark and Jud remembered thinking that, like the other faces, it was not real. His feeling did not diminish its hatefulness, though. In fact, springing at him out of those white flashes, it looked uglier than ever, with a quality of shock, like the instant when one's eye stops on a snake lying close by. Jud refused to acknowledge him for a while and when he did acknowledge him he thought he told him to go away. But he must have done it feebly, allowing, in one of his feverish half-swoons, Meagher finally to prevail over him. It was as if Jud needed him almost as much as he hated him.

"Maybe she won't be able to," Jud said, his own loud voice surprising him.

"Get the proof? She'll get it, you know her. Hire somebody to. Probably done it already. Just waiting, now."

When the lightning flashed this time Jud shut his eyes "I'm done for anyway if she tells. They'd know it was me."

"Not if you don't own up. She can fix that for you. You know she's smart."

"She wouldn't if she could, though. Not now. She said—"

"Yeah, she *said*. Saying ain't doing, though. You know she left that door open for you. You ain't got to do a thing but walk back in."

"It's too late."

"You try it. Who else's she got? She wants you, man. Fact is, I wouldn't even give up on what you been after all this time."

Jud opened his eyes at the wrong instant. It was just when Meagher's face came hurtling out of the dark. He shut them again, shook his head.

"Come on. You just saw her mad. She won't look like that to you next time. Come on. You know how she really looks. Think about being in bed with all that."

But in Jud's mind there was only the face that he had seen last night. He made no answer and after a while he began to think that Meagher had somehow left without his knowing. Again he opened his eyes at the wrong moment.

"Then think about what's going to happen to you. They'll put you down under that pen. If some of these

226

hypocrite Jesus folks don't hang you first. Even that old preacher might not be so 'loving' like you think. Go ahead and tell him. Might as well. He'll be back here before long. With his dead angel, too."

Then it was the Reverend's face. Jud's mind stuck for a moment. "*That* part wasn't my fault. He can't blame me for that."

"Can't, huh? We got plenty of trucks around here. How come all these years and she never stepped in front of one of them? How'd that letter sound to you?"

When had Jud mentioned that? Secretly he felt for the letter. It was still in his pocket. Burn it.

"If it was me I don't think I'd much like to be around here, after that. You and him."

Jud would not be around here. He would be gone . . . far away, hidden somewhere.

"No use to run, though, for they'd catch you. Just make it worse. Don't look to me like you got any choices but just the one. All you got to do is give her that letter."

But he *would* run. "I'll go to some big city somewhere up north." He was on his elbow now and he put his feet on the floor and got up. He stood reeling. He reached out and held to the doorjamb and then, behind him, he heard Meagher's dry derisive chuckle. This was what spurred him through the door and out into the driveway, but then he took only a few more steps. That was as far as he ever got. He sat down on the dead grass at the edge of the gravel and he was still sitting there when first daylight showed itself in the garden.

Throughout that long hollow day Jud waited, and through another flickering soundless night. The thought of fleeing must have come to him a hundred times and always with the same kind of shock, as of recognition, as if he had lifted his eyes and seen a shut door standing open. In fact there were several times when he thought that he was actually, at long last, on his way. He got as far as the door or just a few steps beyond, though one time it was different. Then it was night, late, and he found himself not only beyond the house but almost up to the head of the driveway, still walking, but walking now with that kind of effort that comes at the end of a dissolving dream. Before he turned back he stood for a while in the gap between the hedges, looking out. When he did turn to start back he did it as suddenly as if he had been tapped on the shoulder, and he walked fast, pursued by the feeling that there was somebody watching him through the screen of vines across the front porch.

That was only a little while before dawn and just after daylight Jud heard a sound. It was a car door slamming. Then there were lights in the house and not much later the sound of subdued voices and people going in and out. His room, with the door shut now, was like a corner where he lay hidden, trapped, surrounded by the murmur of voices he sometimes heard as whispers close to his ear. Once he thought the voices were talking about him and he went and stood at the window to listen. But they had stopped. There was only the empty garden lying in the blast of the morning sun. Growing dizzy he sat down. He was trying to think what he would do if a knock came at his door.

A knock did come. This was much later, though, and waked him from one of his spells of sleep. It was his summons, but there were some first blurred moments when he understood only that the light in the room was afternoon light and that a man's florid face was looking in through the doorglass. Then Jud was on his feet holding the door open, suffering the man's scrutiny of his face.

"You all right, son?"

He could nod.

"The Reverend was asking about you, wondering if you was out here. I know you want to come. It's fixing to start in a little while."

Jud managed the nod again, but when the man left him he had to sit down.

His memory of the hour that followed was made up entirely of vivid fragments, with grayness in between. He remembered his judgment on his own face when, laving it with water, he observed it in the mirror. This was what *they* would see. Then the moment, as he entered the living room, when he could not get his breath because of the flowers, banks of flowers right and left whose scent was like a clotting in his nostrils. After that the silence, and the eyes. Whatever propelled him up to that coffin had nothing to do with his will. He thought he was escorted, led by the arm maybe, then left as on stage alone with no choice except to look down at her. He stared at her hands, small and waxen-looking, lying in a whiteness as radiant as a bride's—clean hands, no dirt from the garden. That was all, though it was as if she was watching him from under her lids, trying to draw his gaze up to her face. He never looked: he turned away before he had to look. But the impression, the feeling of being summoned to look at her face, was, and remained, the one that stood apart from all the rest.

The interval at the graveyard also left its impressions. One was of the cedars stirring. Wind, the herald of rain, was stirring them, and there came a single small leap of his blood before the moment darkened again. Through it all he watched the cedars, or else the ground between his feet, or else he sat with his eyes shut. For Lily was there, he knew, masked in one of the solemn faces somewhere not far away. What if his gaze should meet hers? But there was an even stronger reason. In the row of chairs apart near an end of the grave, one figure was the Reverend's. He was not facing Jud, and Jud thought the old man never so much as lifted his head. But there was always the chance he might, and turn and look Jud's way. So Jud stared at the cedars and at the ground and at his own dark eyelids. He did not even know when the Reverend left, but only, at last when the stillness made him open his eyes, that he was gone.

The hours after Jud left the graveyard, walking alone, were like the hours that might follow a sudden and unaccountable reprieve. He kept seeing the road north and the bustling streets of a great vague city he was headed for. It was as if he was on his way, still walking after nightfall, and his stops to rest and let his head get clear were only the small intermissions in his journey. At one point he really was well out of town, walking on the road shoulder. Even turning and starting back did not disrupt his illusion very much. Nothing did, until he found himself in the driveway, passing the house, approaching the door to his room again. It all came back in a single flash of that dry lightning. This was where his journey ended.

But he was wrong, for before the night was over he had come to a decision. Or rather he was brought to a decision, pushed. It was the Reverend. It was late, long after the house lights had gone out, and Jud had been knowing for some time that there was a person in the garden. He was close to Jud's window, once, stopped there, standing a while before Jud heard him move away. Jud stayed on his bed, muffling his breath, and never would have known for sure who it was if the Reverend had not, finally, come to his door. The knock was not much more than touching. Jud made him repeat it several times before he ever moved to answer it.

"Jud." That was all the Reverend said for a minute. The lightning showed him to Jud, wearing no coat or tie, his bright lenses, and his lips not quite shut. He wanted to come in. There was nothing Jud could do.

Once he was seated in the chair the Reverend did not want the light on. Then Jud could see him only by flashes, the balding top of his head clearer than anything else about him, and he began to think that the old man had forgotten where he was, what he had come for. Finally the Reverend said, "You wonder . . . "

This was all he said for a while. Then, "God's just, though . . . whatever it looks like to us, sometimes." This wait was even longer. He had lifted his face and Jud saw his lenses flash. It was not only the Reverend who was visible in these moments. Jud tried to sit less stiffly on the bed.

"She thought a lot of you, Jud. A whole lot." He cleared his throat. "You know that, don't you?"

It had to be answered. He made a noise like "yes."

"Always talking about you. What you could be . . . She said . . . " The Reverend cleared his throat, and the silence after this was the longest of all. He had lowered his head again, because Jud saw, once, the top of it. He never finished the sentence. He said. "I can't believe she's not here with us. Out there." He must have nodded toward the garden. Still later he said, "I was thinking. Just now."

Jud saw that he had looked up again.

"It's going to get so lonesome in that house. You could use that other room, if you wanted to. Would you like that?"

Sometime later Jud managed to say, "I'd better stay here."

"No need to. I'd like to have you for company. If you can stand an old man around. You could still come and go like you want."

"I'd better . . . " But where was the reason he could give? His mind refused to work.

"I'd like mighty well to have you, son."

In a panic Jud said, "You mean . . . tomorrow?"

"Tomorrow'd be fine. Can I look for you, then?"

Jud's yes was something said at a distance from him. It was followed by a flash of the Reverend's lenses, and another when, presently, the old man got to his feet. He said at least a few more husky words, but they left no impression on Jud. Neither did his departure, for Jud could not remember afterwards its happening at all. He remembered the lenses flashing at him. He thought how it would be when the moment came, the moment when the Reverend knew. In Jud's fever that night he saw the lenses like fierce twin suns burning into his eyes, and he dreamed he woke up blind.

22

JUD HAD MADE HIS DECISION IN THE NIGHT, AND IN the morning, at the hour, he walked up the driveway and, passing between the hedges onto the street, turned left as always down the hill. But it was not as always. There was a swimming in his head and even on the steep downgrade his feet went heavily. Also the sky was overcast this morning, shrouding the light. But this, after all these weeks or months of burning sun, only seemed wrong to him and without promise. The low thunder that he heard rumble once before he reached the foot of the hill seemed merely threatening.

He went as usual to Rogan's and sat in his usual corner looking at a breakfast that stirred the beginnings of nausea in his belly. But there was need of food, a day to be got through. And Lily to face, to fool. He forced the bites into his mouth and chewed and swallowed hard and afterwards sat with his jaws clenched, fighting the nausea back. He heard the strokes of the courthouse clock. He was late. Too late, he thought, and he got up quickly from the table.

The low north corner of the courthouse lawn, with its view of Nunn's front door, was as far as Jud got. Retreating he put a tree trunk between him and the sight of it and later, keeping it there, he sank down onto a bench. A fool, on a bench. The letter was in his pocket. Soon it would be too late. What was the reason for it? What, since his refusal would not stop her mouth? Yet he stayed where he was and heard the clock strike nine.

Until late in the afternoon he never got any farther than this, the bench with the tree trunk hiding him from the front door of Nunn's. He retreated and later came back and then retreated again. He did this two or three other times and the last retreat, and the longest, was all the way down to the river. Then it was afternoon. He sat on the bank at the foot of a sycamore tree, in a hollow between big twisted roots, and let the swimming in his head carry him off like drift afloat on the river. Sometimes there was thunder, waking him out of his fits of sleep. With a little stroke of panic his mind would get clear. Hurry. Go to her. It might be too late already. But these spells of clarity kept passing off too soon, before he could get his feet under him, and he would be left caught up again in the slow wheeling tidal motion over the river's face. Until one roll of thunder came louder than the others. He was on his feet. When he got back to the square the hands of the clock had already passed five-thirty and he did not pause until he stood at the front door of Nunn's.

He thought he was too late, for there was only dusk inside the store. Then he saw the milky light in the glass of the little office. He tried the door, found it locked. His key was still there in his pocket, though, and he went in and shut and locked the door behind him. He must have been quiet, for there was no sign of any response from the office. He must have walked quietly, too, because when he reached the open office door Lily was sitting with her back to him and her head bent over the ledger on her desk. His mouth refused to speak. His voice would bring it on him, the shock that her face would be. But he never had to speak, because all of a sudden she started, wheel-

234

ing around in the chair, her face, a fierce white distorted mask, coming at him. He actually stepped back a little.

But it was only her moment of alarm that had made her look, or seem to look that way. Now, recovered, her face was merely cold and regarded Jud through the doorway with a perfectly flat nerveless gaze. He had wanted to speak first, but his lips and tongue would not thaw out.

"What do you want?" she said. Then, "How did you get in here? . . . You still have my key."

"I want to come back," Jud said.

She searched him. She folded her hands and sat back a little in the swivel chair to search him. He had to meet it, though the effort made his head swim, distorting the look of her eyes, making the smoldering irises seem to spin like wheels in the sockets.

"You did hear from her? You got a letter?"

Then he could not face her any longer. His bent head said yes.

"Did she have it . . . the abortion?"

She was waiting. There was a moment when Jud tried to say no. But his head nodded yes.

"I want to see the letter."

It was still there in his pocket: he almost moved his hand. "It's in my room."

"Go get it."

"But it's got my name on it," he murmured.

"I probably won't have to use it. If I do I'll tear your name off. You can tear it off yourself if you want to." She was quiet for a moment, still searching him. "I'll have the proof in a day or two, anyway. Without your letter."

"You'll keep me out of it . . . if I give it to you?" His voice barely made a sound.

"Yes. I'll keep you out of it."

After a moment he said, "But how can you?"

235

"I told you before, the other night. Just trust me. I can fix it."

He could feel the letter against his thigh. But his hand did not move. She would see he had lied again.

"Go and get it. Bring it to the house, it'll be dark by then."

He was standing half in the dark already and suddenly he remembered. "The old man'll be waiting for me," Jud said. "I've got to move in the house when I get back." He thought she was looking at him with suspicion and he added, "I couldn't get out of it. He came in my room last night, I couldn't help it." Then quickly, "I can bring it later, when he goes to bed."

She moved her hands, folding her fingers. The nails on her lamp side gleamed. "All right. I'll be waiting."

"It won't be very late."

"All right."

But he was not dismissed yet, for she kept looking at him in almost the same way. He was about to say again that he would not be late.

"No more 'virtue,' then?" she said.

What could he answer?

"Your skin's more important to you, isn't it?"

He made an effort, but he knew the grin came off as a grimace.

"Of course it is. What use would it be for you to go to prison? That would be stupid." If anything she looked at him more intently, extending the fingers of her folded hands. "You look like it's torn you up, though. You're pale. Are you sick?"

He gave a deprecatory nod. "No. Just . . . "

"Scared? And still upset, I guess." Then she blinked. "You'll get over it, though. You'll see."

Something had happened. At first Jud thought it was

236

inside his own head, a sudden increment of his dizziness that had changed and softened the tone of her voice for him. Then he noticed her face. That was changed too. Her eyes were different and the set of her mouth hinted at a sort of smile. He had still not got it straight when she said, in a soft but this time half-playful voice, "Did you like her better than you do me?"

If he had known what to answer he could not have done it. He was not sure even now that his dizzy head was not playing a trick on him, an eerie trick.

"I'm sorry I was so harsh with you. You were betraying me, though, weren't you?" She did not force him to answer and her voice was still soft when she went on. "I forgive you, though. This once." Then it came, a whisper. "I won't be harsh anymore."

It was not only in her voice, it was in her eyes and she meant for him to see it. But it was a dream.

"Go on now," she said softly. "I'll be looking for you."

These words were part of the dream, too, and so was her cheek where his gaze now had stopped. A movement of her hand waked him up and, turning, he made his way through the dark store and out.

He thought that quite a while had passed before he got back to his room. He knew he stopped several times along the way and one of the stops in particular could have lasted longer than it seemed to. There was a clump of shrubbery near the street in somebody's yard. He had meant only to rest there for a minute and let his head clear, and think. But no thoughts would come. Instead Lily came. It seemed that she had followed him here and now stood looking down at him in a way that brought her face out of the dark. There was light on it, streetlight, through a window. This was the room upstairs above his

237

room and the garment she had on, open down to the cleft
between her breasts, was the dressing robe he knew so
well. Her hands appeared and he saw the robe slowly
parting all the way down to her knees. She was bending.
The dark cold breasts came down on him and the putrid
cheek was pressed against his own. He gave a lunge. He
was on his knees. Then he was on his feet beside the
shrubs, turning left and right to find his way.

There were other stops, the last one between the
hedges where the driveway came out. Then he was back
in his room standing motionless by his bed in the light of
the table lamp. He heard the Reverend's steps coming.
He heard them stop at the door and then the old man's
voice. "I opened up the room for you, son. I'll wait while
you get packed up." Jud answered him but he kept his
back to the door. All while he worked he kept it that way,
avoiding the lamp, imagining that the Reverend watched
him through the door. Finally reaching to turn the switch
Jud held his face aside.

It was like being drawn in the Reverend's wake, sleep-
walking in tracks that led Jud into the house and up the
stairs. In the dark hall at the top, where Jud had never
been before, he held to the newel post, waiting, preparing
a face to meet the Reverend. He did not need it, though,
even inside the lighted bedroom. In the short while the
Reverend stayed, the times when he looked at Jud could
not have showed him anything much but a face through
a watery blur. He wanted to talk. He wanted to stay a
while and talk and he sat down on the chair beside the
door. He did get a few words out: he hoped Jud would be
comfortable here. But most of his words never got past
his throat and he soon fell silent. Mostly he sat with his
head in his hands, while Jud, standing by the window,

watched for the moments when lightning made the garden visible down there. When the old man left, shutting the door, he did not manage even a clear "goodnight."

Jud did not touch the things he had brought up and he left the light burning only long enough to make a show. The darkness made him dizzier than ever. He opened a window and sat down near it on the bed to wait. It was not a minute before the first swoon hovered. He had to fight it off, and soon after that another and another. There was a breeze to help him. He felt the first gust of it with a kind of alarm, as if something strangely out of order had taken place, but after this he met the gusts face-on, gratefully, with his mouth open to draw them into his lungs. The breeze got stronger. Sometimes it made a faint whispering in the windowscreen and now and then it rustled something in the room behind him. He kept turning his head to see what it was, but he could not see anything.

It must have been that in some measure Jud finally did give in to one of those swoons. That would be an explanation for the peculiar rapt intentness that had got hold of him. Hold of his bodily senses, that is, as if they had been raw wounds alive to the most minute of feathery sensations. The breeze from the window felt strong, like gusts straight out of a bellows, making him cold. It was that way with the lightning, too, its brightness almost pain. He could see the garden in the flash, a shock that seemed to bring it hurtling upward toward his window. He covered his eyes finally. Then there were the sounds, the sibilance of the wind in the window screen and behind him the rustling that was like a dry stiff garment shaken. He thought there were other sounds. He *thought*, because he could not tell for sure. They were like sounds in a range too high or too low, just beyond the barrier, exciting his ears like sounds in a memory. They were also a kind of pain and this was what made him finally get up off the bed.

There was wind in the house: that was the secret commotion. Yet he opened his door to listen, stood straining to discern the shape of each small separate sound. The drafts of air were cunning. The sounds were like disguises, deceptions taking the audible form of all those muted stirrings and clickings in the house. More and more, as Jud stood there, it seemed to him that there was not even one whose source he could envision, as if the wind had brought them all from too great a distance. There came a moment, or interval, when he could not seem to remember where he was.

When he did remember he thought he had got turned around. Instead of the hall he was facing the door to his room, which, he reasoned, the wind had blown shut behind him. He could faintly hear that rustling sound through the door, and it came to him that he never had discovered what it was. He opened the door. Instantly, even before he had pushed it completely open, he knew that something was wrong.

It was a white room. This was the effect, of whiteness everywhere, so much so that a moment of lightning was more like a flicker of pale shadows against the wall. Then he saw that the bed, the whitest thing of all, was what gave such an intensity to the room. He blinked at it, as to clear a glaze from the surface of his eyes, and saw it just as before. But it was not as before. Or maybe it was and until now his eyes had simply missed the dim outlines of her body. It was no wonder. From head to foot she was neither more nor less white than the coverlet beneath her. And just as still. He was not aware of moving closer and yet, seconds later, he was looking down at her folded

240

waxen hands. He already knew that she was watching him. But for a little while he failed to notice that she was watching him not from under her closed eyelids but from eyes that were standing open, with a meaning in them he did not pause to read. For that was when he retreated. He blundered in the hall and passing through an open door found himself on the bed again with his heart lodged tight in his chest.

He got up later and put on the light for a moment. That was a curtain rustling in the wind. The wind was real. There were no other sounds but its whisperings and stirrings in the house and, listening, he suddenly remembered. This was also real. It was still there in his pocket, the letter, and Lily would be getting impatient.

Now the wind was a help, a screen over the bumbling of his movements in the dark. Halfway down the stairs he stopped, and stopped again at the foot near the Reverend's door. He felt his way to the kitchen and there let himself out and left the yard by his passage under the hedge.

It seemed a long way. The wind was a confusion, buffeting his face, bending and swaying unfamiliar trees along his path. But his feet took him on, never missing a turn, and then he was standing in her backyard some distance from the house. It was not like a decision he had reached, but this spot where he stopped was as close as he ever got to the door.

Jud was still there when she appeared at the doorglass and stood looking out. She was only a shape framed from the waist up against the light, without any feature but the sharp line of her silhouette. How, then, could he see her eyes and her cheeks and also, at last, another far more striking thing? But he thought he could. He was certain that down the front of her body the dressing robe hung

241

open, inviting his gaze. And he gazed. He stared, in fact. Exactly what it was he was staring at so hard was not clear to him later on. It was not clear even at the time. But he remembered his fear, amounting nearly to terror, and also the impression he kept when finally he had turned his eyes away. It was an impression only of darkness, but a darkness blacker and deeper and colder than any night or any abyss he had ever looked into. He did not look again. Until the light went out he never so much as turned his face toward the door. Then he moved, slowly at first, then faster, hurrying toward the square.

23

IT WAS LIKE A DESIGN, THE WAY THE TRUCK PULLED
up at the stoplight just as he reached the corner. He had
only to lift his hand and the door swung open and the
voice he could not hear clearly over the motor's noise invited him to get in. Trucks on the way north to Louisville
and Chicago came through town pretty often at night
and, in the muddled state of his mind, wanting only to
put this place behind him, he assumed the truck was one
of them. The least attention would have showed him better. Even the driver told him so, but it did not quite come
through at the time. After that Jud was conscious mostly
of being shaken by the truck's motion and small startling
jolts when his head bumped against the window. When
the truck suddenly stopped it seemed to him that this
bumping and jolting had lasted maybe long enough to
take them to the edge of town, yet there were no lights or
houses.

"I turn off here, boy."

In the backwash from the headlights Jud could see the
driver looking at him, and mumbling something, he got
out of the truck. He watched it turn off the pavement and
after a minute disappear down a tunnel of dusty yellow
light. He could not tell where he was. There was nothing
to see, only the obscurely visible pavement stretching
each way and the standing darkness of woods on either
side, pitched by the wind. The moment came when, to be

certain about his direction, he had to recall that he had got out of the truck on this side of the road.

He walked uphill for a while. One truck went by, going fast, limning Jud in its headlights for a few seconds as if he had been a ghost standing there with a pale hand raised. Later he reached the crest of the hill and saw a dim light well on ahead of him. A lone farmhouse? The edge of a town? It was as if the wind had set him down here, walking. The light did not seem to get any nearer.

Finally it did. He passed a dark anonymous house by the road and then another that were dumb witnesses to his progress. The light got brighter. It was very close to the highway, and he soon made out that it was at a gas station or something. It was also at a crossroads. Something, he did not know what, was pressing at his consciousness. But that was when a car came up behind him. He looked around and it was stopping. It stopped beside him, the driver already leaning across to open the door. Then Jud saw his face.

"You crazy?" Meagher said through the open door. "Get in here."

Jud hated his face, his dancing eyes. Without a word he turned and kept on walking down the highway shoulder. But the car came up beside him again, the door still swinging open, the voice hissing at him. "You goddamn fool."

Jud went on, never glancing at him, and still the car stayed at Jud's side. At last he wheeled around and passing in back of the car crossed to the other side of the highway. The headlights went out. Then the car door slammed and he heard Meagher's feet on the pavement coming after him. He tried to walk faster but he could not. It was like fleeing in a dream, gained upon with every step, all but stumbling finally. Then Meagher

244

touched him. Meagher's hand closed on his arm, painfully, like a claw, holding him there, speaking over his shoulder. "You gone crazy, man. They'll have you caught just quick as they miss you. Stumbling around out here sick. Come on, it ain't too late." Meagher pulled at him.

In the light from the gas station window Jud could see over his shoulder the dim glare of Meagher's face. Somehow there was help from that light, or that window— from something. "Let go," he said.

"She's still waiting. *It*'s waiting, man, your time's come. What you been dreaming about all this time. She wants you, man." Meagher yanked his arm.

Turning Jud swung at him with all his might, but he hit nothing. He hit the ground on his knees and heard Meagher cursing him in a low fierce ragged voice. He was expecting Meagher to kick him, but nothing happened. Next there was not any sound but the wind and when he looked up Meagher was gone. Even the car was gone. There was not a soul anywhere, though the light from the window shining onto the empty concrete apron and onto the gravel road beyond was in some way a comfort.

He could not think why the light was a comfort or why, when he had left it behind him, the dark scattered houses he passed affected him in the same way. So did the road he walked on. The road, it seemed was going to be gravel from here on and lead him at last to some place of rest and final safety. Soon there were no more houses and it was lonely, but that did not seem to matter so much anymore. Later, when he noticed how the treeless overgrown fields stretched away to the horizon, he solved it. He was on his way home.

At night along the road between those big ridgetop fields there were not many landmarks visible. But there

245

was one he could not miss, Bethel Church, and as he passed it he began to feel uneasy. This quickly grew worse, becoming anxiety, spoiling everything. His steps went slower and slower. Soon they stopped completely. Everything was spoiled. He was too tired to go on, anyway, and he sat down in his tracks on the gravel road.

Later he began to be afraid. The wind was the first reason, the sound like a whispering in his head or the soughing of breath through barely parted lips. He knew the sound was out there in the brush and briars of the field, but it was too much like an utterance he could not make out and it threatened him. Then, though not right away, he began to understand, or remember. This stopped his breathing and then, almost, the beating of his heart. There was somebody with him. The person was very close, and Jud knew just before it happened that a hand was about to be laid on him. When it settled on his shoulder he did not even jump. He did not even look until the hand moved, slid under his arm and urged him. The face bending over him, Sunk's face, was darker than the sky behind it.

Jud might as well have had no choice but to follow him, walking up the channel between the banks of briars and into the clearing past the shed and up to the dark trailer under the tree. He never heard Sunk knock, though he saw his arm higher than his head reach out to the door. Then Sunk was gone and Jud heard a sound from the trailer and then another one. It was just as if he could see the hand approaching to open the door. He tried to step back a pace or two, but he was not quick enough.

At first he could not see anything at all in the doorway and his arms, that he wanted to raise in defense, hung stiff at his sides. His neck, his throat—he could feel the

246

fierce gaze fastened there. A moment passed, with nothing, not even wind, and then there was movement in the doorway and after that a flickering light that soon steadied itself. "Come on in, boy."

The step seemed too high for Jud's strength, but he managed it. Salter stood beyond and above the lamp, naked from the waist, with shadows between his white ribs. The shadows were under his cheekbones, too, and also in the sockets of his eyes and it was like looking at the phantom of somebody Jud had known once. Then Salter's head moved, his eyes appeared. They were alive. So were his lips. "It was you, wasn't it?"

The light in each eye was like a seed at the core.

"You and that witch. She's took your soul, boy."

Jud put a hand against the wall.

"It's like I had really knowed it all along. For I knowed already she was a witch. Then that little lady come here. I knowed it from what she told me about you. You was serving that witch. And brought that harlot out here to me." Salter paused. Then his voice came again. "*Say* you did."

And Jud said it, though his voice did not make a sound. Propped against the wall, he waited, feeling his heart. But nothing happened. Or nothing except that he looked down at the floor. Salter said, "And I done what you aimed for me to. And more. So I ain't even nothing you need to ask forgiveness from."

For a while after that, though Jud was not ten feet away from him, Salter appeared to have forgotten him completely. As if his body was something very fragile he lowered himself onto the cot behind him at the end of the trailer and began to stare at the lamp. He muttered to himself. Once he looked up and did not see Jud and said,

247

"Pride. Man's pride." He lifted the scarred discolored hand and gazed at it. When he put it down, on his knee again, he said, "They're always laying to take a man in his pride." Then he was looking at Jud once more, seeing him. "That witch send you here?"

Jud shook his head no. There were the seeds of light in the dark of Salter's eyes.

"You still serving her?"

Jud shook his head again. It began to dawn on him only now that there was something wrong, something that Salter's starving body had not told him.

"You wouldn't come. I sent Sunk to fetch you. That little lady come. Come several times. Set right down there." He looked at a box beside his bed. "Right where that harlot set. With her hair shining, wanting to feed me and give me drink for my sickness. Like I was a man fitting for her mercy." He looked at Jud again. "Told me all about you. Worrying about that witch getting you. Only she wouldn't believe it was a witch. I tried to tell her." His eyelids drooped for a moment, then shut, then opened again. It was a blank gaze. "Now she's dead."

His attention had strayed but Jud knew it was not for long. It was like a bird, a hawk circling, already banking in the turn that would bring it back to Jud. What Jud felt when Salter looked at him once more was like the need to lift his arm for a shield.

"What killed her?" Salter demanded suddenly.

"A truck," Jud said.

"A truck." He considered it. "It wasn't no truck."

Jud could not answer.

"It was that witch, wasn't it?"

There was an answer but Jud could not seem to make it out. He thought that if his head would stop swimming he would be able to grasp the answer.

The lightless state he sank into was not so much like sleep as like despair. Yet he dreamed. Meagher was bending over him, whispering. "It ain't too late yet, man. She's still waiting for you, saving it for you." In soft light from her window she was undressing, letting the garments slip from her body, her breasts. But her breasts, laid bare, were bitter darkness against her flesh, making Jud shudder, and he turned his face away. Finally he dreamed of Hannah again. She was seated on the box, as before, her hair by much the brightest thing in the room. It made him think of a lamp burning and the more he looked the more it seemed to give off light of its own. She was leaning close, then closer. He could see how her hair lit up her face and made the dusky blue of her eyes visible. Then he waked up.

There was lamplight and it shone on the box drawn up close to his side. On top of it was milk in a glass and bread on a china plate, all very white like manna in the lamp's rays. The lamp was on the table and Salter was seated there, sitting with his head between his hands. A book, the Bible, lay open under his gaze, but he did not appear to be reading, He was staring, a blind stare. On his forehead the hair, though dry, lay plastered, showing Jud that he *had* been somewhere standing or walking in the rain. Without a shirt. Jud thought of the rain pricking Salter's skin like needles and wet wind in the hollows between his ribs, and he shivered. Even now Salter must be cold—always cold with the wind between his ribs. Jud noticed the blanket covering his own body. "Aren't you cold?" he said.

Salter did not hear: he never stirred. The rain kept on.

"I'm much obliged to you," Jud finally said, a little louder.

"Wasn't it?" Salter repeated in a flat hard voice. "Wasn't it?"

The swimming stopped. "It was me," Jud said.

The swimming did not come back. Everything was as quiet and still as a pool, with never even a breath of wind to riffle it. He was conscious of the bright seed growing in Salter's eyes, but this was not anything to trouble him, either, because he was sinking and would soon be down where Salter could not reach him. A little later he looked up and dimly saw Salter's face and even heard the faint underwater echoes of his voice. After that Jud was too deep to see or hear anything.

It was not so much black down there as it was simply lightless, like having eye-sockets without any eyes in them. But the terror was not the lightlessness or even the knowing that, since up and down and sideways were the same, there was nothing to struggle either toward or away from. The terror was the loneliness. The place was not even a place. It was like a condition whole light-years out of time, eons of remoteness from the slightest hint of any sound or motion. There were not even objects, not even shadows. If he should die and go to hell he knew it would be like that—a kind of starving that never starves, an endless hopeless desperate craving of all his bodily senses.

But he came back. It was like having his eyes suddenly restored to him, though for a long time they did not see much—only some shadows moving close to his face. After a while he felt something, like a ripple of water maybe, lightly touch his forehead, and then he began to feel that everything was all right, he was safe. There was somebody close by, in arm's reach, with gentle hands. Now and again a hand came and brushed across his forehead, brushing the heat away, and each time his mind got a little clearer. Then there was light enough. He knew it was Hannah, seated on the box by the bed where he lay. He knew it at first with a shock that stopped his heartbeat, but the hand, with small calluses, kept coming to touch his head and soon he was not afraid anymore. He seemed to be talking to her, telling or asking her something important, but he never could quite hear the answer. He gave it up, almost contentedly. When he opened his eyes it was daylight.

It was raining. This was the first fact Jud's mind got hold of, drinking it in for a moment before he realized where he was. In the trailer, on the bed. And he knew this almost as one with his knowing that the person seated on the box now was Salter. He could see part of Salter without turning his head and what he could see best was Salter's scarred right hand lying over a knee. Was that what had touched his forehead? It did not look gentle. Then he recalled his image not of the hand lying on his forehead years ago, healing him, but fastened like a claw on Goldie's soft white throat. Shutting his eyes again to feign sleep he lay stiffly waiting for the hand. What came instead was Salter's voice, as if he had got a glimpse into Jud's mind. He said,

"Don't wait on this hand, boy. Ain't none can heal you but the Lord's, if He choose to. This'n can't. Can't heal nothing."

Jud heard him move, grow still again.

"It's something it can do, though."

Jud waited a long time, feeling the strokes of his blood in his throat.

"Done it before. Done it to the wrong one, though . . . Wrong one. And here you are now, boy. And that little

250

lady dead . . . Open up your eyes, boy; it hide."

Jud opened his eyes. He stared at the at the edge of his gaze the hand loomed.

"What did she say back to you?"

He waited for Jud a moment. Leaning most where he could see Jud's face, he re tion.

"Who do you mean?" Jud whispered.

"I was listening. I knowed who it wa her name—Hannah. I heard your wicke got that babe tore from her womb. And th was leaning, looking into Jud's face, his the dark sockets. "But I couldn't hea back."

Jud understood. "I couldn't hear her," l couldn't hear her either."

Salter's eyes blinked and looked away f at the wall for a minute. He stood up. At f he was going to speak again, but he neve to the door and went outside and only t rain was left, falling on the metal roof.

The rain kept falling. Once Jud had to g the door, but he saw nothing except th empty shed and Sunk's ruin of a shack were only the wide vacant fields shroudec of rain. Was Salter out there someplace rain? The wind came up and lashed the the windows blind.

Were they looking for him yet? Jud di then he thought of Lily and then of the thought of the Reverend's lenses like suns too hot to bear, and he shut his eyes tigh

But this did not draw Salter's attention, either, and Jud thought of nights and nights like this, Salter's head between his hands with his eyes blind on the open Bible. Seeing what? Goldie in his hot embrace, or lying dead on the floor? Jud pushed the blanket off him. He stood up shivering in the air and picking up the blanket he took the steps that brought him to Salter's side. Salter did not look up. Jud laid the blanket across his shoulders. Then Salter looked up and at first, because the eyes he lifted to Jud seemed dark and hostile, Jud thought he would throw the blanket off. But he let it lie and kept on looking at Jud, and Jud saw that his eyes were dark but not hostile.

"You forgive me, boy?"

"What for?" Jud said.

Salter never answered. His gaze drifted away from Jud and then back down to the Bible where his hand lay on the page. It was the scarred hand and this instead of the page was where his eyes had settled. Or so Jud discovered after a few moments, because Salter said, "It's some strength left in it yet, though. Enough to stop a wicked mouth from speaking."

It seemed as if Jud's sluggish mind could not digest these words. Except for his image of Salter's hand the interval that followed was almost blank for him. He saw the hand and heard the rain falling. Next he saw Salter's fingers moving, forming, except for the one finger left extended, a crooked fist. That finger pointed to words on the page. "It's right here in the Word of God," Salter said. "Read it."

It was too far away, the print too small.

"Read it," Salter commanded.

Jud bent and looked where the finger pointed. Slowly,

253

while Salter's breath sounded in his ear, the words took shape..

"What does it say?"

At first Jud's lips moved without a sound. Then he mumbled, or maybe whispered, "Ye shalt not suffer a witch to live."

The finger withdrew. Jud saw it bend and fold itself into the crooked fist, the fist on the table now beside the book. Jud drew back slowly and stood upright and the fist was still lying there. But Salter's head had moved. He had looked toward one of the blind black windows and he said, "No use to set here putting it off no longer."

24

"YOU CAN'T," JUD SAID. BUT THIS WAS LATER, AFTER a blank interval in which he stood watching Salter stare at the night-blinded window. Jud waked up and said it, and then he said, "You can't just . . . kill her."

He did not think Salter heard him, not for a while. Then Salter said, "It's laid on me to do." He looked down at the Bible again. "That's why you come here. You was sent. You ain't but His messenger."

Jud groped in his mind. *"He* wouldn't lay sin on you . . . killing."

"It's a witch." Salter's hand came open, then moved and shut the Bible.

"They don't know that," Jud said. "They'll hang you this time."

"Hang me? It ain't man's punishment I fear of. Nor his judgment."

Salter got up from the table. As he did, the blanket slipped off his shoulders and for a minute after that he stood looking down at his starved torso as if he had never observed it before. Then Jud saw that now Salter was showing it to him, too, because Salter's hand came up and tapped at his ribs, pointing to them. "You think I fear of punishment to these here worthless bones? They can leave them hanging till Judgment Day, for all the hurt to me."

Jud realized later but he did not realize then why he said, "It's pride. It's still pride."

"It's the Lord's hand on me," Salter said, and turned and went out the door.

Jud was not sure what he stood there thinking for the next minute or so. It was like something he could not quite get hold of and he kept expecting Salter every second to appear in the door again, coming back. Then he heard, through the rain, a noise, a thud. There was a grinding sound and he realized that it was the sound of the truck being cranked. Salter was starting the truck. A moment more and he would be gone, really gone. To Lily. Then Jud moved.

Coming off the high doorstep he fell and he was on his knees in the rain when the truck's engine came to life with sudden violence. The headlights hit him in the face and seemed to be the reason he staggered as he lunged to his feet, headed for the truck. It had not moved yet. Jud was at the driver's door, pulling at the handle, calling to Salter and hearing himself, his voice, as if this after all was only a thing done in make-believe. He got the door half open, looked into Salter's face. "Get away, boy." The voice, though commanding, did not sound fierce. It sounded almost reasonable, in fact, even while he was pulling against Jud, trying to shut the door. Then the handle yanked loose from Jud's grip and the truck lurched forward.

Jud was running beside it, a hand on the bed. As the truck turned he got one glimpse of Sunk and tried to call out to him. Jud got his hand on a stantion. He was half in tow by now, his feet dragging bounding off the ground, and he made a last great effort, a leap. It was not enough. The stantion broke from his grip and he hit the ground rolling behind the truck.

256

Blindly he jumped up and ran on, chasing the truck for some time after its red taillight had disappeared through the rain. Even then, in spite of his dizzy exhaustion, he kept on walking, just as if there was still a chance he finally could catch up. And in fact he went on somehow believing this all the way back to town. To Bethel seemed no distance. It was like opening his eyes to find himself there and the gas station still open and a car pulled up at the pumps waiting for him. After that it seemed only minutes through the flashing rain, while a man's vexing unfamiliar voice pulled at his attention, before he saw the square and the lighted face of the clock bloom up in front of him. It was not until he stepped out onto the pavement that he realized how much time must have elapsed. He was surely too late.

And he was too late, if not by very much. In the night and the rain and with so many months gone by since he had been here, it must have taken Salter a while to find the house. He must have driven up and down several streets, maybe a lot of them, in the slow rumbling truck, eyeing the houses to one side, then the other, waiting for the one that the Lord's hand pointed to. But he had found it, though the truck was parked a little beyond, in front of the next house, on the wrong side of the street. Possibly he sat there in the cab a little while first, in the dark, communing with the Lord. He would have got out of the truck slowly and walked slowly, back to the house and up the porch steps to the door. He would have paused, first, maybe for a good while. Maybe, before he put the weight of his shoulder to the door, he tried the knob, just to be sure, so as not to break anything if he did not have to. This is the way, after thinking about it, Jud came to imagine his actions. Because he did not think it was all just the crazy zeal of a demented person, a fanatic who was

257

taking the Lord's vengeance in his own hands. There was some of that, all right. Jud had not been wrong when he accused him of pride. But after he thought about the way Salter had seemed back in the trailer Jud decided that he was acting from other motives too. He thought that partly Salter was doing it for him and also for the little lady, Hannah, who had considered him fit for her mercy. A man doing a thing like this for others was not likely to approach it in a blind rage of zeal, with his head down.

That was why Jud imagined him moving deliberately, unlike a man in the hands of the Lord. And Lily's account at the hearing later on supported his vision. She heard Salter break the door open and she heard him blundering around in the dark downstairs, looking for her, but she never heard his voice or any sound of violence. Even when she turned on the light in the upstairs hall and he saw her there at the top of the stairs, he did not come toward her with open violence. He climbed the stairs slowly, just looking steadily up at her, never making a sound except by his breathing. He paid no attention to her warnings. He could not have missed seeing the pistol in her hand, but it might as well have been a toy that could not hurt him. Maybe he thought that it could not, or at least could not stop him. That would have been the part of it that was God's fire working in him. She said he looked surprised when the bullet, one of two she fired, hit him in the chest. His mouth came open, he stared straight up at her like an ox and fell backward down the stairs. He was lying there at the bottom dead, on his back, when she went down and stepped over him and went to the telephone.

He was still there when Jud arrived, though covered by a sheet. There were a lot of people on the porch around the door and when Jud finally wedged his way up to

258

where he could see inside he thought at first, because of the sheet, that it was Lily. He remembered, though, that his eyes barely paused on the covered figure. Thrusting his way closer he scanned the hallway in something like panic lest his eyes fall on Salter standing handcuffed, with an officer holding him by the the arm. Salter was not there. The house appeared empty except for Deputy Redding and the man he was talking to, near where the body lay at the foot of the stairs. Then Jud began to hear the people around him on the porch.

"On those stairs, there. He was halfway up when she shot him," a man in a bathrobe said. Jud stared into his face. From over his shoulder another man's voice said,

"Like he was asking for it. Her standing there with that gun pointing at him."

"Just crazy," a third man said.

But Jud was still staring at the man in the bathrobe. It was a big face, with jowls scraped as clean and slick as a baby's, and it seemed to Jud just then to be full of an appalling wisdom. He tried to think of a question for the man, but he could not seem to do it. The man was nodding, speaking again, and soon Jud understood that there was nothing left to ask, nothing. He stopped looking at the man, stopped listening. For a long time after that he did not do anything but stand staring into the hallway at the sheeted figure lying by the stairs. That was Salter, there. Yet Jud must have been listening, too. At some point in that time his mind recorded a thing that came clear to him later on.

He did not remember when he moved inside, but he did, along with a few other people. Except for Deputy Redding and the man he was still talking to, Jud was the one standing closest to the body. He was still there when they came in with a stretcher and lifted Salter onto it. The sheet slipped off the head and because the face was turned Jud's way he had a straight look at it. Or rather, as it seemed for an instant, the face had a look at him, a dark look of accusation. But that was for only an instant. Jud's first impression gave way to a second one much more decisive, the one that stayed with him after they covered the face again. The eyes were staring, all right, but not at Jud. They were not staring, or looking, at anything and Jud was struck with the thought that if life were to have quit them years ago they could not look now more blankly and finally dead.

Then they took Salter out and when Jud became conscious of himself again he was standing alone in the hallway.

He had started for the kitchen, he thought, meaning to leave the house by the back door. Instead, sometime later, he found himself in his old room, in the dark, on the bed where he had lain so many nights. He even found that he was listening for the movements, the naked footsteps, of Lily undressing above his ceiling. But there were no sounds and the pace of his heart was slow, as though it pumped cold blood. He got up. All the lights were still on but there seemed to be nobody in the house and he went out into the hall and to the stairs. He looked a while for stains on the floor. There were not any. Except that the front door stood open there was not the least sign of disorder in the house. The light in the upstairs hall was still burning. He listened for a while. He put his foot on the stairs and started climbing.

Lily's bedroom was not really a shock to him, though he did not know why, after all his dreams about it. He had never imagined it any way but in such light as the moon gives, with warm carpet for her feet and rich window curtains and a bed made of some dark glossy wood. The coverlet had been a pale tint of pink or sometimes violet, and at the head against the board fleshy pillows lay piled up. But there was nothing: it seemed like nothing. In its bareness it made him think of a sick room just now vacated, the bed unmade and seamed yellow window curtains pulled down over the windows. There were two chairs and a metal stand with a lamp and a dressing table on top of which the few cosmetic items looked somehow wrong. Even the mirror seemed dark, as if it would give back only the dusky image of a face.

Until he turned around he did not think there was anything anywhere on the walls. There was a picture, however, near the door, of a man's face and head. It was surely her father, though at first Jud did not know why he was so sure of this. The features were small and distinguished only by their keenness and the eyes appeared to be dark, either brown or black. It was a cold unpleasant contemptuous face—ugly in fact. Yet Jud saw Lily in it. It was as if he saw, the more he looked, a something impenetrably dark behind it that now was part of his image of Lily and that began, finally, to drain the assurance with which he had been standing here in her bedroom. Then he got a shock.

The shock came in the form of a voice downstairs in the hall, a man's voice. Lily's voice answered and Jud heard the front door shut. Everything happened too fast. He thought of the room across from this one, where he could hide, but it seemed he could not get his feet uprooted from this spot. Then it was too late, because she was coming up the stairs. It was like waiting for an assault, as if the something dark behind that pictured face was about to spring at him through the door.

But the face was white, with startled open eyes and

mouth that did not make a sound for a moment or two. Her lips shut, then opened again. "What are you doing here?"

He could not think of an answer.

"Get out."

He could not move. Then he knew that in spite of the pulse pounding in his head he did not mean to move.

"I can get the police back here. There's one in calling distance. They can put you right now where you're already headed for." But she did not move out of the doorway and it became clear now that she was not ready for him to leave. He knew what was coming. She said, "What made him come here? It must have been you, wasn't it?"

The answer was yes and Jud knew he had to say it. Finally he did, quite clearly, though it seemed to take a while before he actually heard it sound out loud. It was as though somebody else had said it, somebody beside or behind him. But there was a second surprise—if surprise was the right word—waiting for him. This was that nothing had happened, nothing at all. He did not know what he had expected. He only knew that he had looked with sudden alarm at her face and then down at her hands, as though she might have been still holding the pistol. Of course her hands were empty and the look of her face was at least no more than his dreams in these last days had prepared him for. He looked right at her, straight, and nothing happened. And even while looking at her so, he could feel his tongue begin to loosen. He said, "But I didn't mean to."

"Didn't mean to," she said, not as a question. "What *did* you mean?"

"Just to tell him. I didn't mean to send him here."

She searched him and a little scornful smile came on her mouth." No, I guess you didn't. You wouldn't have had even that much guts. It was just to cleanse your little soul, wasn't it?"

"I guess it was," he said.

"And now you've got this on it, too."

Jud did not answer, deliberately. It was an ugly smile, Then he saw, with a kind of dull astonishment, that it was an ugly *face*—hateful, like that picture. The smile faded.

"Now get out of here," she said, stepping back to clear the doorway. "And don't think all this is going to change anything."

He did not move.

"I said get out."

Then he remembered clearly. "They think it was you that sent Goldie up there to him."

Lily just looked at him. There was no trace of the smile.

"I heard them say it out on the porch tonight."

"You're lying." She moved a step closer, back into the doorway. "You're still a lousy liar."

"They'll all be saying it tomorrow. I'll say it too, I'll tell it *worse* than it was . . . if you tell that about Hannah. They won't believe anything you say."

Her mouth tightened and there was a moment when Jud felt something out of his nightmares come back. Then it was gone again. He thought, though only distantly at first, that he could with pleasure drive his fist into her mouth. Or take her by the neck.

"You're still lying. You won't say anything. I've got the proof now, anyway."

Jud never did know whether the interval that followed lasted seconds or much longer. He did remember that at the end of it her face had changed, that it wore an expression he had never seen there before. It was fear. She retreated, and this because he had moved toward her, was

263

still moving toward her. He saw her gaze drop suddenly to his hands and he realized then that his hands were no longer hanging at his sides. It seemed that he meant to use them. At least this was what she thought, because now, backed up against the wall across from her bedroom door, she lifted her own hands to defend herself. Jud often wondered if he really might have done it. He knew that there *was* a moment when, looking into her wolfish eyes, her hateful witch's face, hearing her breath in the stillness, he felt that intention in the stiffness of his half-clenched fingers. He might have done it.

Anyway, something happened. It was not a thing Jud heard or saw or had at the time any impulse to imagine. It was most like a touch on his shoulder from behind, a pale reminding sort of touch. It made the tension go out of his fingers and his hands sink down to his sides. He recalled this later with great vividness, and also the something like regret he felt to see the difference that came at once in Lily's face and posture. The words he spoke just afterwards seemed woefully feeble and short of his desire. "You'll see I'm not lying."

There was nothing more he could say, or do. He simply turned away from her and walked to the stairs and started down. Halfway to the bottom he heard her voice. "Wait a minute."

He did not stop and after a few more steps he heard her call again, in a different softer voice. He was down in the hall and almost to the front door when, from the top of the stairs, she called to him for the last time. This time her voice was harsh, and loud enough to make him nearly pause. "Don't think that's going to stop me."

He opened the door and went on out and down the steps in the rain.

25

THAT WAS THE LAST TIME JUD EVER SAW LILY. ALONG toward the morning of that rainy night he got really sick, hospital sick, and after that it was a couple of weeks before he knew anything about what more had happened. By that time Lily was gone. She had managed, this quickly, to get the store sold, if not yet paid for, and she simply listed her house with a real estate man and left. It was said that she went to live in Nashville. But it was also said that she went to both Atlanta and Chicago and Jud never tried to find out. It was enough for him just to remember her in Hallsboro.

Lily had not been bluffing, as he came to find out, though she had waited until just before leaving town to drop her poison. What with the rumors about her part in the matter of Salter and Goldie, she already had her troubles and did not want any additional ones before her business affairs were pretty well settled. Jud was sure that this was her reason for waiting, because there was not one person in that town whose good opinion as such she cared anything about. He was sure she hated them all—certainly including him, at the last. But she always had known where to be prudent. This was surely why she did not mention Jud's name in connection with Salter's attack on her. She feared that a counterclaim from Jud, accusing her also in the matter, would only muddle beforehand a picture she wanted kept clear and simple.

Of course when her great moment came she mentioned Jud's name, all right. She did it at the store, which was not then hers any longer, on the day she left town. There were half a dozen customers in the store at the time, including one who was a deacon at the Baptist church, and she meant for them all to hear her. She did not even bother to put a decent face on her malice. When the customers just looked at her, probably as if she had been some kind of a toad, she dared them to check her story and named the hospital where Hannah had had the abortion. It was the right hospital. Jud knew it was because Hannah had told him where she was going. But he had never told Lily, and he never heard any evidence that she had conclusive proof of this, or of anything else. It might have been just the violence of her malice, making her reckless, for once. But whether she could prove her assertions or not, there seem to have been no consequences for her. Apparently nobody ever tried to check.

There is no doubt that Lily, if she ever found out the actual results of her revelation, was a good deal disappointed. Of course there was some of what she would have called success. She raised doubts and started some gossip and must have convinced a few people. And—which was maybe her greatest triumph—she caused the Reverend much more than a little agony. Still the effect must have been very disappointing to her. Most people either rejected her story or kept their thoughts well hidden under their hats. It was the kind of thing that Lily never could have believed possible: that a townful of people, out of respect for a woman and out of charity, would ever forego a luscious morsel like this one. But they did.

Of course Lily's character, as it came to be looked at more and more, contributed to this response. And Jud contributed by blackening it further. When he confessed to the sheriff his guilt in the matter of Goldie he made it clear that Lily had inspired him. This explained Salter's attack on her and the sheriff believed Jud. Like almost everybody else he wanted, for Hannah's sake, to believe the worst about Lily. When Jud denied—which is what he did, firmly—knowing of any substance whatever to Lily's claim about Hannah, he was also believed. If people did not believe him, they pretended to. The public feeling against Jud, at least by all appearances, was founded entirely on his treachery toward Salter.

Yet Jud did confess everything, even at that time, though only to one person whose silence he could count on. During his last few days at the hospital, after his mind had got clear, he lay gazing at the blank white wall and thinking and thinking about what he would do. When the Reverend came to see him—he was the one who had brought Jud there—Jud tried to imagine what it would be like to tell him. The Reverend sat on the chair by Jud's bed, under the vase of flowers he himself had brought, and talked quietly to Jud and said a prayer. His face was tired and wasted, its kindliness darkened now and then by little signs of distraction. Somehow he had got wind of the story, which Jud by now had also heard, and he was suffering it. There was one moment when a turn of his head focused the sun on his lenses, very bright, like discs of yellow fire. Then Jud could imagine what it would be like. He imagined the seconds afterwards, the room without a sound, the shape of the Reverend's face a shadow staring into Jud's burnt-out eyes.

But Jud thought he *could* have confessed it to him, because he did confess it to somebody he feared only a little less than he feared the Reverend. He thought he could have and would have except for the agony that he would have laid on the Reverend's soul. That would have stayed with the old man the rest of his life, long, long after the forgiveness that Jud could have counted on from him. So Jud did not confess it to him. He lied. Working hard to show outrage he told him that of course the whole thing was lies cooked up by that vicious woman, who hated everything that was good and hated Jud for confessing the truth about Goldie to Salter. He was sure he left the Reverend comforted, whether the old man's doubts had been very real or not. If the Reverend later remembered having any doubts, his letters to Jud in prison never showed it. He wrote to Jud once a month, affectionate letters, always including some memories of Hannah and Jud together. He died just a couple of years after Jud went to prison.

It was Judge McCloud that Jud confessed to. This seemed right because, after the Reverend, the judge was the closest thing to real authority and also had the power to punish. Jud knew besides that since it was not a matter of legal guilt the judge would keep it secret. And he did. The three years he added to Jud's original five had behind them as technical reason the fact that Jud had broken probation rules. Jud had thought maybe there would be more than three. He had thought this especially while he was telling it, laying the facts out naked on the wide desk between him and the judge, hearing his voice put them there. Without even glancing he could see the eyes behind the black-rimmed spectacles. And there was the silence afterwards. Jud hoped that his life was not going to contain any other minutes like those. If Judge McCloud had reached across the desk and struck him down with something Jud would have welcomed the release.

Jud told me that in the years since then he must have retraced this whole story at least some thousands of times. There were parts of it that had lost a certain kind of reality for him, as if an outer shell had been stripped off, leaving them somehow obscure without loss of perfectly clear detail. His memories of Meagher especially were like this. In spite of everything he was almost persuaded that there never had been such a person. What became of him? Jud had not the slightest idea, any more than he had of where Meagher had come from and why and how. They say that things as real as life can step right out of a person's mind. Maybe Meagher was one of those. Or maybe, even, he came from a place that nobody knows anything at all about.

There were times when Jud thought of Lily in a way not much different. Of course there could not be any question of her reality. Too many people saw and felt it, and Jud was not the only one who kept on feeling it. Even so he often remembered her as if she had existed in a different dimension, like a mirror image. His memory was like that, with no back side to it, no relief. Salter believed she was a witch, and in certain moods it was easy for Jud to imagine that Salter was right, literally. He remembered the way she seized him that first afternoon in the store, the power she had over him. It was more than a figure of speech to say that she took him away from himself. She was *his* witch at least. In fact she was Salter's also. Both of them, smelted in the same fire, were ready and waiting for her when she came.

But if Lily had an ambiguous character in his memory, Hannah did not. He did not suppose anybody, except her father, would have said about Hannah that she was a vivid person in the ways that commonly impress others. She was not pretty or especially smart or clever or any of those things that leave a few people graven in our minds. But of all the memories Jud had, of anybody or anything, hers was the most real, the least ambiguous. It was as if he could walk around and around the memory of her, seeing her from every angle, every way. He could hear her voice perfectly, and he imagined he could recall perfectly every word she ever said in his presence, even the most banal and trivial. He knew why this was so. It was not the words or the voice, it was the way *she* was. She not only said things to you, she gave them to you. And she not only gave them. Somehow she gave them *clear* away, completely and for keeps, like presents to a stranger whom she never expected to see again. That was why Jud still had them. That was why she remained so much alive for him that he could still, four years later, go back and thank her.

In fact the last time I saw Jud, some years ago now, he was planning to do just that. He was then about to leave the prison, because he had been pardoned, forgiven the last four years of his sentence. He did not know yet what he would finally do with his freedom but he did know what his first free act would be. He would take himself back where she was buried and show himself to her and thank her. That was what he had really to thank her for—giving himself back to him. Of course he knew he would not get a reply. But if somehow he should get one, he would then have a question for her. He would ask her why, at such a cost to her, he had had any right to the self she had given him back.